REVENGE OF THE PRODIGAL

REVENGE OF THE PRODIGAL

MICHAEL CAUDO

ISBN: 978-1-7372988-1-6

Cover design and typesetting by riverdesignbooks.com

For my son
Nick

In memory of
Marianne Caudo-Beck
1942 – 2020

TABLE OF CONTENTS

SCUMBAG 101

Saint Patrick's Day, 2022
South Philadelphia

The break-in occurred in broad daylight, sometime before Mrs. Falzone let herself in to check on the dog while Scotty was laying Jilly to rest. Robberies that occurred while a house was empty for a funeral were pretty low but, unfortunately, not unheard of. It was Scumbag 101.

Charles "Scotty" Scottoline's loft sat above a fitness center right off Passyunk Avenue, deep in South Philadelphia. Scotty and Jilly owned the building and rented out the lower level, formerly a transmission repair shop. The building was in the middle of a mixed-use block of rowhomes and a few retail stores that all shared cement backyards too small for anything other than a few potted plants of basil and mint. The yards were separated by cinderblock walls about six feet high and backed up to an alley that let out to Snyder Avenue. The thieves had cut the padlocked chain with bolt cutters, made their way down the alley, jumped the fence, and scaled the wall to the loft, gaining entry through a bathroom window. They appeared to have looted whatever jewelry, cash, and loose valuables were lying around and left the way they came.

"Probably junkies," Detective Jim Corey concluded. He made a note to check for any Ring doorbell footage just in case he was wrong and the burglar (or burglars) had fled out the front. He was six months short of his thirty, and his autopilot had been set on *stay clear of trouble* mode for quite some time. Corey felt bad for Scotty—just buried his life partner and came home to all this. Chances were, he would never recover anything. People tended to be overwhelmed by the violation of their home and the intrusion into their personal space, and Scotty was no exception. He was insured for most of the jewelry, but this was no insurance job. The most expensive items remained untouched in a small safe.

Scotty came down to South Detectives to give his statement. He was cooperative, providing Corey with all the information he needed without hesitation, and his demeanor was consistent with what he had experienced. He seemed a bit odd, which was to be expected, but Corey didn't judge the man for his lifestyle. The job didn't allow for that. Still, something troubled Corey. It was on the last question that Scotty betrayed a small tell of deception. Corey found this strange because it was the most innocuous question of all, yet Scotty stumbled over it. Corey tried to push it out of his mind, but he couldn't shake it. Why would the man struggle with such a throwaway, wrap-up question?

Can you think of anything else that might be missing?

SPIRITUS GLADIUS

CATHEDRAL BASILICA SAINTS PETER and PAUL

Tuesday, April 12, 2022
Holy Week

Meanwhile, Saul was still breathing out murderous threats against the Lord's disciples. He went to the high priest and asked him for letters to the synagogues in Damascus, so that if he found any there who belonged to the Way, whether men or women, he might take them as prisoners to Jerusalem.

Acts 9:1-2 (NIV)

A small group of parishioners waited patiently for their confessions to be heard in the sacrament of reconciliation. At 11:30 on a Tuesday, the average sinner was about seventy-five years old, even during Holy Week. Some of the women gripped rosaries as they waited their turn. Others knelt quietly in prayer, no doubt reflecting on their sins.

What the fuck do these fossils have to confess? Victor Baldassare thought while he sat a few pews back from the penitent horde. *Please bless me, Father, I killed my husband.* Victor amused himself with the thought.

Father Gus was about to jump out of his skin. He kept looking at his watch as yet another parishioner recited the same sins, in the same order, as last week. The priest wanted to tell her to say fifty-two Acts of Contrition and skip the following year, or better yet, just come back when she was ready for Last Rites. Instead, he doled out the same old penance, said a prayer of absolution and sent the woman on her way.

What he was really thinking about was a glass of Johnnie Walker Blue at the Borgata and a progressive jackpot that had thus far eluded him. Football season had crushed him, and he was barely making the interest-only payments on the street loan his tab was converted to. "I don't give a fuck if you gotta raid the poor box and steam open envelopes." That's what Andy Boy had said when Father Gus was short a month ago, and that's precisely what Father Gus did.

The final penitent entered the booth, and Father Gus sensed a more significant figure on the other side of the privacy screen. He heard the kneeler creak under the weight of the next customer.

"Please bless me, Father, for I have sinned. It has been fifty-four years since my last confession."

That caught Father Gus off guard a bit. Quite a few people came in and said it had been many years since their last confession. Some couldn't even remember how long. But it was rare for someone to recite a significant length of time with such precision and not a trace of hesitancy. It was the Lenten season, however, and people tended to return to the church, at least until Easter came and went. The other thing that struck Father Gus was the man's distinct accent. It reminded him of his old friend from the seminary Father Robert, or Boston Bobby as the other seminarians had jokingly referred to him.

"Pardon me, but are you a parishioner here?"

"No, Father, do I have to be?"

"Of course not, my son. I was just curious. You are welcome here. Please continue."

"I have three sins to confess, Father."

"After fifty-four years? Congratulations."

"Well, my last confession was actually my first Penance. That's how I can be so sure."

Father Gus muffled a laugh.

"I'm sorry, Father, but is this funny to you?"

"You're right, my son. It is *I* who should beg *your* forgiveness. Go on, please."

"Vengeance," Victor responded.

"I don't understand," Father Gus said.

"That's my first sin, Father, vengeance. I've committed it. I seek it. I even enjoy it."

"That's a grave sin, my son. 'Vengeance is mine, sayeth the Lord.'"

"Yeah, I been thinking about that. Is it though, his alone I mean? After all, how does God exact vengeance anyhow, other than, say, through famine, a plague, or a bolt of lightning? Through people, right? Sometimes even armies. How do I know God isn't using me as his instrument? I mean, after all, who am I to question?"

Father Gus began to wonder where this was going and who was on the other side of the screen.

"That brings me to my second sin. I've used my profession as a cover for my evil deeds. I've cloaked myself in a position of authority to commit all kinds of heinous acts. You know all about that, right, Father?

Father Gus was about to abandon the confessional and run for the sacristy, but something kept him glued to his chair. Maybe it was some lingering belief in the sanctity of the sacrament. More likely, he was simply frozen with fear. Nevertheless, he did his best to collect himself and maintain his composure.

"This is starting to sound like more than just three sins, my son. Would you like to continue this sacrament later, after you've had ample time to reflect and make a full confession?"

"Nah, I'm almost done. I saved the worst for last."

"Proceed," Father Gus mumbled in resignation and sunk back in his chair.

"I was not my brother's keeper."

"I'm not sure I understand you."

"Sure you do. Like in the Bible. Cain and Abel."

"In what way were you not your brother's keeper?"

"Well, he entrusted his property to me, and I was negligent in its care. I allowed it to be taken from me."

"Was this sinful or simply a mistake?"

"Oh, it was no mistake, Father. It was the culmination of my sinful actions and wicked ways. Now, my brother is suffering from the loss of his property."

"May I ask what kind of property this was?"

"I think you know, Father. It was a painting. Someone lost his painting, and he wants it back."

Father Gus felt his testicles creep up into his abdomen. This wasn't one of Andy Boy's thugs sent to give him a scare. This was something entirely different and infinitely more deadly. And no one, not the police, the FBI, or the pope, could help him out of this predicament.

"What if this property was taken through no fault of the caretaker?"

"Is this my fucking confession or yours?" Victor couldn't help cracking. "Sorry, I shouldn't have cursed in here. But let me put it like this; while I was waiting out there, I was looking around. This is an impressive place. Must be worth a couple hundred million, all the gold and marble and shit. Yet it's still worth less than that painting. I read that the underside of the dome has a mural with a Latin inscription. Do you know what it says?"

Father Gus swallowed hard. "*In omni loco sacrificatur et offertur nomini meo oblatio mundo.*"

"In English, please."

"In every place, there is offered and sacrificed in my name a clean oblation."

"Yeah, that's the one. I like that word, oblation. I like everything about this place. Let me ask you, why does Saint Paul always have a sword? I mean, why would a saint need a sword?"

"That's a common misconception—that he's being depicted as a warrior. Before his conversion on the road to Damascus, he was known as Saul and was a persecutor of Christians. The sword is actually a symbol of his martyrdom."

"What does that mean?"

"He was beheaded."

"What about the other guy, Peter. I recall him using a sword. Cut a guy's ear off or something."

"You seem to have some knowledge of the Bible," Father Gus remarked.

"Well, I was an altar boy once. You might say I followed the path opposite St. Paul's."

"When the Roman soldiers came for Christ, Peter cut off the ear of the High Priest's servant, Malchus. Jesus healed him. It was his last miracle."

"So did God punish Peter? I mean, that's a pretty fucked up thing to do. Yet it didn't stop him from becoming a saint. The father of the Church even. From what you're telling me, Paul was even worse, slaughtering innocent people and then taking on an alias to cover his tracks. And yet look at the place your outfit built for them. Maybe there's hope for me after all. Now I've seen more than a few guys lose an appendage, even an ear once, but I gotta ask you, Father, when's the last time you witnessed a miracle?"

Father Gus was silent.

"That's what I thought. I realize we can't really cover all this here in this booth, so tonight, after you get done grabbing cocktail waitresses' asses and losing all these widows' Social Security checks, you're gonna meet my associate at Angelina's on Georgia Avenue in Atlantic City. You know where it is?"

"Yes." Father Gus was almost whimpering now. "I know where it is."

"Good. Be there at nine. And if I was you, I'd have a detailed plan about how I'm gonna get my brother his painting back. After all, you are your brother's keeper, right?"

"Yes."

"Good. Say it then."

Father Gus paused, unsure if the man really wanted him to say the words. The uncomfortable silence that followed compelled him to err on the side of caution, and he relented. "I am my brother's keeper," he almost sobbed.

Victor Baldassare walked out of the Cathedral and onto Ben Franklin Parkway, where a waiting Escalade picked him up and drove him back to Boston.

MEMBERS ONLY

Caffe Vecchio
Passyunk Avenue, South Philadelphia
Good Friday, 2022

It was now about noon, and darkness came over the whole land until three in the afternoon, for the sun stopped shining. And the curtain of the temple was torn in two. Jesus called out with a loud voice, "Father, into your hands I commit my spirit." When he had said this, he breathed his last.

Luke 23:44-46 (NIV)

Joey "The Kid" Musante sat at the bar of Caffé Vecchio. The Avenue was quiet, and the jukebox and TV were silenced in deference to Christ's agony. Joey wasn't religious in the traditional sense, despite attending Catholic school for twelve years. However, he still honored the conventions out of some nagging sense of obligation instilled by his mother. Maybe it was just superstition, like not stepping on a crack or walking under a ladder, but it was a good a reason as any. The silence was broken by the sound of someone trying the locked door. The sound brought Beto out from the kitchen, and he looked to Joey for instructions. Joey responded by pointing his chin at the door. Beto undid the lock and opened the door only a crack. The shade was pulled down and a small "Members Only" sign dangled from a hook. The sign wasn't meant to be taken literally. The Caffé was still a restaurant open to the public during regular business hours, but Joey had taken to hanging it more frequently since Nick had returned to Lauderdale and Big Gary's health problems and doctors' appointments kept him away from the Caffé.

Beto turned to Joey. "Some guy named Scotty. Says he's looking for Nick."

Joey shrugged his shoulders, but relented when Beto added, "I recognize him. He's from the neighborhood." Joey walked around the back of the bar, fished two Peronis out of the beer box, opened them, and placed them on coasters. Next, he opened the cash drawer of an ancient, decorative cash register and took out the .32 he kept behind the tray, placing it under the bar but within reach. Only then did he nod to Beto to let the unscheduled visitor in.

Scotty stepped into the dimly lit Caffé hesitantly as Beto held the door, then locked it behind him. The man clutched a wool cap in front of him like a small child would hold on to a favorite stuffed animal. He jumped noticeably when the deadbolt clicked behind him and stood there waiting for someone to invite him to sit.

Joey's first impression of the man was one of culture. He was about seventy, slim and well dressed. He wasn't flashy, but his shoes were carefully polished and Joey could see that the plain-looking cap was a Borsalino. Before entering the Caffé, he had taken it off his head, as evidenced by the slight muss of an otherwise impressive shock of gray hair. What Joey noticed most was the thing his mother always said people would notice first about him; the man had manners.

Joey gestured for Scotty to sit. He extended his hand over the bar in greeting and introduced himself. His left hand rested on the beer box for balance and gripped the .32 just in case Scotty's appearance was deceiving: something Big Gary had taught him.

"Joey Musante." He gripped Scotty's hand as Scotty took his place on the stool with the sweaty Peroni set before it.

"Charlie Scottoline. My friends call me Scotty."

The overall impression was that he felt out of place and was trying to make himself disappear, like a man who'd had a childhood that required him to stay out of the way of something…or somebody.

Joey took all of this in. He would have used it to his advantage in another setting, but he felt a little sorry for the strange man. Stranger still, he felt an unlikely admiration. Maybe it was some hidden strength or hard-earned courage that Joey detected. The man had walked into an unfamiliar setting unannounced and that took some balls. A lifetime of snickering and finger-pointing in a tough South Philly neighborhood is going to build some character. The man was apprehensive, that was evident, but he wasn't scared. He seemed to have built up an immunity to that particular emotion. Something greater than fear had driven him here.

RED SKY AT MORNING

Lauderdale-By-The-Sea
Holy Saturday 2022

Nick Di Nobile opened a Michelob Ultra for Ralph and placed it on a soggy coaster on the bar of the Tuscan Tiki. Ralph took a sip from the sweaty aluminum bottle. Nick was working the day shift at his oceanfront bar and grill after the regular day bartender, Ethan, had called out. He was getting ready for the good-natured ribbing his cameo appearance would doubtless trigger among the regulars.

"I can't understand how anybody drinks this shit," Ralph complained to no one in particular.

Nick answered anyway. "I thought you were trying to make weight," he said, trying to lighten the mood.

Ralph "The Rifle" Cappello was a well-tanned, sixty-four-year-old, barrel-chested former middleweight. These days he was tipping the scales at 230—twenty pounds down from his peak weight a few months ago.

"The kid has me on a strict diet. I'm not even supposed to be drinking *this*." Ralph raised his beer while he lovingly eyed the bar menu—for entertainment purposes only. Vinny "The Kid" was helping Ralph trim down and watch his cholesterol and triglycerides. He would pick Ralph up every morning, then they would hit the gym before he shuttled Ralph to the Tuscan Tiki. Most days, they were joined by a few old guys who had come to be known as the Tasker Morris Brain Trust, named after Tasker Morris Ventures LLC. Ralph had formed the company as an instrument for them to pool their money to invest in real estate, hard money lending, and other pursuits—all legal, and mostly ethical.

"Where's your driver today?" Nick asked.

"He prefers personal assistant." Ralph laughed. "How do you like that? Says he doesn't like the connotation that driver conveys."

Nick shook his head. "Guess he'll be demanding a 401k soon."

"He already has one," Ralph responded without a trace of sarcasm. "What's wrong, Nicky? Something on your mind?"

Nick stared out at the ocean while mindlessly drying a glass with a bar rag. Ralph wasn't wrong. Nick had just had a visit from someone he'd hoped to never see again—Anastasia. She was the second scariest person he had ever met. The first was her boss.

"Just drifting off, that's all."

"Well, I guess this place will do that to you. Just look at your Uncle Frank."

It was true. Nick's uncle, Frankie "Stone Crab" Valletto, was a bit wistful these days. It seemed like he was always staring at the horizon and zoning out. Except, while most men presumably gazed out at the future, Frank was searching for a glimpse of the past. Nick had to admit he was sometimes guilty of the same offense.

"I have a theory about that."

"I'm sure you do, Nicky. So why don't you tell me all about it? But first, how 'bout a real drink instead of this dishwater?"

Nick poured him a double Crown Royal and backed it up with an ice-cold Peroni.

"Now you're talking, kid. Please continue."

Nick leaned over the bar. It was only 11:30, but the heat was already becoming oppressive. The Tiki's overhead fans provided little relief and there wasn't much breeze coming off the ocean. Once the afternoon crowd filed in, it would get even hotter. Then, hopefully, a nice onshore breeze would develop and provide a little relief.

Nick launched into his theory. "We all came here from the city. As kids, we lived in rowhomes and everywhere we went, other than those few precious days at the shore, buildings blocked out the horizon. Over time, that does something to your perspective. And then when we get here, we spend the rest of the time trying to adjust our vision, like when you walk into a dark bar on a sunny day. I think that's why my father spent so much time on his boat, looking out at the horizon. He didn't want his vision to become stunted like that, and he didn't want it to happen to me either."

"Your father was a good man, Nicky. He was ahead of his time, God rest his soul." Ralph raised a glass and waited for Nick to pour himself a shot of Crown. They toasted Nick's father, Anthony DiNobile, and downed their drinks. "If it wasn't for guys like him, we might not be enjoying all this." Ralph swept his arm around, his gesture encompassing their surroundings. For Nick, that meant the Tuscan Tiki; for Ralph, maybe all South Florida.

"Uncle Frank always says that even after all his years down here, he's still amazed every time he looks at a palm tree. That's the right attitude. On his worst day, he's still found the magic in this place and never takes it for granted."

"Thanks to you, there's a whole lot of magic jingling in his pockets these days." Ralph raised his Peroni for emphasis. "All our pockets."

"Thanks, Ralph." Nick dug into the beer box for a cold Peroni and popped the cap. "But I couldn't have pulled it off if you weren't there covering my ass—again."

"Nah, kid, you would have figured it out without me. You're craftier than you give yourself credit for."

Nick was referring to an incident many years ago back in the neighborhood when he was a skinny little kid getting slapped around by an older guy on the block. It seemed like a thousand years ago, but a young middleweight named Raphael—subsequently anglicized to Ralph—took offense to the man putting his hands on a neighborhood kid a little too roughly. It was one thing for the older kids from 9th and Morris in South Philadelphia to "toughen up" the younger kids, but this guy was an outsider, and his intentions weren't half as pure. The teenager who would come to fight professionally under the ring name The Rifle had stepped out of the shadows to administer a beating people still talk about. The story having been passed down and embellished, some versions had Ralph killing the guy, but that was nonsense. So, in a world of predictable coincidences, it made perfect sense Ralph Cappello would save Nick forty years later, this time in a scrap with much higher stakes.

Nick thought about the visit he'd just had and when the best time would be to tell Ralph about it. It was going to be a heavy conversation, and Nick wasn't ready to break the mood just yet. Besides, Uncle Frank was on his way, and he needed to hear this too. Nick decided they would enjoy the day for now and he would wait for Uncle Frank to show up before bringing them up to speed. Frank had his own run-in with Anastasia back in Philly, though she'd gone by the name Donna at the time. Even in South Florida, she stood out as an absolute smokeshow. Nick had last seen her on the deck of Dmitry Ivanov's Pershing yacht in Miami on the night Nick turned over the painting, Rembrandt's *The Return of the Prodigal Son*, or "The Prodigal of Passyunk Avenue," as it had come to be known, and walked away with a duffel bag containing four million.

Anastasia could give off the distinct impression that she was hot for Nick. He had to remind himself that quite a few guys got that same impression, and her face was the last thing they ever saw on this earth. Anastasia—Donna? Who knew what her real name was—had come to Miami from Kyiv and started out small, slipping mickeys to unsuspecting guys in nightclubs. They couldn't believe their luck, until they woke up in a hotel room missing their bankroll, watch, and credit cards. Then Dmitry discovered, recruited and trained her, and she graduated to a more potent elixir as Dmitry elevated himself from strip club owner to billionaire.

Nick never thought he'd see her again after that night, and then she'd shown up at the Tiki this morning while Nick was opening with a message: "Dmitry needs a favor from you." The good part was, if Dmitry wanted him dead, there would have been no message. Besides, Dmitry had no reason to be anything but grateful to Nick. As crazy as it sounded, Nick trusted him to be honorable. Dmitry was simply too powerful to require deceit. It wasn't necessary for a man with his influence and reach. He would consider it undignified.

Ralph and Dmitry had their own history. While Dmitry's international connections and unfathomable wealth prevented them from being equals, there was no doubt Dmitry regarded Ralph as a charismatic force capable of bending people to his will. More importantly, Dmitry respected Ralph as a man who kept his word and was loyal to his friends, be they wealthy or poor. Dmitry, himself, was capable of great generosity, his concept of friendship was expansive, and he had proven himself a powerful ally to both Ralph and Nick. Still, both knew the man was capable of unapologetic malevolence in pursuit of his goals, pity was an emotion he had no use for, and he did not suffer fools gladly.

Ralph gazed out at the Atlantic, considering whether it was too early in the day to light a Montecristo #2. The cigar was nestled in the breast pocket of a perfectly pressed, short-sleeve. collared dress shirt. He placed the cigar delicately on an ashtray and admired the wrapper glistening in the sun. The Tiki was just an oceanfront bar, but men of Ralph's age and pedigree simply didn't wear T-shirts in a social setting. He withdrew an S.T. Dupont lighter from his trouser pocket, put on a pair of glasses, read the elegant script engraving on the lighter and tried to mouth the foreign phrase to himself; *Za nashu druzjbu*. He couldn't quite pronounce the phrase correctly, but he knew what it meant: to our friendship. Ralph remembered the day Dmitry gave him the lighter as a gift. It was apparently a big deal to the Russian oligarch, and had cemented their relationship on that day over two years ago. Ralph had always figured he had about a ten percent chance of not coming back from any meeting with Dmitry. Since Dmitry gave him the lighter, however, he'd recalculated his odds to about five percent.

Behind the bar, Nick was doing some pondering of his own. His morning visitor had him thinking of a conversation he had with Big Gary the previous day, in which Gary told him about a visitor of his own. A man had come to Caffé Vecchio in Philly looking for Nick. Nick hadn't thought much of it at the time, but Anastasia's appearance at the Tiki suggested the two visits were connected somehow. Now, he recalled Gary's words about what the man had said: *Something about a painting*.

OUT OF SEASON

Frank wheeled the Honda Civic into the circular driveway entrance to the Ocean Abode. The unassuming resort housed the Tuscan Tiki, home to the Tasker Morris boys. Technically, the Civic wasn't Frank's car. Instead, it was titled to Tasker Morris Ventures, LLC. After Frank's little windfall from "that thing in Philly," he'd had his eye on a used Mercedes S 600, but Ralph had intervened.

"That thing's gonna cost a mint to maintain, Frankie. You choose cars like you choose broads." Ralph insisted on the Civic instead. "Keep the oil changed and this thing is good for three hundred thousand miles."

"But I'll be dead by then," Frank argued.

"Good," Ralph countered. "We'll give it to Vinny after your funeral."

In the end, Frank relented. Tasker Morris was paying the note, after all. Frank just had to be available to run some errands and shuttle some of the Tasker Morris "boys" around. At sixty-four, Ralph was the youngest member of the Tasker Morris Brain Trust, as they were jokingly referred to. Of course, the joke was on everyone else, as the savvy consortium of blue-collar, northeast, inner-city expatriates had amassed a small fortune in real estate and mortgage notes. They had an average net worth of about five million, except for old man Abe, who was probably well into double digits.

Frank tossed the keys to the valet, and Kevin maneuvered the lowly Honda into a front-line spot next to Ralph's Rolls-Royce Wraith. Perhaps better than anyone, the valets had their fingers on the pulse of the South Florida social hierarchy. They served as the gatekeepers of a caste-like system from that entry-level position. Money had a lot to do with it, mainly in the form of tips, but it wasn't the only currency exchanged. Perceived status, charisma, and access were all assets scrolling by on a nonstop, invisible stock ticker on the imaginary South Florida Exchange. Frankie Stone Crab was perpetually low on conventional cash, but when it came to charisma and access, he was a bona fide magnate.

He strolled through the lobby, waved at Rodrigo, the desk clerk, shook a few hands, and held the beachfront door for a well-lotioned family of three. The little boy wore bright blue floats on his arms and a coating of sunblock on his face that made him look like a birthday cake. A palpable sense of wonderment radiated off the kid like plutonium. That door to the pool and beach was like a magical portal to all the treasures his unblemished little mind could imagine. The boy's parents held hands and smiled at Frank. The pungent odor of marijuana wafted from the elevators as a group of college-age kids lined up behind them. The father guided the little boy forward, his hands gently on his shoulders. Frank waved the college crew through like some unofficial ambassador. Frank followed behind, paused at the top step to fire up a Marlboro, and looked out over the view of the Tuscan Tiki and the Atlantic Ocean that framed it. For a fleeting moment, Frank shared that sense of wonderment the little boy possessed. His mind drifted and settled on some random day from his childhood spent building sandcastles on Atlantic City's beach and playing pirates with his cousin Albert. One rare and precious day when all their childhood games were make-believe—before they became real-life brigands.

He inhaled a chestful of smoke, held it for a second, then blew it out his mouth and nose with an audible whoosh. That brief sensation of innocence escaped his body along with the smoke and quickly dissipated into the relentless humidity. Frank heard a splash as the little boy did a cannonball into the pool.

PORCHETTA

Frank walked down to the Tuscan Tiki, which was situated directly beachfront. Sand frequently accumulated in the cracks of the paved stone floor, and occasionally a hurricane brought the ocean straight through. But today, only a gentle breeze nudged the flat screen TVs that hung about the perimeter of the Tiki. They swayed gently, and Frank recalled their bulky predecessors dangling menacingly from chains affixed to bamboo. It made him feel even older than his sixty-nine years.

Today was pig roast day, and the sweet smell of the whole roasted porchetta supplanted the odor of marijuana that seemed to permeate the hotel's interior. The Ocean Abode was an older building and budget friendly to families, but also drew a younger, party-minded clientele. It made for an eclectic mix, but somehow, it seemed to work. The uber-loyal locals were omnipresent and acted like Sherpas for the unsuspecting families, while keeping any overenthusiastic partiers in check. Of course, Spring Break was another matter. Then, all bets were off and outside security, along with uniformed police, was necessary to maintain a semblance of peace. But today was pig roast day, and for the moment, everything was right in Tiki land.

Frank took his place at the bar next to Ralph, who was going through the Tasker Morris mail while sipping a Crown Royal. An unlit Montecristo #2 sat patiently atop a plastic ashtray. Frank gazed covetously at the torpedo and briefly pictured the dark, weathered hands of the Cuban roller who last touched the stick. He looked out at the Atlantic, wondering what the roller was doing this very second. His daydream was interrupted by Ralph's gravelly voice.

"You're not smoking in the Civic, are you?"

"No," Frank answered. "I never do." Frank was telling the truth for a change. *He* hadn't been smoking in the car, but he vaguely recalled the girl he picked up at the cigar bar smoking a few Dunhill cigarettes on the ride to her condo in Deerfield.

"Well, then make sure them cigar bunnies don't smoke anything but your joint in there."

How the fuck does this guy seem to know every little move I make? Frank mused. *He's in bed most nights by 8:30 for chrissakes.*

"She was no cigar bunny," Frank responded defensively, more to stick up for himself than to defend her honor.

"So I'm right then?" Ralph countered.

Frank saw the beginning of a smile start to curl in the corner of Ralph's lips before he suppressed it and knew Ralph was just breaking his balls.

"At least buy me a fucking drink if you're gonna bust my chops already."

Nick walked over and poured Frank a double Crown Royal. Frank stood on the bar rail, leaned over, and kissed his nephew softly on the cheek while gently touching his face.

"What's up, my nephew? Did you save me the ears?"

Ralph paused just as he was about to light the Montecristo. "Are you fucking serious with these ears? That shit is gonna kill you."

Vinny, Ralph's personal assistant, walked up just in time for this exchange.

"My mother—God rest her soul—always said you can eat everything on a pig except the squeal. What can I say? I like them. They remind me of home."

Ralph pointed to an aging bathing beauty. Oblivious to three decades of medical science, she'd slathered her weathered hide with tanning oil. "She's crispy. You gonna eat her too?"

Frank downed his drink and eyeballed Miss Hawaiian Tropic 1983. He fired up a Marlboro, and the cigarette danced in the corner of his mouth as he answered without a trace of sarcasm. "I just might, Ralphie, I just might."

"What part is the squeal?" Vinny asked, visibly confused.

Ralph, Frank, and Nick shared a long look before bursting into laughter.

Ralph shook his head as he got up to use the men's room. "Sick motherfuckers," he mumbled over his shoulder.

"We need to talk," Frank said as Nick poured him another Crown.

"No shit," Nick answered, not realizing they were referring to two different things. "Let's wait for Ralph to come back; this concerns him too."

Frank wasn't sure why Ralph needed to hear that Nick's old flame, Angie, had moved down from Philly and was bartending at the Royal Palm Club in Boca, but he figured it couldn't hurt to wait.

JILLY

Scotty walked out of Caffé Vecchio, pulled his cap down tight, and walked south on Passyunk Avenue. His pace was brisk, and he hugged the darkened portion of the side-walk. Scotty was accustomed to moving in the shadows, head down, his actions honed by a lifetime spent trying to remain invisible. His childhood dreams of becoming a "real artist" were snuffed out by a disapproving father who never missed an opportunity to express disappointment his son possessed no athletic prowess and had no interest or aptitude for following him into the Ironworkers Union. What Scotty did possess were skills that would have made him a first-round draft pick had he wielded a baseball bat as masterfully as he did a paintbrush. But unlike baseball, with its undisputable metrics and averages, the art world is notoriously fickle, dependent upon the subjective whim of critics and gatekeepers.

Scotty's works, though flawless in their execution, failed to inspire. . . or sell. "Workmanlike and derivative," the review read. *Everything is derivative*, he had screeched while reading the review. If that weren't true, there hadn't been an original novel written since Homer penned *The Odyssey*. He'd retreated to a quiet life of menial jobs while continuing to practice his craft in private, each work an homage to the renaissance masters he revered and emulated. His skills did not go entirely unappreciated. A small group of benefactors found his handiwork useful and would occasionally commission a piece. One of those benefactors now watched Scotty from a Sprinter van parked in the Passyunk Municipal lot, a mural depicting a vintage scene of Old South Philadelphia looming in the background. The benefactor sent a text to a number with a 954 area code that read: *Da Vinci leaving* Caffé *Vecchio.* The recipient texted back even more succinctly:

Follow.

Scotty arrived home a few minutes later to his converted loft atop an old transmission repair shop that had been turned into a fitness center. The gym's owner had repurposed some of the vintage signs, making use of the neon wording featuring phrases like "rebuilt" and "repair." Scotty owned the entire building, a double property on Juniper Street he'd inherited from his longtime partner, Giulio De Luca, after his death the previous month. How cruel, Scotty had thought at the time, that he had survived a pandemic that seemed to target them exclusively, only to be felled by a more pedestrian scourge. His wit intact to the very end, Giulio found humor in the irony. He had never run from a fight in his life and battled bravely, right up until he was placed on the ventilator.

At a time and place where it was virtually unheard of, Giulio—"Jill," as his friends called him—lived openly and proudly as a gay man. He was a feared South Philly street fighter in the '70s and '80s, a time when it was recognized as an occupation. He operated a nightclub in Center City and always did the right thing by the powers that be. Neighborhood men cautioned their teenage sons to give the man his respect. He wasn't good-looking by either masculine or feminine standards, but it didn't stop him from driving his convertible around the neighborhood, eyes laden with mascara. When he caught a red light in front of a notorious street corner, there was no whistling or catcalling, just a chorus of "Hey, Mr. Jill" or "How's it going, Jilly?"

Scotty mourned him still. He had lost the love of his life, and with him, the protection he had provided.

The benefactor watched from the corner as Scotty opened the street-level door to a stairway leading to a second-floor loft. The interior door was metal and reinforced. Whoever had gained entry had known what they were doing. They had broken in during Jilly's funeral, the oldest trick in the book, but these were no junkies ransacking a random house. The intruders knew just what they were looking for.

GARY'S GANG

Joey called Gary, saying only that they'd had a visitor. Joey then sent Beto to pick him up. Gary protested at first. His health had been a bit rocky of late, what with the gout and the hypertension, but when Joey said the visitor was asking for Nick, Gary said he'd be ready in ten minutes.

Gary had stepped back a bit from running Caffé Vecchio's day-to-day operations since Nick returned to Florida. Joey'd stepped in, and at first, things went smoothly. Joey was enthusiastic. He had the youthful energy that is typically wasted on the young. Lately, however, he seemed to be channeling that energy into pursuits outside the realm of food and beverage. Aside from Friday and Saturday nights, Caffé Vecchio had started to take on the aura of a private social club. People began to notice, and the suburban clientele became a bit gun shy, as it were.

Beto parked out back, and Gary walked in through the kitchen. Gary had a fifty percent interest in the Caffé now. Nick had also ensured Gary had a little nest egg from the score they made from recovering Dmitry's painting. Health issues had forced Gary to cut back his hours. Nowadays, he mostly came in early on the weekends to make the sauces, do some butchering, and oversee the *pasta e fagioli* the Caffé was famous for. It appeared on the menu as *Virgil's Vazool.* Many dishes on the menu still retained the whimsical names appropriated from art and literature bestowed upon them by Nick's late father, Anthony. Most of them honored renaissance painters, like *Botticelli Bolognese.* Others were named for special customers, and Virgil Corrado, the "mad painter" of Rittenhouse Square, was nothing if not special. The eccentric artist was a close friend and confidant of Anthony Di Nobile, and Nick, Gary and the crew had readily taken him in. He was an integral part of Caffé Vecchio's extended family.

On Mondays, Gary retreated to the upstairs office to do the books and pay the bills. He saw the revenue slipping, but he couldn't do much without putting in fourteen-hour days again, and that was no longer an option. Nick noticed too. They both had long talks with Joey, who promised to buckle down, but little by little, the Caffé was morphing into a hangout.

It was just after three when Gary arrived. Christ's suffering had concluded, and the traditional quiet time was over. Joey turned on the TV, and Alberto, the bartender, walked to the jukebox. Gary's bulk blocked out the light from the kitchen as his shadow crept up to the bar and announced the big man's entrance. Joey was sitting at the bar and exchanged a conspiratorial grin with Alberto as the opening notes of the disco classic "Keep on Dancin'" by Gary's Gang chirped happily from the jukebox. Gary leaned on the bar, shook his head just a bit, and scowled in Alberto's direction. Alberto got the hint and took his place behind the bar, where he poured shots of Crown

Royal for the three of them. They toasted to nothing in particular and knocked back their shots.

Before their glasses returned to the bar, Gary broke the silence. "You do realize I know that y'all fucking with me playing that song every time I walk in?"

Joey shrugged unconvincingly at Alberto, who turned around and pretended he was washing a glass to hide the chuckle he was struggling to suppress.

"You drag me outta bed with this shit, and you still got jokes? Well, I got a joke for you; next time I hear this happy horseshit, I'm gonna "keep on dancing" on somebody's cranium." Gary busted a little dance move to emphasize his point.

Joey got up and spread his arms wide to give the big guy a hug meant to serve as an apology. Gary shrugged it off and pointed at his glass as a cue to Alberto.

"What the fuck was that?" Joey asked, referring to Gary's dance. "The mashed potato?"

This time, Gary took over the toast as the extended version of the song continued to play. "I hated this shit when it came out, and I like it even less now." They knocked back their shots.

Joey draped his arm across Gary's back, trying but failing to reach across the expanse. "Sorry, G, it won't happen again." Then he nodded at Alberto, who got the hint and reached under the bar to turn up the volume.

"Cocksuckers!" Gary barked as he leapt to his feet surprisingly fast, knocking over his stool in the process. He took a playful swipe at Joey's head as he retreated with his hands up in mock surrender.

And that's how it usually went around the Caffé. Some preliminary drinks, a bit of merciless ball breaking, and some half-hearted threats of violence before anyone could get down to the matter at hand. The song ended, and the Delfonics stepped in to save the day. Joey had queued up "When You Get Right Down To It" as a musical apology for the earlier transgression.

Gary began to nod approvingly. "That's more like it. Now we can talk."

Joey began to fill him in on Scotty's visit. Gary stood at the end of Joey's recitation and walked to the back of the restaurant without so much as a word. "Where you going?" Joey called after him.

"I need to call Nick," he responded, pushing his way through the swinging doors.

PRIMA DONNA

Ralph returned from the men's room and reclaimed his seat. He made a big production of using a bar towel to wipe his hands.

"You're out of hand towels again."

"I'll get right on it," Nick said. "I keep telling you to use the inside bathroom."

"I tried; somebody was getting laid in there."

"Probably kids," Nick offered.

"Nice fucking place you're running here."

"You think it doesn't happen at the Royal Palm?" Nick responded a little defensively.

"Guilty." Frank raised his hand.

Ralph just shook his head.

Nick set them up with fresh drinks. Ronnie Cruz had shown up to spell Nick and was handling the other end of the bar. Two waitresses from Commercial Avenue had commandeered the jukebox and were playing some new rap song that was suddenly everywhere. It was a bit raunchy, but Nick liked it. The backing track was a sample from the Stax label. Nick tried to place it; *the Dramatics?*

"Yo." Ralph snapped his fingers in front of Nick's face. "You with us?"

"Yeah." Nick reached under the bar and turned the dial, raising the volume just loud enough to cover the conversation they were about to have. The dancing waitresses reciprocated with a little white girl shimmy and an obligatory "*Wooooo!*"

Nick put his forearms on the bar and leaned forward. "I had a visit from an old friend this morning."

Shit, Frank thought. *Angie's been here already*.

"Sorry, Nick," Frank said. "I was just gonna tell you."

"Tell me what?" Nick smiled and looked back and forth between Frank and Ralph. Ralph shrugged and looked at Nick with his palms upturned, confirming he didn't know what Frank was talking about.

"I saw her a few days ago. She's working at the Royal Palm, bartending at the pool bar."

Nick almost spit out the Peroni he was sipping. "Anastasia is working at the Royal Palm? You didn't drink anything she poured, did you?"

Now it was Frank who seemed shocked. "Donna?"

"Yeah Donna. Anastasia. Whatever the fuck you want to call her. She was here earlier. Wait, who were you talking about?"

Ralph turned on his stool to face Frank, now just as curious as Nick.

"Nobody. My mistake. I'll tell you later. Finish your story." Frank felt terrible now. He had derailed an important conversation, but worse, he dreaded telling Nick about Angie in this setting. Frank figured maybe they could talk later while sitting on the bulkhead, looking out at the ocean at night. At least that's how he imagined it.

"No, fuck that, Unc. Tell me now."

Frank looked at Ralph for some support or guidance. Instead, Ralph gave him a gentle nod. He didn't know what Frank was talking about either, but he was a proponent of ripping off the Band-Aid.

Frank lit a Marlboro and ripped it off with a one-word bombshell. "Angie."

Nick teetered on that moment where your mind is about to acknowledge something but is still holding out for some alternate explanation. He came close to reflexively spitting out, "*My Angie?*" but he caught the words before they crossed his lips and rephrased the question.

"What about Angie?" Nick's voice cracked just a bit, betraying that he had already figured it out.

Frank confirmed it anyway. "Angie is bartending at the Royal Palm. She's been there about a week. I heard she's sharing a condo in Delray."

"Sharing a condo with who?" Nick snapped a bit but caught himself once again. *What the fuck is wrong with you? Why should this upset you, and what do you care who Angie's living with? You have Grace, and Angie doesn't owe you any explanations.* Of course this was all true, but even so, Nick was relieved when Frank said she was living with a waitress from the Trattoria.

"Wait a minute," Ralph interjected. "Did you say Anastasia was here? When?"

Nick had to gather himself. Angie would have to wait. The Anastasia situation was more pressing. "This morning. She had a message from Dmitry—about a painting."

That silenced everyone. Nick used the pause in the conversation to pour three shots of Crown, and Ralph finally lit the Montecristo.

RENDER UNTO CAESAR

ATLANTIC CITY, NJ

Then the Pharisees went out and laid plans to trap him in his words. They sent their disciples to him along with the Herodians. "Teacher," they said, "we know that you are a man of integrity and that you teach the way of God in accordance with the truth. You aren't swayed by others, because you pay no attention to who they are. Tell us then, what is your opinion? Is it right to pay the imperial tax to Caesar or not?"

But Jesus, knowing their evil intent, said, "You hypocrites, why are you trying to trap me? Show me the coin used for paying the tax." They brought him a denarius, and he asked them, "Whose image is this? And whose inscription?"

"Caesar's," they replied.

Then he said to them, "So give back to Caesar what is Caesar's, and to God what is God's."

Matthew 22:15-22 (NIV)

Father Gus was *up* for the first time in a long time, and that warm tingle had taken over. The buzz between his ears resonated through his body, down to his groin, and out his fingertips as they massaged a pair of dice that seemed to obey his every command. He was high on adrenaline and invincibility. The single malt scotch barely took the edge off. On this night, he was infallible. *This must be what it feels like to be God,* he thought. That is, if Jesus ever performed "The Miracle at the Craps Table."

The table had become a blur of chips and money. His mind was firing away with calculations, and at the end of the equation lay Shangri-la. He had pressed and parlayed halfway to the promised land. Maybe the change of casino venue had done him good. He didn't feel comfortable playing at the Borgata after the penitent had mentioned it so casually, like he knew his every move. But none of that mattered now. He had been holding the dice for what felt like an eternity and had piled chips onto every number, hardway, and exotic bet with his winnings. His brain computed every outrageously favorable series of events that would get him to the number. *The Number.* That elusive figure that solved all his problems. He would pay back the money to the church, settle up with Andy Boy once and for all, and make his escape from the penitent. And as far as being his brother's keeper, well, he had only one thought about that, and he uttered it as he threw the dice. "Fuck em."

The first die settled on four. In the split second before the second die came to rest, Father Gus prayed his first real prayer in months. In that millisecond, which seemed to contain an eternity, Father Gus repented. *I firmly resolve.*

. . When had it begun? When did he first veer off the path? He had started out so devoutly. He believed it *all* once. At least that's how he remembered it. He would get back to that place, start over, and sin no more. He just needed this one last favor, this one final prayer answered. This one last…miracle.

"When's the last time you witnessed a miracle?" The penitent's words came back to haunt him, and at that precise moment, the second die came up three.

The croupier swept the table clean and sealed Father Gus's fate with a sickening efficiency. Gus stood there in disbelief, but in reality, he knew there was no *Number*. It was the same pathetic bargain every degenerate gambler makes with fate. He could never walk away. He would never win. Because deep in his soul, he knew what he really craved, what every self-loathing compulsive gambler knew for certain; he deserved to suffer. Down deep, he *wanted* to lose.

He staggered away from the table in a daze. As he crossed the casino floor, the superpowers drained from his body. But his hearing was still good enough to detect the progressive jackpot going off. Everyone was gathering around an old woman sitting at a slot machine. Her oxygen tank was tucked neatly in her scooter. The tubes couldn't hide her angelic smile, and in the chaotic lighting, she resembled one of those ridiculous renaissance cherubs in the Basilica. Father Gus looked on in disgust. She reminded him of one of his pathetic parishioners with their annoying confessions. *She'll probably be dead in a week.*

He walked across to the self-parking lot and took the escalator to the roof level. A waning gibbous moon was shining brilliantly, mocking Father Gus's misfortune. He thought of the pagans that worshiped the sun, moon, and stars and wondered, *What makes us any better? We've spun a more intricate tale, that's all.* His resolve to sin no more had waned faster than the orb. He started his car and wheeled around the lot, tires screeching, descending in a spiral until he was ejected into the Atlantic City night.

He had an appointment with the devil, and the devil doesn't appreciate tardiness.

DUCKTOWN

ANGELINA'S RESTAURANT
ATLANTIC CITY, NJ

Father Gus only had to drive a short distance after leaving Caesars to reach Angelina's. He had spent his childhood summers in this part of Atlantic City referred to as Ducktown. It seemed like a wonderland of possibilities back then. Days on the beach blended into nights on the Boardwalk so gently that only a dinner of chicken cutlets and tomato salad marked the sweet transition. Now, venturing any distance from a casino on foot was risky at best in daylight and downright foolhardy at night. Angelina's was one of the few stalwarts that managed to survive, thrive even, in the countless crests and troughs of the sea of misfortunes that continually battered America's Playground. Father Gus shook his head as he turned onto the block where Angelina's was located. He looked for the makeshift parking lot, wondering if it was still there. The lot was poorly lit but safer than parking on the street. It was a tight squeeze as the unofficial "parking attendant" waved him in and guided him into a spot.

"Pull up a little more, boss—ho!" The attendant had a big smile and wore a tattered reflective vest over street clothes. He spoke in a way that suggested a reassuring familiarity, like Father Gus was a regular and parked there once a week. "Nice job, boss. I'll keep an eye on it. Enjoy your dinner." He didn't ask for a tip, but Father Gus knew the drill. Maybe it was a tip, maybe it was extortion. *Was there even a difference?* Father Gus thought as he handed over a five, touching the man's hand in the process and feeling the roughness. He looked at the man's face up close for the first time. He had a scar that extended from his forehead but spared his right eye, which reminded Father Gus of that actor from *The Wire* and *Boardwalk Empire.*

The man saw the look and played along. "Thank you, Father. People round here call me Chalky."

Father Gus was caught off guard. "Do I know—"

Before he finished, Chalky smiled even broader, his grin rivaling the mocking lights of that progressive jackpot. He pointed to the *clergy* placard in the rear window of the Hyundai.

Chalky reached for his phone and watched as Father Gus walked away toward Angelina's. *Enjoy your dinner, boss.* The grin was gone.

Father Gus walked through the front door, which opened to a bar separate from the dining room. He wasn't sure who he was supposed to meet, but the last person he expected to see was Andy Boy and one of his goons sitting at the end of the bar. Andy was in the middle of telling a joke to the bartender and hadn't noticed him walk in. Father Gus turned on his heel, calculating the odds of this being a coincidence as he reached for the door. His hand was on the knob when he heard that unmistakable gravelly voice. "Yo, Padre."

His head dropped forward a few inches as he manufactured the best smile he could muster and turned to face his Lord and Creditor. "Andy!" Father Gus did his best to feign pleasant surprise. Unfortunately, his performance wasn't going to win any awards.

"Don't *Andy* me, get the fuck over here." The joke still hung in the air, and Andy never got to deliver the punchline. Or maybe he did. "Don't tell me—you're here to give communion to some shut-ins. No, that's not it. Last Rites, that's it." The bartender slapped the bar in laughter, and the goon folded his arms over his chest and smirked at Father Gus.

His brain was firing away like he was at the craps table again, but he couldn't come up with a good story to tell Andy. He certainly couldn't tell the truth, that he was here to meet some predator from Boston who was possibly more carnivorous than him. So he did the next best thing; he told a half-truth he knew would upset Andy and therefore have a chance of being believed.

"I was at the casino, Andy. I was trying to win some money so…you know."

Andy grabbed him by the back of the neck, not entirely roughly, more like a father would grab his teenage son. "Sit the fuck down." Andy's hand deposited him on a red Naugahyde stool inches from his own. "Borgata?" He wasn't hollering now; he was whispering in that scratchy way that could be even more sinister. Except he wasn't mad, not especially.

"Nah, Caesars. Figured I'd change my luck."

"Oh yeah? How'd that work out for you?"

"Well, actually I—"

"Stop. We both know how it worked out."

Father Gus just nodded.

"Can you just have a fucking drink like a human being instead of a degenerate for a minute and have a normal conversation with me? Fake it if you have to."

Andy motioned to the bartender. Father Gus ordered a Dewar's and water, while Andy drank a martini with an anchovy garnish.

"I have an idea how you can settle up with me and go forward to sin no more."

Andy nodded to the goon, who took the hint, excused himself to a post at the jukebox, and punched up a few songs. The first tune was "Darlin' Darlin' Baby" by the O'Jays, and it made for an odd soundtrack to the plan Andy laid out. It was risky, and Father Gus sometimes struggled to follow because Andy intentionally left certain parts out. *Still,* Father Gus thought, *it just might work.* It didn't matter anyway; he was out of options.

Andy, for all his bluster, was at his core a practical man. He couldn't remember the last time he actually needed to hurt someone. That was just messy and brought unwanted attention. More importantly, it didn't get you your money. He lived by the advice his mentor had instilled in him all those years ago: *you can shear a sheep many times, but you can only skin him once.*

SLOW LEAK

Father Gus left Angelina's feeling somewhat relieved. The penitent's associate had been a no-show or, more likely, saw him sitting with Andy Boy and decided to scrap the meeting. He hadn't noticed anyone at the bar that fit the bill, but you never can tell. *Fuck him*, Father Gus thought. He had a plan now, and Andy would provide a little cover in the short term—and when you're a con man, the short term is all that matters. He had another thought as well; tomorrow, he was going to find a Gambler's Anonymous meeting. Maybe, in some indirect way, his prayer *had* been heard. He had an inexplicable sense of well-being he hadn't felt in years. He considered walking straight down Georgia Avenue and jumping into the ocean — born again. Instead, he walked the half block to the parking lot, buoyant. His mood soon sunk lower than the deflated rear tire of his Hyundai.

"Ain't that a bitch." Chalky jumped off his barstool perch at Father Gus's approach, as if noticing the flat tire for the first time. "Look like you got a slow leak there, boss." Chalky shook his head and held his chin between his thumb and forefinger. "You got one of them donuts in there? Maybe I could change it for you, get you on the road."

Father Gus looked at the sagging tire. He couldn't remember any leak, but vehicle maintenance wasn't exactly high on his list of priorities. He could hardly recall the last time he changed the oil. "I'm pretty sure there's a spare in there," he said as he popped the trunk with his remote.

Chalky leaned over into the trunk, pulling on the liner that covered the spare tire beneath. He howled a bit as he reached for his lower back with his right hand and eased back out of the trunk, still hunched over. "Motherfucker." Chalky leaned on the bumper and straightened slowly, although not completely erect. "Sorry, boss. Bad back from my football days—AC Vikings. Creeps up on me now and then."

Father Gus looked annoyed as he traded places with Chalky at the trunk. His brief exuberance had been swept away even faster than the dealer had cleared his chips. He leaned over at the waist and reached into the trunk, balancing himself with his left hand and tugging at the liner with his right.

Chalky was still rubbing his lower back when his right hand slipped under the reflective vest, and in one deft move, a barrel was placed with precision at the back of Father Gus's right ear. *Pop*. Father Gus tumbled forward into the trunk. *Pop—pop—pop*. Three more shots followed in quick succession. It wasn't exactly a foreign sound in the neighborhood. Chalky tossed the gun into the trunk and lifted Father Gus's legs, folding the priest in like a beach chair. He slammed the trunk with two gloved hands that Father Gus hadn't even noticed.

"Sorry 'bout that, boss," Chalky whispered over his shoulder as he walked north on Arctic Avenue toward the inlet area of Atlantic City known as Gardner's Basin. The faux columns of Caesars loomed to his right in the distance. An electronic billboard mimicked a giant slot machine. The wheels tumbled in place, reflecting a progressive jackpot. Chalky decided he would treat himself and his lady to a fine meal at Morton's. Then, the next day, he would collect the other half of his payment from the man his North Philly cousin had introduced him to. Reem said he was with the Italians, but Chalky thought the boy looked Irish.

THERE BUT FOR THE GRACE OF GOD GO I

Grace walked up to the Tiki carrying a few bags. She was back a bit early from visiting her mother in West Palm. The trio's conspicuous silence at her approach set off her unerring radar.

"What are you hoodlums up to?"

Nick suppressed a smile. Ralph and Frank answered "nothing" in unison, making them all look even guiltier than they were.

Frank and Ralph rose from their seats to greet her with hugs and kisses. They were decades her senior but treated her with the deference her beauty and wisdom demanded. Even after all these years, Nick continued to be in awe of her. He couldn't believe his luck, knew he didn't deserve her, and suddenly felt pretty guilty about his mini-breakdown over the news about Angie.

Nick stepped out from behind the bar as Grace placed her shopping bags on a stool. She had come bearing gifts, as always. She was never happier than when she was giving someone a gift. He knew little about her childhood, as Grace wasn't one to cry about her rough, poverty-stricken upbringing. As he watched her eyes light up as she handed

Frank an amethyst crystal she had chosen especially for him, Nick glimpsed that little girl on a Christmas morning many years ago, all her disappointment washed away. Grace had converted all that hurt into making those she loved happy, especially Nick. She protested just a little when Nick kissed her and scooped her up in one motion, carrying her to the beach. Ralph blew an approving plume of smoke from the Montecristo, and Frank placed the crystal in his pocket. He watched as his nephew carried his lover to the water's edge, feeling a mixture of pride and satisfaction. His thoughts drifted back to an afternoon many years ago, when Nick was a little boy and he had wiped his tears and handed him a little magical trinket of his own. It was only a rock, but Frank felt sure it contained just as much magic and power as the crystal Grace just handed him. He glanced over at Ralph, who was sitting back on his stool, arms folded over his midsection, the #2 dangling from his lips. Ralph undid his arms and rocked his heft forward. They clicked glasses like proud parents.

Lo spazio tra. That's what Nick's dad, Tony, would call such a moment—the spaces between. One of those fleeting slices of time between the action that contain what really matters in life. They seem to evaporate before you fully appreciate them, but they always come back, sometimes years later. Maybe in a dream or a spell of déjà vu. And just as Frank was thinking all this, Ralph interrupted his reverie with a well-timed, "What the fuck are you looking at?" Frank hadn't realized he'd been staring into Ralph's eyes the whole time. He had been transported back to that day on Mountain Street in 1976 when Ralph The Rifle had cemented his reputation as a neighborhood legend.

"Nothing," Frank responded. He knew Ralph was only joking. As far as Frank was concerned, the legend lived on.

Nick placed Grace down gently on the beach. She had managed to pull off her wedges as Nick carried her, and they dangled from her fingers. Nick's loafers were full of sand, and he turned them upside down and banged them together as they took a seat at the water's edge. They looked out at the cruise ships on the horizon, Nick held her hand, and they were quiet for a while. He enjoyed the break from the action, not to mention he was a bit winded from the effort and needed to catch his breath. *I need to get back in shape.* Nick thought he still looked pretty good for fifty-two, but it got a little tougher every year. He looked over at Grace; she was ageless. Each year seemed to bring out another layer of beauty in her. The faint lines starting to appear on her face only made her appear more exotic; at least, she appeared that way to him. Nick wasn't sure anymore if he believed in God. Sometimes he felt guilty about it. Other times, he figured if there was a God, he should have done a better job at making himself evident. But as he looked over at Grace, Nick felt gratitude for a universe that would bring her to him, and he felt what he guessed people meant when they referred to love. And if there was no God, well, this would have to suffice.

"I saw how you looked at me up at the bar," Grace said. "You don't have to feel sorry for me, Nicky. We've all had sadness in our lives. It's only when we resist the suffering and cling to unhealthy attachments that we become miserable."

"What's that?" Nick asked teasingly. "Buddhism?"

"It's the *truth,* Nick. It doesn't require a label."

Nick no longer wondered how she always seemed to know what he was thinking, but sometimes it still spooked him. *What else does she know*?

"I wonder if he's out there," Nick asked. He was thinking of his father and the ashes he had spread out over the ocean from the jetty in Brigantine. He watched as a wave crept up, flattening and dissipating at their feet. What was left of it slid back down the slant of the shoreline and was swallowed up by the next. Three more waves came and went before Nick answered his own question.

"Sometimes, I think I feel him. I hear him whispering one of his crazy sayings. I used to fight it, now I find myself straining to hear them. I despised those memories, the sad reminders. I think we resist them because they show how far we've strayed from innocence."

Grace listened intently but didn't answer right away. A few more waves passed before she grabbed a handful of sand from behind her. She allowed most of it to run from her hand, like some hourglass on fast-forward, until only a few grains remained.

"How many grains of sand do you think are in my hand?" she asked.

Nick wasn't sure if it was a serious question.

"How many on this beach, in front of your little tiki bar?"

"Millions, I guess," Nick answered.

Grace nodded. "Now, how many in Florida? On the east coast? On the Earth?"

"Billions. Countless."

"Countless," Grace echoed. "And for each grain of sand on Earth, there are ten thousand stars in the sky. Now think of our place in a universe of that size."

"Insignificant," Nick responded.

"No." She leaned forward and locked eyes with him. "That is where you're wrong, my love. We aren't insignificant at all. On the contrary, we are indispensable. Your energy, my energy, your father's—it's all an integral part of that equation. Do you remember what they taught us about energy in school? It is neither created nor destroyed, only transformed from one form to another. Every element of your body, my body, comes from stardust. So when you think of your father, the energy your brain expends to conjure that memory, that is where your father lives. So yes, my love." Grace nodded out toward the horizon. "Your father is out there." She placed her hand on Nick's chest. "And more importantly, he's in here."

BROCCOLI RABE

Andy Boy sat in his warehouse office sorting through the mail that lay scattered across his desk. An envelope partially obscured the headline of the *Philadelphia Inquirer* that read, *Priest Murdered in Suspected Gangland Hit*.

A second-generation huckster, Andy had taken his father's business from a pushcart stand in the Italian Market (still referred to simply as "9th Street" by the locals) and grown it into a medium-sized regional wholesaler. Andy had stood vigil at that outdoor stand throughout his childhood and teen years, frequently next to the boxes of broccoli rabe they were known for. The brand name emblazoned on the boxes, "Andy Boy," became so associated with his presence that it soon became his moniker. Today, almost no one around him was aware of this etymology, save a few old-timers and the federal government. So, he wasn't surprised when a special agent from a branch of said government pressed the buzzer at the loading dock and announced he was there to see Andrea Caposecco.

"What can I do for you?" Andy's gravelly voice sounded even more garbled over the buzzer intercom.

"We just have a few questions," Special Agent O'Connell answered.

"Well, I got nothing to say." Andy couldn't resist adding, "Except you must have your head further up your ass than that reporter from the *Inquirer*."

O'Connell couldn't help smiling at Andy's quip. It was precisely what he expected from the man. Andy was from the old-school, low-key, entirely predictable mold. Which is how O'Connell knew without a shadow of a doubt Andy had nothing to do with the priest's murder. What he did know, however, was that someone had gone through an awful lot of trouble to make it look like he did.

"Andy, I'm not here about the priest—not how you think. This is off the record." He was met by silence. O'Connell gave it some thought. He glanced over at the surveillance camera beneath the loading dock overhang. He knew Andy was watching him. He gestured to his young partner, Special Agent Merriweather, to wait for him in the car. The younger agent begrudgingly complied. O'Connell pressed the buzzer again. "Andy, there's been a credible threat, something we picked up on a wire. We're obliged to make you aware of it. You know the drill."

O'Connell was fibbing a bit. There had been no threat, not recently at least, but he thought it might pique the old-timer's interest. Not because he cared about any danger necessarily, but because Andy might be tempted to figure out who was talking out of school about him. O'Connell's hunch had been correct. The door buzzed and clicked open. He pulled on the steel door, but Andy was already standing in the entryway.

"This is far enough. Tell me what you came here to say."

"If I could just come in for a minute—"

"No way, kid. This ain't a two-way conversation, and I don't want nobody getting the wrong idea. The only way you and I end up in a closed room is if I'm in cuffs." Andy put his hands out in front of him. "So unless you got a pair of bracelets for me, this is as far as we go."

This is my kinda guy, O'Connell couldn't help thinking, letting his admiration leak out just a little. Andy had lived up to all his expectations. *Fuck it*. He decided to take a chance.

"Fuck that priest." O'Connell spat on the loading dock after he said it. "I figure he got what he had coming. Probably diddled the wrong guy's grandson or something." O'Connell was pleased to see that Andy registered a hint of surprise at his remark. He kept going. "And fuck them guys from Boston too." He let the last comment hang in the air, then turned to walk away. The power had shifted.

"Wait a minute," Andy called after him. "What guys from Boston?"

O'Connell extinguished his smile before he turned back to face Andy. One look and he knew he had the old man's interest. O'Connell sensed he was about to cross over a line he might not be able to come back from, but he had already made all the calculations and assessed all the risks. So, O'Connell did what most men with a set of balls would do at that moment—he threw all those calculations and assessments out the window.

"The ones after the painting, Andy. The ones who tried to set you up for Father Gus."

Andy had already written off the money Father Gus owed him. In reality, the priest had paid off the principal long ago. He almost felt bad for him. At least, as bad as you can feel for a degenerate clergyman. But with Father Gus now out of the picture, Andy had lost an important game piece on his board. He needed another pawn.

"Let's take a walk," Andy said. "But just to be clear to you"—Andy gestured with upraised arms and spun in a 180-degree turn—"and to anybody else who might be watching or listening, this ain't no proffer session. I'm strictly listening."

"Understood," O'Connell confirmed.

They walked off the dock and down a one-way street that dead-ended at a weed-strewn field. There, O'Connell told Andy everything he knew about the painting and the Boston crew. Andy occasionally grunted at a significant revelation, and O'Connell took that as a tacit acknowledgment. He asked for nothing in return. O'Connell wasn't interested in hearing what the old man had to say. No, now that he had been bestowed with this newfound knowledge, O'Connell was more interested in watching what Andrea Caposecco would do with it.

JUST ANOTHER DAY IN PARADISE

Nick and Grace walked back to the Tiki, where Grace said her goodbyes to the boys and kissed Nick. She squeezed his hand and held it a second longer than usual as she pulled away.

"Be careful, my love," she said before she headed back to the condo.

Ralph had smoked the Montecristo down to the band, which he carefully stripped off and deposited in a plastic ashtray. Frank was talking to Ashley, one of the new cocktail waitresses. Even from a distance, Nick could see the folded-up hundred in his palm. Vinny was sunning himself at a table outside, legs outstretched, waiting patiently for his next assignment. He didn't have to wait long.

Ralph draped an arm around Nick. "You ready for that talk now?"

"Sure thing. Right after my uncle finishes making a donation."

"A donation to what?"

Nick pointed at his uncle with his chin. "The 'Hot Young Cocktail Waitresses Who Would Never Fuck an Old Man Foundation.'"

Ralph grunted, but had to admire the old man's determination. *Good for you, Frankie*, he thought. *Fortune favors the bold.*

Nick used the old man's gambit as an excuse to linger a few more minutes. Some Philly guys were staying at the resort and had set up camp at the other end of the bar. They had commandeered the jukebox and "It's Gonna Take a Miracle" by the Royalettes had just started. No way Nick was walking out on that tune. He sent a round of drinks over, picked out the loneliest looking guy in the crew, and raised a glass in his direction. Nick's instinct was right. A fat guy stuffed into a Grumpy's Tavern T-shirt reciprocated. At that moment, with those lyrics swimming around in his head and mixing with the alcohol, Nick's resolve began to wane. His brain started making calculations while his heart made justifications. He was on the brink of a relapse, not for drug or drink, but for something just as deadly. They could have driven anywhere to talk, but it suddenly seemed a good idea to head over to the Royal Palm Club. Vinny pulled the car around, and Ralph didn't protest when Nick called out the destination. It was inevitable, he figured, and better they went with him.

"Take the beach," was all Ralph contributed. Ralph avoided the faster albeit less scenic routes these days. Not long ago, he had chided Frank for the same quirk. *Maybe I am getting old*, the sixty-four-year-old thought to himself.

Nick brought them up to speed about Anastasia's visit on the ride up to Boca, but he was having trouble focusing. He noticed he had a couple of missed calls and a text from Gary. *Give me a call. Somebody came by to see you.*

Suddenly, I'm a pretty popular guy, Nick thought.

Frank used the time to do a little texting of his own, first to Denroy, a doorman at the Royal Palm Club and a trusted confidante in the Tasker Morris Brain Trust sphere of influence.

What's up, Frankie? You coming over?

Be there in a half hour, nephew. Who's working the beach bar?

Knuckles and Fritzie. You need something?

Frank sighed, satisfied Angie wasn't working and relieved that he didn't need to come up with some diversion to delay Nick's inevitable collision with Angie Romano, who was more a towering inferno than an old flame. Frank might have lost a few steps, but he was still nimble enough to realize Nick needed time to elapse between his revelation about Angie and some half-assed reunion. Down deep, Nick realized this too, but the song had put him over the edge. He had come to recognize music as a kind of trigger and sometimes joked he would be the first guy to check into rehab for an R&B addiction. *Hi, my name is Nick, and I'm an audioholic.*

All good, nephew. See you soon, Frank texted Denroy back. Denroy responded with a brown thumbs-up emoji, and Frank settled back in his seat. He closed his eyes, satisfied that he had averted a clash of the titans for one more day. His nephew needed time. *I took care of that*, Frank thought. Nick also needed to get drunk. *I can definitely help him with that*, Frank concluded.

"What the fuck are you smiling about?" Nick asked.

"Nothing, Nicky, just grateful for another day in paradise."

"Fucking psycho," Ralph quipped as he stared out the passenger window. Palm trees and gilded mansion gates whizzed by as they made their way north on A1A to Boca. They weaved their way through Deerfield and caught the bridge at Camino Real. Nick used the time to text Gary.

Yo, Big Man. Call you in a few. Everything okay?

Yeah. For now. But I think you need to get up here. It's about a painting.

I should have known, Nick thought. He stared across the Intracoastal at the Royal Palm Club and his attention shifted. *What the hell is Angie doing here?*

The bridge closed and they crossed over. The guard at the Royal Palm Club gate recognized Ralph in the front seat, but Frank never missed a chance to flash his card. The membership was a little perk Ralph and the Tasker Morris boys had bestowed upon him after his help recovering "The Prodigal of Passyunk Avenue."

Denroy greeted them at the door with a big smile and a conspiratorial wink directed at Frank. Ralph palmed him a hundred, and Frank placed a Padron Anniversario in his breast pocket, securing it with a gentle pat. Nick had that old, sick feeling in his stomach like a softball lodged below his heart. He rubbed at the spot involuntarily, as if massaging it would make it go away.

"You okay, Nick?" Vinny asked. "Can I get you a water or something?"

"Thanks, Vinny. I'm okay. I could use a drink, that's all."

Denroy came jogging to catch up with Frank. "I almost forgot. I've been holding this for you. You dropped it sometime ago, and I picked it up. Then I heard you were in Philly and had a heart attack. I recited the prayer for you every day. I've been meaning to return it to you."

Frank held the St. Michael prayer card and ran his thumb over the familiar creases where the lamination had come apart over the years. He handed it back to Denroy.

"You hold it, nephew. I was meant to drop it, and you were meant to pick it up."

Denroy didn't argue. He tucked it next to the Padron, clasped his hands in front of him, and bowed a little. "Thank you, uncle. I knew you would come back in one piece."

"Well, then you had more faith than I did," Frank quipped. He kissed Denroy on the cheek and increased his shuffle to catch up with the crew.

"You done playing kissy-face with Bob Marley?" Ralph jabbed.

"Fuck you. Denroy's a good kid. Better than them stumblebums that hang around your shithole bar," Frank shot back a bit too touchy.

Ralph cut a side-eye at him and mumbled out the side of his mouth in a machine gun cadence meant to be heard only by Frank. "You wanna fuck my girl, that's one thing, but don't bad-mouth my bar."

Ralph was a bit sensitive when it came to Blaine's Tavern. It was the first business he had acquired when he came to Florida from Philly. For a man not prone to emotional attachments, he was more than a little sentimental about Blaine's. It was where he went to be alone, to commune with an old version of himself that no longer existed, to touch a bar that didn't seem like it was created for a theme park.

Frank worried he had gone a bit too far, but then Ralph draped his arm around his old friend as they walked out into the sun of the Royal Palm Beach Club, and for a moment, they were teenagers on the street corner again and everything was right in the world.

Nick could only wish he felt the same.

CARAVAGGIO

On Herod's birthday, the daughter of Herodias danced for the guests and pleased Herod so much that he promised with an oath to give her whatever she asked. Prompted by her mother, she said, "Give me here on a platter the head of John the Baptist." The king was distressed, but because of his oaths and his dinner guests, he ordered that her request be granted and had John beheaded in the prison. His head was brought in on a platter and given to the girl, who carried it to her mother. John's disciples came and took his body and buried it. Then they went and told Jesus.

Matthew 14: 6-12 (NIV)

Scotty walked to the kitchen section of the loft and made himself a double espresso. He looked around at a house that had stopped feeling like home now that Jilly's booming voice no longer filled the empty spaces. The intruder had left their home feeling violated. It wasn't the theft so much as the fact someone had wandered around their space uninvited, touching the items carefully collected over a lifetime. More than material things, the intruder had robbed Scotty of the residual intimacy that had lingered after Jilly's death. Try as he might, he could not remove the blemish. Like a canvas that had been painted over, the ghost image would always remain lurking beneath.

Scotty stood at his workstation and gazed at a blank canvas. He ran his fingers over the badger hair brushes he handmade specifically for his craft. The priceless ancient pigments still sat dutifully on a shelf, thankfully untouched. The lapis lazuli, cinnabar, and lead white were as valuable as the paintings themselves. Next to them was a container of a substance composed of phenol formaldehyde, once known as Bakelite. It was instrumental to his craft. The thief had displayed a lack of sophistication in skipping over these items, which partially explained his ultimate blunder.

Scotty first learned of Bakelite's use by the famed Dutch forger Han van Meegeren. During the German occupation of the Netherlands, van Meegeren sold a "Vermeer," *Christ with the Adulteress*, to Reichsmarschall Hermann Göring, the notorious Nazi looter of priceless works of art. After the war, it was recovered from a salt mine, along with other Dutch cultural treasures. Van Meegeren was charged with aiding and abetting the enemy, charges that were later dropped after he was able to prove the painting was not a Vermeer but a van Meegeren. He was convicted of forgery and fraud but became a Dutch national hero for scamming the Nazis. Van Meegeren died before serving his sentence.

Like Scotty, van Meegeren had been rejected by an art world that had become obsessed with cubism and disdainful of the Renaissance style of the Old Masters. Both men also suffered under fathers who mocked their sons' interest in painting and used it as fuel for relentless abuse. The mental abuse and beatings only served to steel Scotty's resolve. Even as his father's belt was in mid-arc, he would fix his eyes on an item in the room—any inanimate object would do—and compose a still life in his mind, planning it down to the brush stroke and plotting his escape. Each lash of the belt formed a layer of varnish that, while obscuring the masterpiece beneath, ultimately served only to preserve it.

Scotty was suddenly possessed by a burning desire to create an original piece. Well, mostly original. His analytical ruminations about a way out of his predicament merged with his creative force, joining to form a rough sketch of a composition. His thoughts wandered to Caravaggio, the tortured genius of Rome. His troubled personal life, filled with endless brawling and duels, culminated with his murder of Ranuccio Tommasoni, a notorious gangster from a powerful Roman family. The dispute was rumored to be over Fillide Melandroni, a Roman prostitute who modeled for Caravaggio. Tommasoni was her pimp, but to Caravaggio, she embodied all the beauty and innocence of the Madonna. He portrayed her in many of his paintings, sometimes as a saint, other times as a courtesan. The tension between the sacred and the profane became a hallmark of his paintings. That tension vibrated across centuries and found frequency in Scotty's soul.

Caravaggio had been forced to flee Rome and spent the rest of his life in exile after being sentenced to beheading, a sentence that could be executed by any sword-wielding citizen. He fled to Naples, then Malta and Sicily. He continued to produce paintings in exile, hoping to win the favor of powerful patrons who would procure a papal pardon for him. Many images portrayed biblical scenes of beheadings wherein Caravaggio depicted his own face on the severed head. Perhaps it was his twisted sense of humor, a desperate attempt at levity, or a gory plea to spare his life. He never received the pardon. It was from this painful story Scotty found inspiration for the piece.

Scotty assembled his tools and fetched three items that would serve as source material for the subjects of his painting. One was a painting gifted to him by his friend and fellow painter Virgil Corrado. The subject was a hauntingly beautiful woman sitting alone at a sidewalk table and raising a glass to an empty seat. The painting was framed in pink cherry blossom trees and was titled *Sakura*. The second item was a photo taken of him and Jilly a few years ago at Caffé Vecchio. It was New Year's Eve, and they had decided to celebrate at the Caffé. Jilly had been friends with the late owner, Anthony Di Nobile. It must have been taken seconds before the clock struck twelve. A large African American man Scotty recognized from the neighborhood stood in the foreground. In the background, congregating at the bar, were a group of revelers. A female figure stood out, her face bathed in a light intruding through the front window. Scotty couldn't be sure, but it appeared to be the momentary flash of fireworks exploding on the Avenue. It made her face glow like Titian's *Venus of Urbino*. He was certain she was the same woman painted by Virgil in his *Sakura*. The sheer coincidence should have blown him away, but Scotty had come to accept the mystical as commonplace in both art and life. He believed, like many, there was no such thing as coincidence. Next to her was a man Scotty never met but knew by reputation. It was the same man he'd gone seeking earlier at Caffé Vecchio; the man Jilly had always told him to go see if things ever went sideways.

Scotty opened a book of Caravaggio paintings, the third source item he needed, to the page displaying *Salome with the Head of John the Baptist*. As he began to make a preliminary sketch, looking back and forth between the photo, the book, and Virgil's painting, an idea started to form.

Scotty went to the massive walk-in closet, which was the size of a guest bedroom, walked to the back of the closet and selected a raucous, vintage Versace shirt that Jilly loved to wear. He rubbed the fabric to his cheek and clenched his eyelids shut. He hadn't been able to bring himself to pack up Jilly's belongings, and the collection of shirts was displayed as a memorial. Scotty parted them like a curtain and placed his thumb on the fingerprint sensor hidden behind the shoe rack. A hidden door, which encompassed the entire rear wall, clicked open and Scotty gazed lovingly at the framed treasure secreted within. A spotlight triggered by the door's opening brought the figures to life.

A plan took shape. Like Caravaggio in exile, he would paint his own profane masterpiece for a powerful patron.

But unlike Caravaggio, he sought neither riches nor pardon. Scotty began to laugh uncontrollably.

He returned to his workstation with the canvas, took it out of its frame, and began to paint. The image that emerged was a familiar one, except he inserted the likeness of Virgil's woman, the same goddess from the Caffé Vecchio photo, as Salome. To Scotty, the singular most chilling aspect of the Caravaggio was neither the stern gaze of the executioner nor the overt blood and gore, but rather the indifference on Salome's face—eyes averted, like a little girl already tired of a new toy. The Baptist's head had scarcely been placed upon the platter, yet her visage displayed the unique combination of equal parts disgust and boredom.

Scotty focused his attention on the macabre subject matter of the painting. He applied his brushstrokes effortlessly, like Michael Jordan making a layup. The head on the platter gradually began to take on the unmistakable likeness of Nick Di Nobile.

The emptiness left by Jilly's death, the invasion of their sanctuary, a lifetime of ridicule all began to fade away and was replaced by another sensation. Like a double shot of Don Julio 1942, the fiery burn gave way to a warm, comforting glow in his belly—the exquisitely delicious taste of revenge.

THE WIZARD OF SOPPRESSATA

"No thief, however skillful, can rob one of knowledge, and that is why knowledge is the best and safest treasure to acquire."

L. Frank Baum, *The Lost Princess of Oz*

The benefactor pulled away from the curb. There was nothing left to be accomplished that day, so he drove back to the cheese shop. The shingle hanging above the store was identical to the script on the side of the Sprinter van: *Scopa Italian Specialties, Fine Cheeses and Meats.* The shop's phone number began with 465, but the weathered sign retained the original HO5, pronounced "Howard Five." Nino saw no reason to change it, and in fact had it replicated on the side of the van. It was more a testament to stubborn pride than an attempt to be quaint. The sign had endured over the years, weathering the seasons like a stubborn anachronism, standing watch over Passyunk Avenue—just like Nino. Occasionally, an "influencer," new to the neighborhood, would take a selfie in front of the sign and post it along with a pithy hashtag, racking up thousands of "likes."

A small bell situated over the door rang as he entered his sanctuary. He strolled among the hanging soppressata and provolone. Gloria, his longtime assistant, was at the counter waiting on Vincenza, a neighborhood woman who had been shopping there since Nino opened the doors some forty years ago. She greeted him warmly, and Nino reached behind the counter for a bottle of his homemade wine. He pushed into her hands, even as she resisted.

"Buona Pasqua, Jenny." Nino called her the name she was known by in grade school, making her blush. He remembered what a beauty she was as a teenager, and when she smiled, he could still see her standing in the schoolyard, brushing the hair away from her face.

Where the fuck has the time gone? It was a question Nino asked himself more frequently these days. It gave him a newfound sense of urgency in his affairs, especially concerning a certain painting. He bid Jenny farewell and nodded toward Gloria as he retired to the back room, indicating that he would now be available for visitors. Each afternoon, Nino would entertain several visitors. Some needed help with a traffic ticket, others maybe a zoning issue, and still others required a short-term loan. Nino charged only modest interest, never made a loan of more than $500, and if the borrower failed to pay, he simply never lent to them again. He held no formal city government position, and what separated him from those who did was one significant difference; he got things done.

Nowadays, Nino spent a lot of time trying to forget things, or at least pretending he didn't remember. The past hurt too much, so he did a good deal of shoulder shrugging, sometimes accompanied by a *"Whaddaya gonna do?"* When a meeting ran too long or became uncomfortable, he simply rose from his chair, retrieved a small parting gift—some olives, maybe a small soppressata—and gently steered the supplicant toward the door in a way that seemed so natural they didn't realize what was happening until the little bell rang again and they were standing outside, clutching salumi. Then Nino would retreat to the back room and perform his magic. He acted on each request immediately so he didn't have to remember anything. He would unfurl a rubber band from a stack of business cards the size of a small brick and locate the right one. Sometimes the individual was no longer at the number, and Nino retired the card. When the right connection was made, he recited some secret phrase or ancient incantation until the supplicant's problem was usually solved. The oblation would come later, sometimes not for years. Next to the stack of business cards was another, more solemn brick. This one was composed of prayer cards from funerals Nino had attended. In the last few years, it had swelled to a size that rivaled its mate. Nino had made a vow to himself a long time ago—when the prayer card brick eclipsed the business card brick, he would close shop. He estimated he was about fifty prayer cards away.

Nino flipped through the business cards until he found the one he was looking for. Old and yellowed, the corners were soft and splitting. Nino smiled at the memory of his old friend as he peered down at the card through his bifocals. Caffé *Vecchio, Anthony Di Nobile – Proprietor*. He glanced over at the brick of prayer cards but resisted the temptation to retrieve Tony's card. Still, he said a brief, silent prayer, made the sign of the cross and kissed his fingers to the sky at its conclusion.

Gloria appeared in the doorway. "You okay, baci?"

Gloria and Nino called each other *baci.* It was their special term of endearment. A little code between secret lovers, although it was the worst kept secret in the neighborhood. There was no reason to pretend anymore. Nino's wife had passed away fifteen years ago, and the children were grown and had moved away. None of them had any interest in working in the cheese shop, and Nino couldn't blame them. Still, they both clung to the clandestine nature of their affair, despite its transparency and the neighborhood's indifference.

"I'm fine, baci. I just need to make a call. I'm thinking we'll go out to eat tonight. Somewhere on the Avenue."

Gloria rolled her eyes a bit. She could never get Nino off the Avenue. She made a smoochy sound with her lips and turned. Nino smooched an air kiss back. *Maybe one day I'll sell the shop and we'll move somewhere far away*, he thought. Gloria would laugh if he said it out loud, but more and more these days, he was starting to mean it.

His ability to make problems disappear, solve neighborhood disputes, and help a needy family celebrate Christmas was why although everyone called him Mr. Nino to his face, out in the neighborhood, he was referred to by a loftier title. Whispered over backyard fences and invoked *sotto voce* from barstool to barstool, it was spoken with reverence and without a trace of sarcasm. When someone needed something "fixed" in South Philadelphia, there was only one person they needed to see. He lived above the cheese shop on Passyunk Avenue—Nino Scopa, *The Wizard of Soppressata.*

NON-FUNGIBLE TOKENS

Nick lagged behind the crew to check his phone. Gary had texted again, and Grace had forwarded an inspirational Instagram post. As he thumbed through the messages, he heard someone call his name from a poolside cabana.

"Yo, Nicky!"

Nick turned to see Brett Cole waving him over. He glanced over at the Royal Palm Beach Bar, steeling himself for the image that might await him there. He let out a breath he hadn't realized he was holding as he saw Ralph shaking hands with Fritzie and Knuckles behind the bar. There was no sign of Angie. He couldn't decide if he was relieved or disappointed, and suddenly he felt like getting really fucked up.

Brett was a nice enough guy. A bit socially awkward maybe, but essentially a decent fellow. He had sold some software start-up for enough cash and stock options to keep him knee-deep in Bugattis for the rest of his life. He'd tried to explain it to Nick—something about an algorithm—but the more detail he went into, the less Nick understood. And even though his unborn grandchildren would never fly commercial, there remained a distinct sadness about Brett. Despite all his wealth and the trappings that went along with it, down deep he was still a kid on the playground, desperately waiting for someone to pick him for their team.

"How's it going, Nicky? Can I pour you a drink?" Brett gestured toward a bottle of 1942.

"I'm good, Brett. Good to see you. Sure, why not."

Brett poured Nick a generous measure.

"To the algorithm," Nick said.

Brett liked Nick's toast and clicked Nick's glass. "The algorithm."

They drank, and Brett pulled up a seat for him.

Ralph looked over from the bar and gave him a little shoulder shrug as if to say, *What the fuck are you doing*? Nick waived and gestured with a finger to indicate he would be over in a minute.

Brett had multiple laptops set up in the cabana. One was open to a page displaying what looked like a stock chart. The other screen seemed a bit incongruous and featured what could best be described as a group of cartoon characters, rather amateurishly drawn.

"What's this, another algorithm?" Nick asked.

"Not exactly, but it's related. Have you ever heard of an NFT?"

"NFT? I don't think so. What is it, a stock symbol?"

"No, it stands for non-fungible token. It's the future, Nicky. It's going to be bigger than cryptocurrency."

"That stuff is out of my league, Gates." Everyone at the club—most people in Boca for that matter—called Brett "Gates," as in Bill Gates. He seemed to like it.

"No, it's not. See this?" He pointed to one of the characters. "I sold one last month for three million."

Nick took another sip of Don Julio and paused for a second to gauge whether Brett was fucking with him. "You're not joking, are you?"

"I never joke about money, Nicky, you know that."

Nick knew that to be true, still, he couldn't understand what exactly Gates meant. "I'm not sure I get it. What did you sell? Where is it?"

"I sold the image, a jpeg."

"A jpeg? Couldn't anyone just copy it? Then they would own it."

"No, they wouldn't. Not the original. Blockchain technology assures that. Anyone can copy it, but the original can't be replicated. Unlike traditional art, it's forgery proof. That's the beauty of it."

"I'm sorry, you lost me. This is more confusing than the algorithm."

Brett laughed. "Don't feel bad. You're not alone. In fact, some people refer to it as a non-*explainable* token. This part you'll appreciate, though. Someone recently sold an NFT painting for sixty-nine million."

"Sixty-nine million? For a jpeg?"

"I'm buying one now, Nicky. You want a piece?"

"Too rich for my blood, Gates."

Nick finished his drink and gave Brett a friendly parting hug, then walked out of the cabana and into the sunlight. He waved back at Brett, feeling good that he spent some time with him. He knew what it was like to be lonely, unwanted even. Gates had no shortage of hangers-on and leeches but few real friends. *That's the curse of outrageous fortune*, Nick thought.

Gates hollered after him, his finger hovering over his laptop's touchpad. "You're in for a hundred thousand, Nick. If we lose, I'll cover. But we ain't losing."

Nick laughed and threw Gates a reverse peace sign over his shoulder, unsure whether he was serious.

When he arrived at the bar, Vinny had the music turned up and the Main Ingredient was singing about "Rolling Down a Mountainside." Nick took a seat between Ralph and Frank. Fritzie poured him a 1942 with an Amstel Light behind it. He was ready to finish telling them about Anastasia's visit, and Gary's text.

Back at the cabana, Gates executed a few clicks to the tune of five hundred thousand dollars, and just like that, Nick Di Nobile owned twenty percent of an NFT painting without even knowing it.

BENEVOLENT ORBS

"Why are we even getting involved in this?" Joey asked.

Gary looked at him for a long time before answering. "I didn't say we are. But we need to run it by Nick."

Joey walked behind the bar, took two Peronis out of the beer box and opened them, placing one in front of Gary before taking a swig.

"You got a problem with that?" Gary asked. He was plumbing the depths of those deep-set eyes for the truth before Joey could respond. Lately, as Joey had grown, becoming sharper, craftier, Gary would imagine he was talking to Nick at that age all over again. Joey had all of Nick's charisma and confidence, along with an additional trait Gary could only attribute to Jimmy Musante—the father who'd died before Joey was born. He hadn't decided yet whether it was a gift or a curse, but in addition to that big, beautiful heart, Joey possessed a characteristic he'd neither asked for nor knew precisely how to manage. When the situation required it, Joey could be unflinchingly ruthless.

Joey crossed necks with Gary's Peroni like the swords of two musketeers.

"No problem at all."

Gary stood abruptly, causing his stool to teeter for a moment, then swept up the Peroni in a beefy palm and shuffled swiftly toward the jukebox. For a big man who wasn't getting any younger, Joey never stopped marveling at his speed and grace.

"Good, now we can play some songs." Gary stood before the jukebox and nodded at Joey to indicate he had honors. "Call it, kid."

Joey thought about it for a second as he looked over at Big Gary, who was as much an uncle to Joey as Nick. Joey trusted him with his life and had lost count of the times he'd saved him from one scrape or another. He thought about it carefully, all the while looking at Gary's face bathed in the jukebox light; he looked like a figure in one of Tony Di Nobile's many paintings that still lined the Caffé—weathered but dignified.

"Zoom," Joey finally called out, a song by Fat Larry's Band, an underground South Philly favorite from 1982 that had done pretty well in the UK and Australia. The group had another local hit with "Act Like You Know," a song that found success many years later on a soundtrack to the video game *Grand Theft Auto: Vice City*.

Gary smiled, appreciating the call. He knew Joey meant it as a nod of respect and deference. Joey walked over and draped a lanky arm over Gary's shoulder. The two of them let the song pour over them like warm maple syrup. They took turns picking out the rest of the set.

That was the power of Caffé Vecchio. It set its own agenda and didn't like being rushed. The paintings that stood as guardians around its perimeter demanded careful deliberation and exacted a hefty price for haste. The jukebox worked in conjunction with the paintings as a sort of hourglass, counting off the requisite time before one embarked on a mission, whether it concerned treasure, a woman, or an adventure. This latest mission promised to involve all three.

"Something I been meaning to talk to you about," Gary said once they were seated back at the bar with fresh beers, having made their offerings to the gods of R&B.

"Shoot."

"I can't help noticing the place has changed a little since I been away tending to my health."

"Changed how?"

"Let's just say the atmosphere seems a bit edgier."

"It's always been edgy, even back when I first started DJing here. I remember Tony saying something about that being the secret sauce that kept people coming back." Joey was getting a little defensive, and Gary sensed it.

"I hear you, and you ain't wrong. But that's a fine line you straddlin." Gary cocked his head toward the jukebox and pointed his finger skyward, as if the music was being pumped in from the heavens. And with Stevie Wonder singing "As," maybe it was. "You hear that?"

"Hear what?"

"Exactly," Gary responded cryptically.

"I don't get it." Joey turned to the bar and sipped his beer, betraying the impatience of his youth.

"That's my point—you don't get it. What you *don't* hear is just as important as what you *do*."

"So?" Joey responded weakly, knowing a lecture was coming. Secretly, he was looking forward to it. Like every fatherless boy, Joey both resisted and embraced the wisdom that came from the father figures who orbited around him. Some hovered reliably as the moon, others hurtled by like asteroids, threatening an impact that never materialized.

Gary, like Nick, and Tony before him, was a benevolent orb of the first type, bringing order to Joey's occasionally chaotic universe. The goodness inside him rose and fell like a King Tide, depending on his proximity.

"What you're listening to is the musical equivalent of restraint. Stevie's holding back, making you want to hear more. Something Tony used to call "the spaces between." He ain't filling up this song with a bunch of unnecessary notes and shit. He's giving your brain the room to fill in the gaps for yourself. Just like Tony cooked these recipes, not all heavy-handed with the spices." Gary swung his arm around to take in the paintings. "Just like these guys were stingy with they strokes."

The big man stood up. Joey spun on his stool to face him, thinking he knew what was coming next. Gary didn't disappoint. He stuck out his thumbs, pointing them at his chest as he began to gyrate in time to the song. "Just like this guy makes love."

Joey suppressed a laugh, feigning disgust. "That ain't something I really want to think about. You had me at the paintings. Continue."

Gary kept dancing, a little more subdued but pretty smooth. His moves displayed the very economy he was waxing about. "What I'm trying to say is people come here for the food and maybe to brush up against a little sense of danger—not to actually *be* in danger. So maybe pull back on the whole social club vibe and have your crew give up their seats at the bar for customers—especially *new* customers. Capisce?"

"Capisce," Joey answered, knowing Gary was referencing a recent Yelp review. A suburban family had turned on their heels, abandoning their reservation after feeling like they "... had wandered into the Ravenite, circa 1990."

As the song built to its crescendo, Gary slid sideways back to his stool, gliding gracefully along the black and white checkerboard tile, his lesson and his dance routine punctuated by a double clap as he reclaimed his seat in perfect time to the music.

THE THORN

ROYAL PALM BEACH BAR, BOCA RATON

Nick wasn't sure if he was disappointed or relieved Angie wasn't working that day at the Royal Palm. He took a sip of his 1942 and conjured up an image of her behind the bar, reaching into the beer cooler, shaking up martinis, the sun peeking under the thatched roof and sparkling in her eyes.

"Yo, Nick." Ralph snapped his fingers like an impatient hypnotist and ended Nick's trance. "That's the second time today. You're starting to remind me of a guy that used to hang around the Paradise back in the day. He was always gazing off like he was somewhere else. Then, one day he just froze up like that. We had to check him into Hall-Mercer on an involuntary hold. After that, he was never the same. Started singing the same song over and over again on a loop." Ralph looked over to Frank for confirmation. "You remember the guy?"

"Johnny. Johnny Spells, we called him. I don't remember his real name, but I remember the song—'Hello Stranger' by Barbara Lewis. I still can't hear that song without thinking about that sorry fuck. Last I heard, I think he stepped in front of a bus."

"That's a beautiful story, gents," Nick said. "Thanks for sharing. I'm fine though and there's no buses around here."

The Royal Palm Beach Bar was a kind of upscale tiki bar. If Nick's Tuscan Tiki was ever replicated in Epcot, it would look something like the Royal Palm. Despite their differences in net worth, their respective guests were basically the same. They were all players in the same drama. The Royal Palm was simply a swankier stage. Nick was having a hard time coming up with a plausible series of events that would bring Angie here. Although he had no reason to expect otherwise, he was a little hurt that she had moved thirty miles up the beach and hadn't so much as texted him. He was consciously aware of the negative influence attachments had throughout his life, and Angie had always been the hardest attachment to let go of. The Avenue back in Philly ran a close second.

"So, what did she have to say?" Frank returned to the subject of Anastasia.

"It's about the other Rembrandt," Nick answered.

"The one with the boat?"

"*Christ in the Storm on the Sea of Galilee*. Anastasia said Dmitry located it, supposedly in Philly."

"Naturally," Ralph chimed in. "It probably never left. I heard rumors over the years, but it was mostly bullshit. Some lowlife trying to be relevant, claiming he saw it in some warehouse or shipping container. I even remember some bar rag claiming she saw it in some church basement."

"Uh, that last one might not have been far off the mark," Nick said.

"What's that supposed to mean?" Frank asked.

"Anastasia mentioned something about a sexton."

"What's that, some kind of stripper?"

"If it was, *you* would know." Ralph threw a lemon wedge at Frank.

"It's someone who works for a church doing maintenance, repairs, cleaning. Anastasia said the painting was stashed in a church in Philly for years until a sexton recognized it and helped himself to it."

"Did she happen to mention who this guy was?" Ralph asked.

"No, just that he lived near the Avenue and someone had broken into his house recently."

"Dmitry?" Frank asked.

"No, that's the problem. Someone else knows about the painting, someone just as rich and powerful as Dmitry."

"Who's richer than Dmitry?" Frank shrugged in a show of skepticism, but Ralph had already figured it out.

"The guys that wear sheets."

"The KKK?" Frank asked.

Ralph looked at Nick and turned his palms up. "You see what I have to deal with? No, you fucking lunatic. Not the KKK, the guys with the oil."

Knuckles put an iced bucket of Peronis on the bar and popped open three, placing them on coasters. Vinny had made his way over to a lounge chair and sunned himself like he didn't have a care in the world.

"So what's this all mean to us," Frank asked.

Nick answered for Ralph. "It means maybe Dmitry has competition."

"What else does that tell you, my young friend?" Ralph asked, engaging Nick in the Socratic tutelage he reserved only for worthy protégés. Nick thought about it for a second. If Dmitry was no longer the biggest, baddest bully on the playground, it had a number of ramifications for Nick, Ralph, and the rest of the Tasker Morris Brain Trust. Nick tried to seize on the most salient of these. Finally, he concluded, "It means he needs us more than ever, maybe even more than we need him."

It was precisely that power shift Ralph was referring to, and he raised a toast to Nick's critical thinking.

"Exactly," he said as he took a fresh Montecristo from his breast pocket and lit it with the S.T. Dupont lighter Dmitry had given him. Ralph respected Dmitry and would never think of double-crossing him. The Russian had never done anything to deserve such disloyalty. More importantly, it simply wasn't in Ralph's makeup. What did enter Ralph's mind was another angle, a dangerous gambit that would require discipline, deception, and a great deal of risk.

"One of us has to pretend we've gone over to the other side," Ralph said.

"What? No way, Ralph. I've stuck my neck out plenty already. Plus, no one would buy it," Nick responded.

"Don't underestimate yourself, Nicky. But I wasn't talking about you." And with that, both men turned to look at Frank, who suddenly looked like he had lost his hard-earned tan.

"No way. I'm too old."

"That's exactly why it's *gotta* be you, you fucking desperado," Ralph said. "You go back home and make a side deal."

"Side deal with who? I don't know no fucking *Arabs*." Frank pronounced it with a long A.

"No, but you do know the De Rosas," Ralph said.

"There are no De Rosas left in South Philly; I saw to that." Frank couldn't help boasting.

"That's where you're wrong, Frankie. The Rose had a nephew."

"He did?" Nick interjected. "I never heard of any nephew."

"None of us did," Ralph answered. "He's some fucking blueberry farmer from Hammonton, but ever since The Rose was kind enough to shoot himself in the eye, this kid's been strutting around the city like some delusional heir apparent. He's managed to put together a half-ass crew of third-string castoffs and some cowboy from Boston. So now he thinks he's the Prince of Passyunk Avenue. Some website reporters started calling him 'The Thorn,' and apparently, he likes the name. Fuckin world's upside down when the street follows the internet."

Frank nodded. "Lot of money in them blueberries."

Ralph stared at him for a good five seconds while retrohaling the Cuban smoke. "That's what you take out of this? The kid's not an actual farmer, you fucking wacko, it's a figure of speech."

How the fuck does he know all this shit? It was a question Nick found himself pondering more frequently these days, but he knew better than to question the veracity of Ralph's intel or his sources. If a dog took a shit on Passyunk Avenue, Ralph knew about it in Boca before the turd turned cold.

"What can I tell you, Ralph?" Nick said. "Sometimes life imitates art."

"I'd hardly call what that reporter writes art," Ralph snarled.

I don't know, Nick thought. *Some of that stuff is pretty good writing*. He wisely kept that thought to himself.

Frank downed what was left of his glass of 1942. He wasn't sure what The Rose's nephew had to do with any Arabs, but a lifetime of impulsiveness in pursuit of elusive glory caused a switch to flick in his head. "Okay, fuck it. What's our first move?"

Nick had forgotten for a moment just how brave his uncle could be. He admired him for it, even though he knew it was driven mainly by desperation.

"First thing we do, "Ralph said, "is go to Home Depot."

"Home Depot?" Nick looked puzzled. "For what?"

Ralph and Frank shared a brief conspiratorial smirk at Nick's expense for not sniffing out the old joke. Ralph threw a beefy arm around Frank's neck and hugged him roughly while answering Nick's question.

"To pick up a wheelbarrow for this old hoodlum to push his balls around in."

Nick laughed, and the three men clinked the necks of their Peronis.

"Whaddya say we get out of this dump and head over to a respectable bar?"

Ralph was referring to his old dive bar, Blaine's Tavern. A dark bar sounded like a pretty good option to Nick, especially since he had finally convinced Ralph to install a jukebox in the place. He was tired of thinking about Anastasia's visit, the painting, and what increasingly seemed like an inevitable trip back to the city. He was looking forward to continuing his day in a drearier setting, one more conducive to his sentimental mood. A nice, dark cave to visit with old demons and conjure old hurts anew.

"Vinny!" Ralph barked, rousing him out of his sun-worshipping slumber. "Make sure the car's out front."

Vinny jogged ahead, and the three of them sauntered along the perimeter of the pool. They must have made for a curious sight to the unsuspecting vacationers peering at them cautiously over the top of their downturned sunglasses. Three distinct versions of South Philly aristocracy plopped down in the middle of South Florida opulence.

OCCAM'S RAZOR

That day when evening came, he said to his disciples, "Let us go over to the other side." Leaving the crowd behind, they took him along, just as he was, in the boat. There were also other boats with him. A furious squall came up, and the waves broke over the boat, so that it was nearly swamped. Jesus was in the stern, sleeping on a cushion. The disciples woke him and said to him, "Teacher, don't you care if we drown?"

He got up, rebuked the wind and said to the waves, "Quiet! Be still!" Then the wind died down and it was completely calm.

He said to his disciples, "Why are you so afraid? Do you still have no faith?"

They were terrified and asked each other, "Who is this? Even the wind and the waves obey him!"

Mark 4:35-41 (NIV)

Scotty first started working at the Basilica in 1997. It was a pretty good job for him, considering that Jilly covered all their expenses. The couple owned quite a bit of real estate, including the building that housed their loft. For Scotty, it was something to do during the day and made him feel good about having some spending money jingling in his pocket. Mainly, he could save up for vacations with which he would surprise Jilly. He enjoyed being around the church, tending to the furnishings, statues, and paintings. The irony was not lost upon him that he cared for a church that technically excluded him, but his connection transcended dogma. He attended mass and received communion daily, finding an odd comfort in the rituals and relics. For an agnostic, he was a pretty good Catholic.

One of his duties as a sexton was to catalog and maintain the sizeable collection of art gifted over the years. Most of it was junk—cartoonish statues and velvet-Elvis-quality oil paintings donated by well-meaning parishioners. The donors hoped it bought them a few years less in purgatory.

During a routine inventory the previous year, before Jilly became ill, Scotty came upon an interesting copy of Rembrandt's *Christ in the Storm on the Sea of Galilee*. His first inspection was relatively cursory. The lighting was dim and the paintings were stacked two or three deep, so he only glimpsed it behind two other works he had tilted forward. He jotted down a notation that he would later enter onto a spreadsheet. He was familiar with the original and its theft from the Isabella Stewart Gardner Museum in 1990. The painting portrayed a beloved biblical scene,

Christ calming the waters on the sea of Galilee as the disciples clung to the vessel, certain of drowning. Countless copies had been made, as it was a favorite of the Church, so he wasn't surprised to see it in the Basilica's collection.

That night, he lay awake thinking of the painting. The Basilica's basement had been dark, and he had only glimpsed it for a moment. Still, he detected something subtle through the grime and varnish—a single brush stroke. It was composed of a lead white pigment and depicted the foamy crest of a breaking wave. For a skilled forger like Scotty, reproducing a painting was simply a matter of replicating technique. The acquisition of age-appropriate canvasses and rare pigments was far more complicated than the actual act of painting. What he couldn't get out of his head was the recklessness of that singular stroke, the absence of the hesitation usually apparent in the act of imitation. In its place stood a brash confidence indicative of the uninterrupted transference of energy from hand to canvas. The thick application of paint known as the *impasto* technique, employed masterfully by Rembrandt and Titian, was evident. The stroke was totally devoid of self-consciousness. It was a butterfly masquerading as a caterpillar.

When he finally drifted off to an uneasy sleep, Scotty dreamed he was on a boat. The sky was Mars black, and the waves were building. He turned to see Jilly asleep at the rudder. He tried to shout a warning, but the foam from the waves filled his mouth. He tried to run to him, but the waves surged over the transom, pushing him back. Finally, Jilly stood. He appeared defiant and unafraid. Jilly folded his arms in front of him and stood solid as a rock despite the shifting deck beneath him. He smiled at Scotty. Jilly may have appeared fearsome to most, but to Scotty, his face resembled an angel from Botticelli's *The Madonna Della Melagrana.* Just when the storm seemed to have subsided, a huge wave crashed over the stern in a burst of water and foam. When it dissipated, the deck where Jilly had stood was empty and the vessel was rudderless.

Scotty bolted upright as he awoke from the nightmare. He got out of their bed as quietly as possible and walked gently to the area of the loft reserved for his studio. He stood at a blank canvas, and with only the light of the moon pouring through the window, he began to sketch. He needed to get the rough outline down while the dream image was fresh in his mind. The freehand skeleton would assure that the subsequent strokes retained his vision. But to perfect the forgery—Scotty resented that word, but he had to admit that's exactly what it would be—he would require the original standing beside it.

Scotty had been wrong about most things in his life, with the notable exceptions of Jilly and art. This is how he knew, beyond doubt, the painting he'd seen earlier that day was no copy. Like the voice of Dinah Washington singing "Easy Living," Jilly's favorite song, it was distinctive. Singular. *Inimitable...* almost. The key in any replication is to mimic down to the imperfections—the scratchiness of the record, the static, the layers hidden beneath. He found himself in a trance.

His thoughts wandered to the Gardner theft and the stories he had heard over the years. He thought of Father Gus—his vices poorly hidden—and the strange visitors at the Basilica with strong Boston accents. Occam's razor is a theory that posits entities are not to be multiplied beyond necessity, meaning no more assumptions should be made than required. The shortest distance between point A and point B is always a straight line. And in this case, Scotty concluded, that line went straight from Boston to South Philly.

Scotty couldn't be sure how much time had passed when he finally came out of the trancelike state, but daylight had begun to leak into the loft. The composition was rough, but the sketch had started to come to life. The boat heaved and fell, and the disciples desperately awaited Christ's intercession—and Scotty's brush. He covered the canvas and stepped away to brew some espresso in an old-fashioned stovetop pot that Jilly preferred.

As Scotty sat at the kitchen table waiting for it to percolate, on a yellow legal pad he began to sketch out a plan to liberate the painting from the Basilica's dusty basement.

BLAINE'S

Oakland Park, Florida

Nick walked into Blaine's and was momentarily blinded by the Vantablack darkness. The contrast between the sun-drenched world outside and Blaine's cavern-like interior made it feel like you were stepping into a black hole. The bar was lined with hard-core regulars who had long since given up trying to escape its gravity. Walter Jackson's plaintive wail on "Suddenly I'm All Alone" beckoned from the jukebox. Nick pulled up a stool and knew he was home. Frank was still outside having a smoke, but Ralph sat down beside him. Low-cut Cathy, the day bartender, produced an ice-cold Peroni that hit the back of Nick's throat like a shot of freon. Vinny walked over to the jukebox.

"You touch that thing, and I'll kill you," Ralph barked. Vinny raised his hands and walked backward from the machine. "You're up, Nick." Ralph sensed that Nick was in one of his moods. He took a twenty off the bar, slapped it in Nick's hand, and sent him to the mound with the confidence a manager reserves for his ace. On the walk over, Nick began to put together a playlist composed of songs written and/or produced by Van McCoy. A Philly-based songwriter and producer, McCoy was best known for "The Hustle," for which he won a Grammy. It was McCoy's lesser-known works, however, that had their hooks in Nick, one of them being the Walter Jackson song playing presently.

Nick started with "When You're Young and in Love" by the Marvelletes, followed by "Right on the Tip of my Tongue" by Brenda and the Tabulations, then "To Each His Own" by Faith, Hope and Charity. He was about to top it off with McCoy's masterpiece "Walk Away from Love" by David Ruffin, but couldn't bring himself to play it, even after all these years. It was a heartbreaking number, with all of Ruffin's post-Temptations anguish on display, made all the more poignant by the horns and strings that heralded his last foray into the top ten. A passionate, tearful kiss before parting. For Nick, it encapsulated all the fleeting nostalgia and unfulfilled promise of star-crossed love. He had been ducking the tune for years.

And so Nick began the little unspoken game he played with the crew. He would play a string of seemingly unrelated songs as they tried to decipher the common thread—in this case, McCoy.

Settled in at the bar in the dark comfort of the tap room, Nick became enveloped by nostalgia. The songs and liquor soothed him like old friends, and he began to unwind the tale as Anastasia had told it. An unholy alliance had taken root in South Philly. Dmitry's rivals had found common ground with the Di Nobiles' old nemeses, the De Rosas. Apparently, one of the Rembrandts stolen in the Gardner heist had been stashed away in a church for safekeeping, until it went missing. Now, a priest had turned up dead and *Christ in the Storm* had changed hands once again. As Nick recited the words, the story began to sound even more ludicrous to him than when Anastasia first told it. For a painting that had remained invisible for almost thirty years, it was suddenly changing hands faster than a hot Rolex. If it wasn't for Gary's call about the strange visitor to Caffé Vecchio, Nick might have doubted the whole thing. Then there was Anastasia herself—Dmitry didn't send her lightly. It wasn't a request, and if Nick refused there would be consequences. The warm ooze of his surroundings had taken on the viscosity of a tar pit, and Nick was starting to feel like a T. rex. He needed to escape for a minute.

When he walked out to get some air, he was surprised to find it dark out. The songs, drinks, and conversation had conspired to form a collective blur. It wasn't quite a blackout, but it was dangerously close. Nick hadn't had one since. . . well, for a long time.

Vinny joined him. "You okay, Nick?"

"I'm good, thanks. Think you can run me over to the Tiki?"

"No problem. You ready now?"

"Let me go back in and say goodbye to Ralph and Frank."

Vinny jogged across the street to get the car, and Nick stepped back into the bar. He hugged his uncle and leaned down to give Ralph a kiss of respect on his cheek. Ralph spun slowly around on his stool. He hiked up his pants as he stood and gripped Nick firmly but lovingly with both hands on either side of Nick's face.

"You ready for this, kid?"

Nick thought about it. "Well, I wasn't ready last time and that worked out okay, so I'm sticking with 'no.'"

"Good answer, kid. Overconfidence has been the downfall of more than a few of my friends."

"Well on that chilling note, I guess I better get some rest."

"Frank's booked on Spirit. You're booked on American."

"Hey," Frank piped up. "Why do I have to fly Spirit? I'm older."

"Exactly," Ralph fired back. "Don't worry; if you die in Philly, I'll fly you back private."

"Great. My first private flight, and I'll be in a box."

"Fuck that. You'll be in an urn, you old fuck. I'm not paying for a casket. Now give your nephew a kiss. After tomorrow, you two are on opposite sides. Once you get to the city, things might not be so cozy."

Nick didn't give him time to think. He grabbed Frank by the back of the head, pulled him in close, and kissed him on the cheek. He whispered in his ear.

"I love you, Unc. Be careful around them snakes."

"I love you, Nicky. You be careful too; sometimes them snakes are closer than you think."

Nick knew his uncle was right.

THE GHOST OF DAVID RUFFIN

The Tuscan Tiki, Lauderdale-by-the-Sea

Sometimes, events happen in life that are too bizarre to be written off as mere coincidence. The universe hiccups and the consequence is an occurrence that defies all known laws of physics and probability. As a result, the human brain kicks into defense mode and flips some internal switch to make the experience explainable—and forgettable. It's the reason déjà vu is so slippery and fleeting. You've glimpsed some truth you weren't meant to see, so the brain immediately starts firing in a sequence to make you forget the experience. Nick had encountered this phenomenon a few times in his life. The last time was on board Dmitry's yacht, *Mishka,* when Dmitry told the story of first seeing Rembrandt's *The Return of the Prodigal Son.* Dmitry had tied off a cosmic thread that stretched across continents and over decades. It was a tie that bound Dmitry to a man he never met, Nick's father, Anthony Di Nobile. And it was a tie that continued to bind Nick to the Russian, an unspoken obligation to a dead father and loyalty to a stranger that, in a weird way, had become his surrogate.

Vinny dropped him off at the front door of the Ocean Abode Resort right on time for Nick's next brush with the supernatural.

Nick stumbled into the Tiki in one of his sullen, indulgent moods where it was usually best to go home and sleep it off. The alternative was to surrender to it and ride the wave of self-pity until it crashed on the familiar rocks of regret. Tonight, Nick was resolved to hang ten to the bitter end.

It was uncharacteristically quiet at the Tiki, and only a few regulars remained seated at the far end of the bar. Nick was relieved to see his trusted bartender and friend Ronnie Cruz at the helm. Nick needed someone around from back home, and Ronnie fit the bill perfectly; a reformed crew boss from the badlands of North Philly serving a self-imposed penance, one piña colada at a time. He knew the value of silence.

"*Jefe.*" Ronnie greeted Nick warmly but without expecting a response. Instead, he poured Nick a Crown Royal and backed it up with a Peroni. He then busied himself with the remote, changing the channel for an invisible patron.

Nick was seated at the end of the bar closest to the beach. How had his world become so complicated again in two short days? He looked out at the ocean for an answer, but the moon had retreated behind the clouds and the sea reflected nothing back. More troubling was how readily he had waded right in. Maybe he secretly willed these crises into his life in some perverse law of attraction scenario. He knew that's what Grace would say. That thought reminded him that he hadn't checked in with Grace since he walked into Blaine's hours ago. He pulled out his phone to text her that he was okay, but he struggled to come up with an innocuous enough message, so he decided it was more prudent to just call her in the morning given his present state.

Nick took a long pull from the Peroni. He stared at the empty shot glass but couldn't remember knocking it back. The jukebox had mercifully been playing some benign Top 40 when he'd walked in, and he felt grateful. Ronnie refilled the shot glass. Nick heard the almost imperceptible click that indicated someone was skipping songs on the jukebox. It was late enough in the evening not to be a major faux pas. On a busy day, with competing crews of musical taste vying for control, it could cause a full-blown riot.

The first five piano notes announced that the ghost of David Ruffin had followed Nick from Blaine's to the Tiki and was about to exact his revenge. *Bah Bah Boomp-Boomp-Boomp*. To Nick, it sounded like Jacob Marley dragging his chains in some Motown version of *A Christmas Carol*. The inside of his skull felt like an oversized cabasa jolting back and forth in time to the song—*shooka-shooka-shooka-shooka*. His head drooped forward involuntarily, and he stared at the bar for a moment. Then a violin string soared toward the sky and was punctuated by a mallet striking a glockenspiel situated somewhere between Nick's stomach and heart.

His mind scrambled to come up with a reasonable explanation. Maybe one of the Philly crew staying at the resort was a David Ruffin fan. Perhaps one of the guys at Blaine's had cracked the code and followed Nick over to the Tiki to play the audio answer. Except everyone close to Nick knew the song was verboten at the Tiki. It was the equivalent of asking Sam to play "As Time Goes By" at Rick's Café in *Casablanca*. Nick looked up at Ronnie. He was drying a glass with a worried look on his face, staring toward the jukebox. Nick took a deep breath, stood up, and placed both hands on the bar to steady himself. When he turned, it wasn't Frank or Ralph, or even one of the Philly delegation that greeted him, but the only woman he knew who was more dangerous than Anastasia, albeit in a slightly different way.

Walking toward him, backlit by the jukebox and shrouded by palm fronds, Angie Romano smiled at him like her presence at the Tiki was an everyday occurrence. Nick was tempted to come up with something clever to say to cover for what must have been a pretty stupid look on his face. A variation on the Bogart line from *Casablanca* came to mind—*of all the tiki bars in all the towns in all of South Florida*—but he thought better of it. He wouldn't have gotten it out anyway because Angie had quickly covered those last few yards and planted a kiss square on Nick's lips while draping her arms over his shoulders.

Nick collapsed back on his stool.

"*Jesús.*" Ronnie rolled his eyes worriedly and started to cut some limes to appear busy.

"I was at the Royal Palm today," was all Nick could manage.

"I know. Don't you think I got a call?"

"Fritzie?"

"Nah, Knuckles."

"You make friends quickly."

"It's not my personality."

"Oh, I don't know, Angie, you can be pretty charming when you want to. You charmed me, didn't you?"

Angie had to smile at that remark. "You always do this, Nick."

"Do what?'

"Turn it around, make it about you." Angie paused, catching herself. "I'm sorry, Nick, let's start over. I come in peace."

"Is that why you played that song?"

"Let's talk about it, Nick. Except you haven't been a very good host. Do I have to make my own drink?"

Ronnie, who was glued to a TV pretending not to listen, immediately began mixing a cocktail. Without asking, he prepared the Tiki's version of a Negroni, topped off with a bamboo skewered mango slice. Angie looked amused.

"I see my reputation precedes me. You been talking about me, Nick?"

"Only in my sleep."

Angie raised her glass in Ronnie's direction. "You two kids sleeping together?"

"Roommates in the asylum," Ronnie stated succinctly as he retreated to check on the regulars at the other end of the bar.

"Now that's a good bartender." Angie clicked his Peroni.

"He's more than a bartender. He saved my life once."

"And now you owe him?"

"Something like that. Not quite so dramatic, but yeah, basically."

"Nobody owes anybody anything in this life. That's how people get into trouble—staying in situations too long out of some misplaced loyalty."

"Loyalty is never misplaced. If someone takes my loyalty for granted, it's their flaw, not mine."

"Wow. You've become quite the philosopher down here. It must be the ocean view." They both looked out at the ocean for a few seconds, as if to test Angie's hypothesis.

"And now *you* have *your* very own ocean view in Boca. Congratulations. You should have reached out."

"Why? Did I need your permission?"

It's how their conversations always went—lighthearted sniping, until one of them became defensive and said something hurtful.

"I'm sorry, Nick. I didn't mean it like that. I just haven't seen you for so long, and I guess I'm a little nervous."

"You? Nervous? That would be a first."

"How 'bout we start over? It's nice to see you, Nick. You look great."

"I'm drunk."

"Good. Me too."

"You look beautiful. I'm glad you're here. All I meant to say was, I wish I knew you were moving down. I would have helped."

"I know that. That's *why* I didn't tell you. I appreciate it, but I wanted to get settled in on my own first, without anyone's help. Then I planned on coming to see you."

"And?"

"And here I am."

Nick thought about it for a second. This was usually the part where he said something clever and witty and mean. Instead, he took a deep breath, sipped his Peroni, and said nothing.

Angie finally broke the silence. "Here we are, two old friends sitting by the ocean on a beautiful night. This is the kind of scene we only dreamed about back home when we were kids, yet here we are all tortured and twisted up for no good reason. I'll go play a few songs, you have your friend freshen up our drinks, and then we can sit on the beach and stare out at the ocean. How's that sound?"

With everything that had occurred the last couple of days, all the bombshell revelations about the painting and The Rose's nephew, somehow this moment seemed the most terrifying. It had been a long, crazy day. Nick had drunk way more than he should have, gone down some truly dark holes, and needed a good night's sleep to prepare him for the dangerous journey he was about to embark on. The wise choice was obvious; thank Angie, respectfully take a pass, and go home. So, he answered Angie the only way he could.

"Sounds great."

Nick walked down to the bulkhead steps and took a sand-strewn seat while Angie worked the jukebox. Ronnie was at his side in a flash with a beer and a Negroni.

"You okay, *jefe*?"

"I'm good, my brother. Just an old friend."

"Okay, if you say so. I'll be right up there if you need me. But can I ask you something?"

Nick could never refuse Ronnie. "Of course. You never have to ask permission."

"That toast your Uncle Frank makes sometimes—the one you only pretend to join in but don't actually drink to. Is she the wench? I mean the girl?"

Nick knew what he was referring to, the old toast from *Gilda*, a Rita Hayworth movie. Frank had repurposed it—*Disaster to the wench who did wrong by our Nicky.*

"The very same," Nick answered. "Good lord." Ronnie looked to the sky, then shook his head. "I'm going to start closing up. I'll walk you home when you're done with your talk."

"We Go a Long Way Back" by Bloodstone began to play as Angie sat next to him. She could have sat in the center of the steps but wedged herself into the narrower space between Nick and the railing.

"So . . . how do you like Florida?" Nick said like he was chatting up some newly transplanted northerner who had accidentally wandered into the Tiki.

"I like it just fine. Guess you had the right idea all those years ago."

"It hasn't always felt that way."

"Take a walk down to the water with me. I want to show you something."

Nick got up, dusted off the back of his pants, and kicked off his Ferragamos. He held them by the heels with two hooked fingers of his right hand after switching the beer to his left. They walked to the waterline in silence, but Nick thought, *if she asks me how many grains of sand are in her hand, I'm just gonna dive in and swim out until I drown.*

They took a seat just before the sand became wet and looked out at a dark sea. It wasn't long ago that Nick had strolled out of the ocean at this very spot, and Grace had leaped into his arms. Everything seemed so certain and uncomplicated then. His thoughts drifted back to another day many years ago when he and Angie sat just like this on a Texas Avenue beach in Atlantic City. It had felt like they had their whole lives in front of them. Before things unraveled. Before The Rose killed Jimmy.

"See how the waves crash out there, Nick?"

He nodded.

Angie waited a few seconds. "And the way they just fade to nothing at our feet?"

"What about it?" Nick asked.

"I was watching the waves the other day in Boca and thinking about us."

Nick's ears became feverishly hot, and a lump developed in his throat at her use of the word "us" as it pertained to the two of them. He no longer thought the concept even existed to her. A person can remain alone with their thoughts for so long that it starts to feel like they only exist to them.

"I was thinking we shouldn't waste time mourning all the loss in our lives."

"I'm not sure I understand." Nick couldn't figure out if she was talking about the two of them, or Jimmy, or both. "How do you get that from looking at the waves?"

"A wave starts out with such fury. It builds and builds until it crashes with a roar."

"And then?"

"And then it settles down and makes its way gently to the shore. Except, that's not the end. A wave never really dies, just recedes and regroups until it builds the strength to crest again. The wave is the part we see, the ocean's reaction to the wind and the tides, but the force that creates it . . . that never goes away."

Nick thought he knew what she was getting at, but he wasn't used to Angie speaking so metaphorically. It was like she had undergone some kind of transformation. Angie seemed to read his thoughts.

"You're not the only person capable of change you know."

She had a point. Nick had a bad habit of being a little self-centered when it came to their *relationship*. He felt like he was being unfaithful to Grace for even thinking of the word in that context. *Nick and Angie. A concept once taken for granted that no longer existed.*

Angie sensed Nick wilting under the weight of her words. "Hey, I'm sorry if I got too heavy there. We're *friends*, right? There's nothing wrong with that."

The Dell's "The Love We Had (Stays On My Mind)" began to play. Marvin Junior, the baritone Ruffin affectionately referred to as "Iron Throat," delivered an earthy wail that landed square on Nick's solar plexus. He leaned forward and blew out a breath, seeking relief that did not come.

"Friends," Nick stated after he caught his breath. "Definitely . . . friends." Angie held his hand. It made his whole body tingle, and he kept reciting the word over in his head. *Friends—friends—friends.* "Can I ask you something though?"

"Sure," Angie said. Her voice betrayed, for the first time in their conversation, fear of what the next question might be.

"Are you a Buddhist now or something?"

Angie smiled at him. She got up and turned back toward the Tiki, signaling their little talk was over. She was still holding his hand and gave him a little tug so he'd follow. She answered Nick without a trace of sarcasm. "Buddhist? Nah. I'm fucking Sicilian."

PUSSY OR HEALTH

Andy sat at his desk at Caposecco Fruit and Produce and pulled a bottle of Seagram's VO out of a file cabinet drawer. He splashed a generous pour into a cloudy rocks glass and placed it on a desktop calendar to sop up the excess. The glass landed randomly on Easter Sunday and formed a caramel-colored crescent moon around its perimeter.

He raised the glass to his lips but was interrupted by a light knock at the door. Andy spun on his chair to view the black and white monitor covering his office door. He recognized the man, a driver for Athens Hauling—nice kid, Billy *something*. Athens handled the garbage and recycling for Caposecco. It was a once defunct company that rose from the ashes of Rosa Waste Management, a company that faded into obscurity following the death of its owner, Bobby "The Rose" De Rosa. The Rose was gunned down in a daring New Year's morning assassination that had become the stuff of South Philly legend. There was no shortage of theories about who had shot The Rose in the eye.

To say The Rose's death was no great loss to humanity was an understatement. A running joke at the time was that at his funeral there wasn't a wet eye in the whole place. The murder remained unsolved, and the bankers box containing the case file over at Homicide had collected an impressive layer of dust. De Rosa had muscled the former owners of Athens out of their carting business in the eighties following the suspicious federal indictment of the Manos brothers. No one had suspected at the time that The Rose was the unnamed informant feeding the FBI false information about the Manos brothers, and anyone else who stood in his way. So it seemed only fitting that the consortium that filled the void left by De Rosa's death retake the Athens name. Andy and his partners owned fifty-one percent of the stock, and he had insisted that the surviving son of Manos, Leo, be given a ten percent stake gratis. That was just Andy's style. He adhered to a self-imposed code of honor that demanded such concessions.

Andy reached under his desk and pressed the button that let the man in.

Billy Fitzsimmons walked gingerly over to Andy's desk, as if he feared leaving a trail of desperation on the floor. Andy gestured for him to have a seat while he reflexively reached for a file containing Athens invoices. Andy was meticulous about keeping his invoices current, even when they were from a company in which he was the majority owner—especially then.

Billy shrunk into the old, cracked cushion of the office chair. This wasn't some carefully appointed boardroom of a Center City start-up. On the contrary, Andy's office was a no-nonsense affair in keeping with the demeanor of the man at the helm. Also, unlike most of those flashy start-ups, Caposecco consistently generated big fat gobs of money, decade after decade. Billy had removed his baseball cap upon entering the sanctum and gripped it in his hands, which were presently situated between his knees. Andy sized up his posture and put away the folder. In its place, he slid another cloudy rocks glass, which he gripped on the inside with two sausage-like fingers. He poured Billy a measure matching his own and extended his own drink over the desk. Billy picked up his glass and clinked it against Andy's. Andy took a satisfying sip. Billy downed the contents in one gulp that made his Adam's apple dance spastically.

"Pussy or health?" Andy inquired.

"What?" Billy looked puzzled.

"You're here because you have a problem, right?"

"Yeah." Billy was treading carefully, not wanting to insult the man.

"That's what I thought. So which is it, pussy or health?"

Billy thought for a minute before answering. "Actually, it's about money."

"So, pussy then." Andy acted relieved. "That's good. Pussy, I got a shot at helping you with; health, not so much."

"I'm not sure I understand, Mr. Caposecco. I'm sorry. I owe someone money. How is that a pussy problem?"

Andy unscrewed the cap and patiently poured him another glass. He had delivered this lecture many times.

"All money problems," Andy said, pushing the glass across the desk, "are at their core pussy problems. Driving a flashy car you can't afford? Pussy problem. Wife made you buy a big house and you're behind on the mortgage? Pussy problem. Borrowed money from a loan shark to impress a piece of ass that's a little out of your league with some extravagant gift? Big pussy problem. So, which one is it?"

Billy looked even more pitiful than when he walked in. His eyes were focused on the floor as he whispered, "The last one."

Andy rapped on the metal desk with his knuckles to get Billy's attention. Billy brought up his gaze to meet Andy's stare. He was surprised to find a glimmer of kindness in Andy's deep-set eyes. The area around them was as weathered as a Spaghetti Western cowboy, but the pupils retained the mischievous glint of a Catholic schoolboy.

"Relax, kid. It's a common ailment, rarely fatal. I've made worse mistakes myself." Andy laughed like he was remembering some bittersweet misstep from his past—because he was. He recovered from his brief reverie to pose the most important question yet. "So, was she worth it?"

"I wouldn't know," Billy answered, clearly embarrassed at having to make this confession.

Andy raised his eyebrows, incredulous. It was as if he himself had been snubbed. "What the fuck is this world coming to?" Andy poured two more doubles. "What's the damage?"

"Thirty." Billy made quick work of his drink.

"Thousand? Jesus Christ, kid. I gotta see a picture of this broad."

"Well, it didn't start out at thirty. I borrowed ten and bought a used Rolex Datejust for nine."

"You should have come to me for the watch, kid, but whatever. Then what?"

"She wouldn't accept it. Said I was a sweet guy, but she didn't feel that way about me."

"Ouch. Been there. What happened next?" Andy poured two more VOs. This was becoming a pretty good story, and he appreciated the distraction if nothing else.

"I got drunk, pawned the Rolex for five. Lost that, plus the thousand, at the Hard Rock, got down another ten on football, borrowed to cover that, now I can't even cover the weekly juice, and it just keeps growing."

"Pussy problem." Andy confirmed the ruling.

"Pussy problem." Billy finally nodded in agreement with Andy's initial assessment. "I've already paid back the principal plus—"

"Stop." Andy cut him off. "Don't go there. That ain't the deal you made, so if you want my help, let's not start off like that. Would you say that if you owed it to me?"

"No, sir, you're right, Mr. Caposecco. I'm just frustrated, that's all."

"It's understandable. And call me Andy. So, I have to ask, to whom do you owe this ungodly sum?"

"Some guy that hangs around the Paradise Bar. Acts like he owns the joint, buying drinks for everybody, always has a crew of guys around him."

"Does this big shot have a name?"

"Lenny De Rosa. Everybody calls him The Thorn."

"Sounds like a scary guy." Andy had never heard of him. He knew the last name, of course, but that didn't mean anything. He would have to ask around and see if this "Thorn" was affiliated with anyone or just some rogue free agent. If it turned out to be the latter, Andy would extend his standard deal; Billy could pay Andy half the outstanding debt, in exchange for which, he could inform his creditor that he had paid the debt in full—to Andy. And *Mr. Thorn* could come see Andy if he had a problem with the arrangement. That would usually be the end of the affair, the age-old method for flushing out independent operators. Sometimes, Andy took it a step further; he always saw the future opportunity presented by an individual in need of sponsorship and the licensure Andy could bestow. The carrot was always more profitable, but it didn't work without the threat of the stick waiting in the wings. Of course, there were always a few who thought the rules didn't apply to them. Didn't believe in the stick . . . until the very moment it got shoved up their ass.

Andy wasn't worried about Billy paying him the discounted amount. He could pay Andy out over time, conventional interest. It was all pure profit anyway, and Andy could take it right out of his pay. After all, Billy worked for *him*, whether he knew it or not.

Andy told Billy he would need a few days to follow up with him. If this *Thorn* was fronting for one of Andy's friends, that would be the end of it, although Andy might lobby for a little relief for the kid. Otherwise, he would proceed with the alternative.

Billy thanked Andy, shook his hand with both of his, and turned for the door. But before Andy buzzed him out, he had one more question for this tortured soul.

"Hey, Billy, you never finished the story. What's the name of the succubus who brought you to such dire straits?"

Billy stared somewhere over Andy's head and froze, like the very head of Medusa hung there, daring him to utter her name. Then, figuring he no longer had anything to lose, Billy tempted fate one last time.

"She used to bartend at the Paradise, but I heard she moved to Florida. Angie Romano."

Andy sat in silence for a few minutes after Billy left. He meditated on the past few days' events: Father Gus turning up in his trunk outside Angelina's; Agent O'Connell's visit; the Boston angle; the painting. He thought about the missing Rembrandt, the ship tossed about in the storm. It got him thinking about Caffé Vecchio, his old friend Anthony Di Nobile, and his son, a good-looking kid named Nicky. He remembered the kid sporting around an absolute dime piece back in the day. An angel face but built for speed. Biagio Romano's granddaughter, Angela. These were far too many coincidences for a man who didn't believe in coincidence.

Andy needed some answers. He pressed an intercom button that connected to a desk phone inside the warehouse. Dino answered.

"Bring the car around to the loading dock. I need you to drive me somewhere."

Dino backed the Escalade down the loading dock, facing out alongside a set of stairs, and waited for his boss.

Andy washed his face and hands in the powder room attached to his office, then fixed what few hairs he had left on his head with some pomade and sprayed them down with an old can of Consort. Andy needed information. He needed to run these seemingly unconnected events by someone he could trust, and at his age, that was an ever-shrinking list of people.

He got in the passenger side of the Escalade.

"Where to, boss?" Dino stared straight ahead, still in his white refrigerator coat. For no discernable reason, the name tag was embroidered *Ted* in red script.

"Take me to see The Wizard."

Dino pulled the Escalade out of the loading dock headed west on Packer Avenue, then north on 7th toward Scopa's Cheese Shop.

Special Agent O'Connell picked them up on Lawrence Street and followed them from three cars back. Dino parked next to the fireplug on the corner and walked Andy to the door. A little bell jingled as they entered, and Gloria escorted Andy to the back room while Dino waited out front. Nino Scopa was rearranging his funeral cards into a macabre tarot deck. Andy felt grateful not to reside there yet. His old friend stood to hug him, and as they embraced, The Wizard whispered in his ear.

"What took you so long?"

BUONA PASQUA

Nick woke up with the kind of headache he thought he had left in the past. Now it was back like a vengeful ex. It receded for just a moment, only to be replaced by that sick feeling in his stomach that posed the age-old question: *Did I do anything last night that I'm gonna regret?* It was the blaring alarm clock ringing in the skull of every drunk. *I'm no better*, Nick thought as he scrambled to make the justifications that could only make sense to an alcoholic. *Is that what I am?* The soul searching would have to wait. He had more pressing matters to attend to, not the least of which was what promised to be a long, painful conversation with Grace. *I don't know why she doesn't just leave me.* The pity parade was kicking in, so Nick jumped in the shower in an effort to drown out the voices.

They were having Easter dinner with Ralph and Frank, and Grace was probably prepping everything at her place in Pompano. He needed to get over to help, make like everything was normal, before dropping a bombshell on her. He was about to do what he had promised her he would never do again—go back to South Philly.

It was a promise he had made to himself when he first left, then broken three years ago. He had returned to settle his late father's estate and ended up embroiled in a deadly race to locate a painting hidden by Tony DiNobile for decades, Rembrandt's original version of *Return of the Prodigal*, which had been stolen from the Isabella Stewart Gardner Museum in 1990. A painting made all the more valuable by the notion that it didn't exist.

Nick was trying to convince himself he was going back to protect Caffé Vecchio, to make sure Gary and Joey were safe. But the uncomfortable fact gnawing at him suggested something even stronger was propelling him back, and he wished it weren't true. The undeniable truth was he craved the action.

This impulse was supposed to be inconsistent with the *new* Nick, the one liberated from the chains of the old hurts, no longer a slave to those unhealthy attachments. But in reality, recovery from those attachments was every bit as tricky as recovery from addiction to substances. You had to work at it and were never entirely free from their enticing claws. They beckoned, deceived, and dissembled, cloaked in seductive explanations and convenient justifications. Like every addiction, Nick's had its unique triggers.

It is said that relapse is part of recovery. In that case, Nick was standing at the precipice of relapse with a gun pointed at the back of his head. As he stared into the abyss, he rationalized his inevitable leap. This particular pistol had a hair trigger, and the trigger had a name—Angie Romano.

Nick's thoughts had wandered off under the warm rain of the shower. He switched the control to cold and stayed under it for as long as he could stand it. The shock caused him to gasp, and he hoped it would steel him for the unpleasant task of explaining to Grace why he needed to break his promise.

He dressed quickly, downed a double espresso, and drove north on A1A toward Grace's condo, stopping briefly to pick up Frank along the way. Since his windfall from the role he'd played in recovering the Rembrandt, Frank had managed to move into a respectable two-bedroom condo in Casa Lido, a two-story structure off Commercial but east of the bridge. It was a tidy building, and Frank liked the idea that he could walk up the outside steps to his unit without entering through a lobby. Something about dealing with a doorman rubbed Frank the wrong way. It reminded him of the time he had spent sneaking around The Royal Palm, navigating its layers of security. Sometimes, he still woke up in the middle of the night feeling like a trespasser. He would get up, put on all the lights, and walk around the condo. He would touch his belongings and examine the contents of his fully stocked refrigerator to assure himself he really lived there. Living like an ordinary citizen still felt foreign to him because deep down he didn't believe he deserved it.

Nick parked below his unit, next to the Civic, and beeped once. Frank peeked out from between the blinds and raised a finger, indicating he'd be out in a minute, which would be closer to fifteen minutes for Frank.

He emerged ten minutes later, lit a cigarette after locking the door, puffed furiously as he walked down the steps, then extinguished it on the ground before getting into Nick's Bentley.

"Buona Pasqua, nephew."

Nick was about to say something like, *you're gonna be late for your own funeral*, but pulled it back when he thought how close the old man had come to death protecting him. Frank's cologne overwhelmed the Bentley's interior as soon as he shut the door.

"Jesus Christ, Unc, you smell like one of them cigar bunnies. What is that, Hai Karate?"

"It's Tom Ford. You wouldn't know nothing about it. Blanca bought it for me for Christmas."

"Blanca from the Ambassador?" Nick asked, referring to a cocktail waitress at the cigar bar in Boca.

"The very same. She doesn't work there anymore; she's selling real estate in Palm Beach, and I referred her first customer."

"Palm Beach? She owes you more than a bottle of cologne."

"Don't worry, we're square. She's a great kid. Calls me her uncle."

"So does the bathroom attendant at Primo." Nick smiled, and so did Frank as he pinched his cheek. "Buona Pasqua, Unc."

With those pleasantries out of the way, Nick pulled back onto A1A and they drove the rest of the way to Pompano as Sinatra lamented about the girl he lost to the "Summer Wind."

THE FALL OF ICARUS

Easter Sunday

In Breughel's Icarus, for instance: how everything turns away
Quite leisurely from the disaster; the ploughman may
Have heard the splash, the forsaken cry,
But for him it was not an important failure; the sun shone
As it had to on the white legs disappearing into the green
Water, and the expensive delicate ship that must have seen
Something amazing, a boy falling out of the sky,
Had somewhere to get to and sailed calmly on.

From "Musee des Beaux Arts"

W. H. Auden

Ralph was the first to arrive. He brought a selection of wines, including a 1997 Opus One. But he was most excited to sample the bottles of homemade wine Vinny had driven back down on his last trip.

Vinny was the designated driver for a few of Ralph's and Frank's snowbird friends. He would shuttle their cars south at the beginning of the "season" and back home at its conclusion. He was compensated pretty handsomely and always brought back a bonus shipment of various goodies Ralph had arranged for—homemade wine, soppressata, cheeses. Some of this you could get your hands on in Florida, but the fact it came from back home gave it a special aura that made it seem like it tasted better. *What is taste anyway?* Ralph thought. *A sense like any other, influenced by any number of factors; ambiance, company, setting. Maybe that's why everyone remembers their own mother's cooking most fondly.* Ralph liked that theory. It made him feel warm and satisfied, one of the dividends of a life well lived. Well, mostly well lived. With that thought, Ralph got up from the sofa.

"Hey, Grace, mind if I sit on the balcony until those two hoodlums show?" It was rhetorical, as Ralph had already pulled back on the slider and the ocean breeze was blowing in. He had a bottle of homemade in one hand and a small water glass in the other.

"Of course not." Grace smiled. "Make yourself at home."

Ralph paused for a moment. "How 'bout you, gorgeous, care to join me?" Ralph's invitation was directed at Grace's mother, Adriana, standing sentry at the stove and the Easter ham pie baking within. He jiggled the bottle in his hand for emphasis. Adriana was wearing an apron and had a kitchen towel draped over her shoulder that she snapped at Ralph to shoo him away.

"What, and inhale your smelly cigars? No, thank you. I'd rather sweat over a hot stove."

What a beauty, Ralph thought. *A little older than I'm used to, but madone, what a woman*. Ralph had considered asking her out on a proper date but figured she wouldn't be interested in keeping company with an old ex-con.

For Adriana's part, she feigned disinterest, but on one level, she was flattered. It had been years since Grace's father had passed, and while she would never let on to Grace, the truth was she was lonely. Her flippant remark belied the fact that she found Ralph exceedingly charming, confident and, well, sexy. She pushed this thought out of her mind as soon as it intruded and made a covert sign of the cross as she mumbled, *forgive me*, under her breath. Adriana stirred a pot that required no stirring. She used the towel to pat away the beads of sweat that had accumulated on her brow, convincing herself they were the product of a hot oven.

Grace was setting the table when Nick and Frank arrived. Nick moved behind her, embracing her in a hug and kissing her neck. She tried to break out of his grip, feigning disinterest, but his kiss filled her with a warm floating feeling. She turned to kiss him, nibbling lightly on his lower lip.

"I heard that's how your Ukrainian girlfriend likes to play."

Nick knew she was only joking, but the butter knife she was jabbing under his rib cage gave him cause for doubt.

"I love you, Grace. Happy Easter." He hoped that would diffuse the situation.

"You fucking better. Buona Pasqua." She turned back to the table and thrust her bottom against him as she leaned over to continue placing the silverware. Nick wasn't sure if she was being clumsy or sexy, so he went with sexy. He playfully grabbed her by the waist and pulled her to him. Grace pretended to protest. Finally, she jabbed him in the ribs with an elbow, and Nick let go, realizing she hadn't been pretending. Grace had a way of keeping him in suspense that hooked him from the day they met.

"Break it up, you two," Ralph boomed as he walked in from the balcony. A swirl of Cuban smoke followed him in on the ocean breeze, and Adriana peeked out disapprovingly. He kissed Nick on the cheek and motioned him over to the kitchen island. "Did I ever tell you guys you're my favorite couple?" He said it loud enough for Grace to hear, but more for Nick's benefit than hers, as he sensed Nick was about to be in the doghouse after breaking the news of his travel plans.

Grace looked at him suspiciously, seeing right through his ruse. "Only a million times. What do you want this time?"

Ralph didn't answer. Instead, he grabbed a bottle of Maker's Mark and set to muddling the ingredients for three Old Fashioneds for the three Philly throwbacks. Vinny called them the three OGs once, and Ralph gave him a backhanded love tap on the cheek. It was light enough to be joking, but his pinky ring caught him on the tooth and Vinny didn't make the same mistake again.

"You tell her yet?" Ralph whispered.

"I'm still breathing, ain't I?"

"Good point." Ralph gently placed a single large ice cube in each glass, finished by a generous pour. He stirred each drink methodically and finished with three orange peels. Frank joined them and they clicked glasses.

"Here's to the ones that had the sense to walk away," Ralph proposed.

"Salute," Nick and Frank reciprocated, and they drank.

"Not us," Frank stated the obvious.

"Not us, Frankie. Not us," Ralph confirmed.

They finally sat for dinner, and Frank led with a prayer that started off well enough but somehow veered into an airing of his grievances with God and life in general. Ralph was about to intervene when Gloria stepped in to salvage it with a beautiful prayer of thanksgiving.

The rest of dinner was uneventful. Ralph regaled Adriana with some stories from the old neighborhood. She chuckled at his colorful tall tales, at first out of courtesy, but eventually found herself laughing uncontrollably at these improbable fables of high adventure and the mythical characters who populated the South Philadelphia of his youth. By the time Ralph got to the story about a mute number writer whose name had suggested a goat in his lineage, she had one hand on the table and the other on her midsection as she gasped for air, tears in her eyes from laughter. Nick thought Ralph must have been getting pretty drunk because every word of every story was true. Nick finally stepped in when it sounded like he was about to tell an especially sordid tale involving a donkey.

Decorum having been re-established, Nick excused himself to the kitchen to help Grace with the dishes and molest her just a bit. Alexa was streaming a soothing "Philly Sound" playlist that acted like the perfect digestif as Jean Carn lamented "Was That All It Was." Nick's good mood was interrupted by the thought of the discussion he needed to have with Grace. In reality, it was less of a discussion and more of a pronouncement. He was trying without success to quell the rising dread and guilt. Nick had hoped to wait until Ralph and Frank left, but something about the way Grace was acting suggested she already sensed something was up. He settled in next to her at the sink and helped load the dishwasher with plates that already looked clean as Grace began to tell a story of her own.

"Are you familiar with the story of Icarus?" Grace asked as she wiped the countertop.

"I think so. From Greek mythology, the boy with the wings?"

"Yes, that's the one. The boy with the wings."

Nick wasn't sure where this was going, and it didn't sound good, but he had little choice other than to play along—he probably deserved whatever was coming.

"You should like this story; it involves a painting. Icarus had a father named Daedelus. He thought it would be a great idea to make some wings out of feathers and wax so the two of them could go flying around. He warned Icarus not to fly too near the sun, but being young and a fool, Icarus just couldn't help himself. His wings melted, and he plunged into the ocean, killing himself."

Nick knew the story, of course, but the way Grace delivered it was blunt and unadorned with any flowery touches. Nick was used to hearing stories crafted with a scalpel, but Grace used a sledgehammer. As suspected, she had already figured out his plans before he had a chance to share them—as always.

Hoping his tan concealed any blushing, Nick tried to normalize the conversation.

"You said something about a painting."

"Yes, thank you for reminding me." Grace was toying with him now like a lioness swatting at a cub—lovingly, but with just enough force to bolster her authority. "It's called *Landscape with the Fall of Icarus*. It appears to be a rather boring painting when you first look at it. A man plows a field in the foreground and would seem to be the focus of the painting. A shepherd tends to his flock, and some ships sail off toward a city in the distance surrounded by cliffs."

Nick vaguely recalled the painting, but it involved a poem by W.H. Auden describing the scene. He was trying to remember the name for a written work that described a visual art form. An image of Achilles's shield and Homer's Iliad flashed across the silver screen in his mind.

"Are you listening to me?" Grace's voice brought him back to reality.

"Yes. I'm sorry. I was thinking about something."

"Oh, well think about this; in the corner of that painting, down near the bottom, two skinny legs are poking out of the water. You would hardly see them unless you knew to look for them. They belong to that fool Icarus, and no one notices—not the farmer, the shepherd, or anyone on the ship."

Nick wanted to get this over with. He would have preferred her just slapping him in the face, but that wasn't Grace's style.

"I guess that fool is me?"

"I don't know, Nick, that's for you to figure out. One thing the painting doesn't cover, though. I bet you somewhere outside the frame, in some small village or something, a woman waited patiently for his return and mourned him when he didn't."

Nick had it with the charade and the allegory. "Do you want me not to go?"

Grace paused for a long moment before answering. For once, she actually considered laying down the law, but she knew it would only delay the inevitable.

"That's your decision. I can only give you this piece of advice—just because your father built the wings doesn't mean you have to put them on."

"Ekphrasis," Nick blurted out.

"Excuse me?" Grace's eyes became larger. The lioness was showing her fangs.

"I'm sorry. I just remembered the word. It's when a writer is describing a painting or statue. Like in the Icarus painting."

"That's nice, Nick. I'm glad you figured that out. You better get going. I think you have some packing to do."

"Don't let me leave like this, Grace. I need to know you're supporting me."

"I've always supported you. You just need to be honest about who you do these things for."

She was right. *Who am I doing this for? Dmitry, Ralph . . . my father?* It didn't matter at this point. He didn't have the luxury to indulge in that analysis. He had committed, the wheels were in motion, and he had given his word. And on a level he usually didn't allow himself to plumb, he had to admit it excited him, invigorated him, just like the old days.

"You ready, kid?" Ralph was at his side, a beefy hand on his shoulder.

"Born." He borrowed Vinny's standard response.

He hugged Grace for a long time. She kissed him tenderly, touching both sides of his face, her fingertips like butterflies. Ralph stood holding a half-opened door. Frank was already in the hallway. Nick finally released her from his embrace. Grace took a step back. Her eyes were dry, and her mouth had the remnants of a smile as she wound up and slapped Nick across the face, producing an audible crack.

"Oof. You okay, kid?" Ralph asked, barely suppressing a laugh.

"Yeah," Nick answered as they walked down the hall. "I deserved that."

"Yes, you did." Frank weighed in as the elevator doors closed.

THE BLUEBERRY PRINCE

Leonard De Rosa sat at the bar of The Paradise surrounded by a haphazard crew of miscreants bound more by individual ambition than loyalty. They clicked glasses and draped arms around one another, professing brotherly love, but each would betray the other without hesitation if the price was right. The justifications could wait for later, and each knew the other felt the same way. But in a strange fashion, the notion had a deterrent effect because they all distrusted one another equally, and no one deluded themselves that their bond was anything loftier. All of them save for their de facto leader.

The Thorn was a true believer, an outsider unburdened by years of witnessing betrayal layered upon betrayal. Like a self-assured autocrat, he believed this pack of wolves actually liked him. What he misapprehended was the true nature of the alliance. Theirs wasn't an autocracy so much as a kleptocracy. The minute their association outlived its profitability, the rules would evaporate. But for the moment, The Thorn held court. His subjects fawned about laughing riotously at his jokes, but behind his back, they partnered off and tested one another on the state of play, feeling out the usefulness of the man they derisively referred to as "The Blueberry Prince."

Foremost among them was an old Boston-based hood known as "Fenway Phil." He wore a peaky scally cap with a green shamrock embroidered on the back, which was now facing the front, as he always wore it backward. Phil was run out of the North End decades ago. He wasn't even from Boston, hailing from New Haven, Connecticut, but none of that had occurred to The Thorn or his crew.

There was one person in the Paradise that night who knew all about Fenway Phil's pedigree, or lack thereof; he knew how he got his sentence reduced too. That man sat on a stool across the room facing in the opposite direction, playing a poker machine, pretending to slap the "Hold" and "Deal" buttons with a mixture of gusto and disgust. At the end of the week, a man would come to the Paradise, empty the hopper, and bring the proceeds to the Caposecco Fruit and Produce warehouse. This collector wore a white refrigerator coat with the name Ted embroidered in red script on the left breast, but his real name was Dino. He was seated at the opposite side of the bar as The Thorn and his crew. He pretended to be engrossed in a basketball game on the television behind the bar, but he was listening intently to the reckless banter of the crew, making mental notes and piecing together a hierarchy. Dino sat close, but not too close, to the man playing the poker machine.

That man owned the poker machine he was pretending to play, delivered the produce used by the kitchen, removed the trash thrown in the Athens Hauling dumpster, and held the promissory note secured by the bricks and the liquor license. Andy Caposecco peeked through a small mirror on the wall behind the poker machine. He had a perfect view of Leonard De Rosa and company. None of them gave him a second look. He was indistinguishable from any other old rummy chasing a buck on a rigged machine. They wouldn't have noticed him at all had he not improbably hit a royal flush that caused the machine to rattle off credits like a tommy gun. The bartender walked out from behind the bar, knocked down the credits and paid the odd little man for his win. Andy tipped the bartender generously, put on his jacket, and walked out the back door. Dino waited a few minutes and walked out the front door. He joined his boss, who was already waiting in the passenger seat and pulled away from the curb onto Passyunk Avenue.

Special Agent O'Connell sat patiently in the Acme parking lot across the street. He smiled as he watched Dino and Andy Boy leave the Paradise through different doors and drive off together. There was no need to follow. Andy had figured it out pretty quickly. Everything was going according to plan and all Andy Boy needed was a little nudge in the right direction. O'Connell sat there for a long time thinking of what that nudge might consist of. He wasn't sure what would do the trick. But as he put the car in gear and drove around the neighborhood, he found himself passing by Caffé Vecchio and impulsively pulled over into an open spot. He was still unsure of the plan but figured this was a good enough place to start.

He walked into the storied Caffé, took a seat at the bar and ordered a glass of the house Chianti. He had heard all of the stories associated with Caffé Vecchio, but this was his first actual visit. Looking around the room, he took in all the paintings hanging over the tables on the perimeter. The Caffé had a familiar feel. Like an old leather jacket, it had taken on the character of its owner. Any blemish or imperfection only added to its aura. He understood how his predecessor had developed such an affinity for it. The Caffé, as well as the rest of the neighborhood, had detected Special Agent Sidney Del Ciotto's foulness and spit him out like a bad clam. The FBI followed suit soon after. Del Ciotto's apparent fentanyl overdose and the subsequent revelation of his unholy alliance with The Rose had closed the book on a scandalous affair that never officially saw the light of day. The scandalous images anonymously sent to the FBI from a Kyiv internet café saw to that.

One of the paintings in particular caught O'Connell's eye—a reimagining of Rembrandt's *Prodigal in the Tavern* with the face of Anthony Di Nobile standing in for the Old Master's self-portrait. It was segregated from the others and appeared to have been placed in a position of honor directly above the jukebox. O'Connell rose from his stool and walked toward the men's room. Like one of those cheesy images of a blue-eyed Christ, the Prodigal's gaze seemed to follow him as he walked across the black and white tiled floor.

Gary peeked out from the window in the kitchen door. Beto was preparing a Botticelli Bolognese but sensed something was wrong.

"Everything okay, boss?" he asked.

"All good, amigo," Gary answered, but his furrowed brow betrayed him.

Gary watched as O'Connell walked to the men's room. He positioned himself behind the bar, telling Alberto to take a cigarette break.

O'Connell was focused on the paintings as he walked back from taking a leak. He wiped his hands on his jacket—Gary made a mental note to replenish the hand towels—absorbed by a particularly hideous scene of a beautiful woman beheading a man for no apparent reason. It was a copy of Caravaggio's *Judith Beheading Holofernes.* His face registered genuine surprise when he finally got himself settled back in at the bar and looked up to see that a large African American man had replaced the kindly bartender who had poured his Chianti.

"Gruesome, ain't it?" Gary said, scowl still intact.

"Excuse me?"

Gary didn't answer right away. He reached behind him. O'Connell looked on nervously, even patting his hip covertly, assuring himself his sidearm was still there. It was a nervous tic he hadn't indulged since his days at the academy. Gary turned around, wielding a bottle of the house Chianti, and refilled O'Connell's glass.

"The painting. I saw you looking at it. Kinda nasty, right?"

"Yes, I suppose so." O'Connell took a sip of his wine, which was uncharacteristically filled to the rim. A rivulet escaped down the side and dripped onto the bar. The agent silently cursed this betrayal of his newly evident unsteadiness.

Gary wiped it up with an efficient swipe of a bar rag. "No worries, my man. Happens to the best of us. I find these days it helps to take a deep breath and then let it all out before squeezing the trigger, so to speak." He glanced toward O'Connell's right hip, giving an almost imperceptible nod as he said it.

O'Connell couldn't help but be impressed by this giant black psychic behind the bar of a South Philly Italian institution. *Fuck it*, he thought. He had been running on pure instinct these days, and it had served him well so far. He stood and extended his hand.

"Special Agent William O'Connell."

"No shit." Gary gripped his hand. Not too hard, but O'Connell swore he felt the man's thumb and finger touch around the back. "You here on official business?"

"No fucking way."

"I didn't think so." Gary walked out from behind the bar over to the jukebox. He looked up at Tony Di Nobile's face in the *Prodigal in the Tavern* for advice, but his old friend just smiled and raised his glass. "What kinda music you like?" He stared straight at the jukebox, but O'Connell knew he was talking to him. The big man didn't wait for him to answer before following it up with a multiple choice question that limited his options. "Funk, Soul, or R&B?"

"How 'bout 'Walk On By'."

Gary looked up. The scowl was back and seemed to ask, *You fucking with me?*

"That's a trick request." Gary paused before the follow-up question. "Dionne Warwick or Average White Band?" Gary purposely dragged out the last option, savoring each syllable.

"How about D Train's cover?" O'Connell snapped back without hesitation. The Burt Bacharach composition had been reinvented and recorded by everyone from Isaac Hayes to Cyndi Lauper.

"Shiiiiiit," Gary mumbled to himself. He tried not to use his standard response anymore, ever since that actor on TV made like *he* invented it.

Gary punched it up on the new internet jukebox. Joey had finally retired the vintage old girl while Gary was convalescing. He had erupted upon first discovering its absence and was only slightly appeased when Joey assured him it had only been relocated to his office. It had been in Caffé Vecchio so long that Andy Boy from Athens Vending insisted they keep it as a gift.

"Alright now." Gary resumed his position behind the bar, sensing this man was somewhat different from that scumbag Del Ciotto. "You got your drink, and I played your song. So let me give you a little advice. This a free country, and you welcome to drink and eat here any time you please. But if you're looking for information, you come to the wrong place." Gary poured himself a Maker's Mark over one large ice cube.

O'Connell saw his opening. He raised his glass to Gary. Any traces of his initial uneasiness had faded, his hand now as steady as his gaze. He looked the big man dead in the eyes. "Information is exactly why I'm here. Except I'm here to deliver, not receive."

Gary was starting to put it together. First Scotty's visit, then that priest turning up dead in AC. Now this friendly neighborhood G-man.

"You ever heard the saying, 'Beware of Greeks bearing gifts?'"

O'Connell downed what was left of his wine and smiled. "Well then, I guess it's a good thing my people hail from County Cork." And with that, O'Connell told Gary the same tale he'd recited to Andy Boy. A story of betrayal, double-crosses, a dead priest, and a stolen painting.

STARTING AT THE END

Nick's flight was delayed. He considered heading to the bar for a drink but thought better of it. There would be plenty of time for drinking once he got to Philly. It was inevitable. The moves he needed to make, the company he needed to keep, alcohol was an indispensable piece of the puzzle. An accouterment more integral than any knife or gun. The trick was to drink just enough to blend in and put people at ease but not so much as to dull his senses or impair his judgment. The balancing act was getting more challenging as he got older. It had served him well in the early days, roaming the streets and hitting all the hot spots. Now, at fifty-two, it had long since begun paying off in diminishing returns.

He walked over to Hudson News and scanned the paperback racks, skimming over the new crop of mystery and thriller novels. He picked up a few and read the taglines and synopses, but they just increased his already sky-high level of anxiety. Maybe the fact he was already living inside a plotline more improbable than the most ambitious of the fictional offerings contributed to this sensation.

Nick picked up a pebble grain leather journal and ran his thumb over the cover. The surface had the comforting feel of a once familiar object, like the stitches of a baseball when you haven't held one for years. It had a satisfying heft to it, and he cracked it open. The blank pages produced a gentle breeze on his face as he leafed through them like a fresh deck of cards. He had no idea what, if anything, he would write in it, but he found himself walking to the register and purchasing the journal, along with a pen.

At first, he simply wrote his name and phone number in the space provided. He closed the book, did some deep breathing techniques, then looked around the terminal and its inhabitants, imagining each of the travelers with their own notebooks, their own dramas, soul-crushing comedies, delightful tragedies. *What's so special about my story*, he thought. He had become numb to what most people consider an epic adventure. Adventure is as much a luxury as any other privilege. Still, like all opulence, it soon becomes drudgery to the adventurer. Nick imagined himself some bored Ulysses, demanding to be bound to the mast so he might experience the sirens' song, so he might *feel* something. *Is that what I've become? Some washed-up adrenaline junkie, bouncing from one contrived crisis to another? An ant in search of an odyssey? All to distract me from what? From myself? From growing up?*

Grace would say he was stuck somewhere in his past. Maybe that was it. Maybe no matter how far he rolled his boulder up the hill, all he really wanted was to let it roll back down and start back at the beginning, where everything seemed so right, so good, so . . . pure.

Nick never considered himself much of a writer. Sure, he could tell a story. Not nearly as entertaining as Ralph, or even his Uncle Frank, who could still command a room with his staccato delivery, the words pouring out of his mouth as effortlessly as smoke rings. Certainly not like his father, the master of many mediums—music, art, cuisine. Yet with all his skills, Anthony Di Nobile could never connect with the only audience he ever cared about reaching, not during his lifetime at least. Not until Nick had recovered the painting his father kept hidden for him all those years and gazed upon the image that had brought them both to tears, and those tears finally bound them together.

Nick opened the journal. He took the pen in his hand and placed its point on the first line of the first page . . . and wrote nothing. He didn't know where to begin, but for some reason, *the beginning* didn't seem quite right. That felt pretentious, as if his journey had somehow been more important than anyone else's. So he started at his destination instead, a place he hadn't realized he wanted to be, not until this moment. He wasn't quite sure how he would arrive, but something told him writing it down was the first step toward getting there. The pen moved fluidly, as if of its own will. Before Nick fully realized what he was writing, a word appeared in his Catholic school cursive at the top of the page. It was the destination his subconscious had been willing him toward all his adult life. A place he hadn't been able to voice in spoken word but managed to scrawl by virtue of this trance. A single word.

Redemption.

Just writing that one word seemed to cause a shift inside of him. Willing that one word onto the page made him feel a little less like a bystander in his own life and more like the author of his own story. It made him think of that conversation with Grace a few days earlier about the grains of sand on the beach and his place in the universe. Nick had grilled her a little, suggesting how ridiculous it was for men and women to believe they had free will in such a vast galaxy where even time was relative. Grace had answered him in her unique style, blending science with mysticism. Something about elegant design, string theory, and how more than one potentiality can coexist with another. Somehow, she made this all sound perfectly feasible. *"Just because God knows what you're going to do doesn't mean you don't have a choice,"* was how she put it, and it made perfect sense now.

Her words rang in his ears as he walked down the Jetway and onto the plane.

FUCKING FABULOUS

Nick was expecting Gary to pull up in the Fleetwood, just like old times, so he was slightly disappointed when he received the big man's text. *Not feeling good, pretty boy. Joey picking you up. C u tonite. G.*

He walked out of the terminal and texted Joey. *I'm outside Terminal B. You close?* Joey texted back after a minute with an imprecise, *On my way.* That could mean Joey was leaving the cell phone waiting lot or that he just got out of the shower. Nick took a deep breath and decided to let it go. He settled for a thumbs-up emoji.

Joey pulled up fifteen minutes later in a black Range Rover. The tint was so dark that Nick didn't realize it was him until he beeped. Nick hesitated for a second, expecting Joey to get out to greet him and take his bag. Joey had lowered the window, and Nick could hear that he was on a Bluetooth phone call. The liftgate popped open, signaling Nick to toss his bag in the back. For the second time in fifteen minutes, Nick did some deep breathing. *I should have called an Uber.* He wasn't even out of the airport, and already he felt his blood pressure rising. He got in the passenger seat and was overwhelmed by the combination of air freshener trees and too much cologne. Joey was still on his call. Nick finally gave him a stern look, and Joey got the message.

"I gotta go. I just picked up my Uncle Nick from the airport." A young female voice responded, "Hi, Uncle Nick, when do I get to meet you?" Her voice was annoying enough to guarantee she must be beautiful. Nick was about to respond courteously when Joey answered succinctly for him, "Never, *ciao,*" and hit the disconnect button.

Nick looked at his nephew. "Me? I've been fine, flight was great. How 'bout you?"

Joey snorted an embarrassed laugh. "I'm sorry, Unc. How are you?"

Nick leaned over, and Joey hugged the man who was his father's best friend and gave him the respect he deserved. Nick held him close for a few seconds, with enough force to remind him of their respective roles. Joey got the message and gripped his uncle a little tighter. "Love you, Unc. Sorry I didn't help you with your bag."

Nick pulled back and took his first good look at him in over a year. He looked older, more confident, and for some reason, that alarmed him. He thought about himself at that age and remembered how long wisdom lags behind the certainty of youth.

"I love you too, Joey, that's okay. Now can you take that toothpick out of your mouth? You almost poked a hole in my cheek."

Joey flicked the toothpick out the window, and they both laughed.

"I have something for you, Unc." Joey tapped the touch screen and queued up a track. "It's a little mix I've been working on, and it made me think of you. I've been playing it at the Caffé on old-school night. I save it for late in the set and everybody seems to like it."

Old-school night, huh, Nick thought. The Range Rover's speakers reverberated with a beat from a Post Malone song that wasn't half bad. It gradually became layered with a funky bass line that triggered some wicked déjà vu in Nick. The mix transitioned with the aid of some lofty strings and horns to a post-disco swan song from the Phillysound songbook. The song's title and lyrics coupled perfectly with the plaintive voice of the soulful chanteuse, Jean Carne.

"Was That All It Was." Nick pronounced the title as a statement rather than a question.

"I found the 12-inch version in my father's vinyl collection," Joey explained.

"I'm glad to hear that. I was starting to think you gave up on the music."

"Nah, just been busy, Unc, but I always make time for it. I'm still spinning one night a week at the Caffé."

"Good for you, Joey. Your father would be proud."

Joey didn't answer, just stared ahead, briefly checking the rearview and side mirrors to distract himself from Nick's compliment. He grabbed another toothpick from the cupholder and placed it in the corner of his mouth, switching it back and forth with his tongue until it dangled just right. Nick realized it might have been a bit too soon to go there with the kid, remembering how *he* had squirmed uncomfortably whenever someone would preach to him about his own father's mythical attributes, most of which had remained invisible to him throughout his youth. He decided to change the subject to lighten the mood.

"What the fuck is that smell?" Nick inquired about the overpowering scent that had enveloped him since he got in the car.

"It's Fucking Fabulous," Joey answered.

"I beg to differ," Nick responded.

"No." Joey laughed. "That's the name of the cologne—Fucking Fabulous by Tom Ford." Joey pulled the bottle out of the console, displaying it to Nick.

Nick's thoughts went to his Uncle Frank, who would arrive later that afternoon. He suddenly started to feel very old, the way only a younger guy could make you feel when he clues you in on something new that you were previously oblivious to. Nick considered that perhaps he had switched roles, and Joey probably regarded him the way Nick had once thought of his Uncle Frank. For the first time, he began to question whether he was up to the mission they'd cooked up.

"Give me that," Nick said as he snatched the bottle out of Joey's hand. He doused himself generously with the scent, making the sign of the cross with the bottle as he sprayed.

"What the fuck are you doing, Unc?" Joey was looking at him like he had lost his mind.

"Anointing myself."

"Are you feeling okay?" Joey asked.

Nick's head bobbed back and forth as he reached for the volume control, turning it up.

"Fucking fabulous," he answered.

LEONARDO

Scotty took a step back to inspect his work. He was at that stage where any additional brush strokes would only detract from the composition. He liked to paint with music in the background, usually Sinatra. Something about The Chairman's breath control and flawless enunciation of the lyric gave him comfort. Today featured bossa nova selections from Sinatra's collaboration with Antônio Carlos Jobim. He occasionally found himself applying a flourish of red ochre or lapis lazuli in an elegant synchronicity of pigment and lyric, his brush strokes as economical as Francis Albert's baritone.

As "Change Partners" played in the loft, Scotty put the finishing touches on the face of Angie Romano as Salome. This technique wasn't anything Scotty had learned anywhere, rather something that evolved from his adolescence when he sought refuge in art and music from an indifferent father and an uncaring world. The music infused his paintings like a wood cask flavors a stately bourbon with gentle undernotes that complement the profile without overpowering it.

Scotty never forgot, however, that he was a hunted man. His initial theft of *Christ in the Storm* made him a loose end in a deadly conspiracy he hadn't bargained for, and his continued existence was a luxury its present possessors could not afford. Like Caravaggio in exile seeking the protection of the Knights of Saint John, Scotty sought refuge at the only place he could think of—Caffé Vecchio. He hoped the humble gift of his painting would touch Nick Di Nobile and bring him under protection. He had stopped in on Saturday night and had dinner, an exquisite Bistecca alla Fiorentina that rivaled the dish he had last enjoyed with Jilly in San Lorenzo Square. It was an impressive cut, much too large for one. He took most of it home and shared it with Leonardo, their Italian Greyhound. Nick hadn't arrived yet from Florida, so Scotty left word with the bartender—"Please let Mr. Di Nobile know Charles Scottoline stopped by to see him."

The music had shifted in tempo as the night progressed. Candi Staton's "Young Hearts Run Free" started up. Joey, the young man Scotty had met at his last visit, was seated at the corner table, a beautiful young thing at his side. She appeared to be permanently affixed to his neck, releasing only intermittently when a patron approached to shake Joey's hand or whisper in his ear. As a result, Scotty thought it best not to interrupt, but his visit hadn't gone unnoticed. A waiter arrived at Scotty's table with an anisette, nodding toward Joey, who was extending his own anisette in a toast. Scotty's own father drank the liqueur nightly. The smell of it, mixed with the cheap stogies Vito Scottoline smoked, haunted his memories. It was why he hated pizzelles to this day—all he could taste was the anise. Yet there he was, raising his glass and knocking back the drink with a smile on his face. It burned in his stomach, along with all the other childhood traumas that cut like tiny razors. They stung at the moment, but the callouses that developed over the wounds allowed him to perform the labors his art required.

Scotty hadn't set out to steal a priceless masterpiece. While he was about 95% certain the painting was authentic, he couldn't completely rule out that it wasn't simply from *a follower of* or *in the manner of* Rembrandt without bringing it home for a more thorough inspection. *One doesn't stumble across such a find and simply move on.* After completing his authentication, he vowed to return the painting to its rightful owner, the Isabella Stewart Gardner Museum. Perhaps the notoriety from returning Rembrandt's sole seascape would spur interest in his own works. He wasn't committing a theft so much as performing a public service, Scotty justified his actions, as most people do when they are about to embark on a morally questionable course of action.

But when Father Gus turned up dead, he realized he was deluding himself. The painting belonged to him. It was his destiny, perhaps even some karmic payback for a lifetime of having his talent overlooked. He would never surrender it voluntarily. The universe owed it to him. Well, the universe must have been listening, and the calculation changed following the theft. Someone else knew about his actions, and they wouldn't rest while he was still breathing. He had begun carrying Jilly's old Ruger whenever he left the loft, which was less frequent. He had the uneasy feeling that he was being watched.

Scotty doubted he could even muster the courage to pull the gun, much less fire it. After all, he had wielded the brush, while Jilly had wielded the sword. His only hope was that his meeting with Nick would go as planned, and he would find sanctuary at Caffé Vecchio. His old friend Virgil, The Mad Painter of Rittenhouse Square, assured him that such a gambit would work and promised to advocate for him. The mercurial artist's eccentricities were exceeded only by his immense talent. Like Scotty, his gifts had gone largely unnoticed, save for a few savvy collectors willing to deal with his bizarre behavior. Virgil had insisted Scotty meet him at Holt's Cigar Company to finalize the plan.

BROTHERS OF THE LEAF

Holt's Cigar Company had been around for over one hundred years. Its flagship store is located on Walnut Street in Center City, Philadelphia. Scotty wasn't a cigar smoker, nor was Jilly, so he'd had no reason to visit before today. Lately, however, he was going places and doing things he wouldn't have dreamed of before Jilly's death. The theft and resultant fallout had forced the introverted painter into situations and company he had previously shunned. He did his best to overcome his anxiety and pulled on the brass handle of the outer door leading into Holt's.

Scotty was surprised to find within not a smelly, stodgy cigar shop, as he had imagined, but a rather well-appointed outer showroom of expensive humidors, lighters, and various accoutrements of the cigar world. A gorgeous red Elie Bleu humidor caught his eye.

"Beautiful, isn't it?" A nattily dressed salesman had materialized at his side, close enough to be attentive but not so close as to be overly solicitous.

"The color, what is it called?"

"Red sycamore, with eight coats of varnish. The interior is Spanish cedar. Each humidor is made in France, and

Elie Blue offsets its CO2 emissions by planting a tree for each product sold."

"Fascinating," Scotty said, in response to the wondrous shade of red, as opposed to the company's laudable climate policy.

"Four thousand, including a beautiful analog hygrometer, of course."

"Yes, of course. But I don't smoke cigars," Scotty felt compelled to confess guiltily. But to his surprise, the salesman wasn't put off in the least.

"That's not so unusual. We sell to many customers who purchase gifts for Brothers of the Leaf; Sisters of the Leaf as well," he added without a trace of sarcasm as he extended his hand. "Arturo. A pleasure to meet you."

Scotty shook his hand and introduced himself. Upon hearing his name, Arturo's eyes brightened in recognition. "Ah yes, the painter." Scotty's surprise must have registered, as Arturo immediately followed up with, "Virgil's friend. He's waiting for you upstairs in the lounge. He left a package for you if you'll wait just a minute." Arturo retreated to the inner sanctum of the shop, which consisted of the cigar shop proper and acted as a giant walk-in humidor. He returned quickly with a box of Arturo Fuente Opus X cigars in a gift bag and placed it on the counter in front of Scotty.

"How do I get to the lounge?" Scotty asked.

"When you walk out, it's the first door to your left. The stairs lead to the lounge, and Sophia will greet you at the landing." Arturo stood at the counter, hands tucked behind his back as he bowed slightly.

"Thank you." Scotty took the bag from the counter and began to head for the door. Arturo called after him, his voice taking on an apologetic but urgent tone.

"Mr. Scotty, I'm so sorry, there's a small matter left to attend to."

Scotty couldn't imagine what matter of business he might have with this pleasant man but soon divined what Arturo was loath to say out loud when he handed him a leather check presenter, adding by way of explanation, "Virgil instructed me to provide you with the bill. My apologies if there has been some confusion."

The beginnings of a reluctant smile began to appear on Scotty's face. He should have known. There was something comforting about the predictability of an old friend, no matter the cost—especially since both predictability and old friends were in such short supply of late. Scotty placed his Amex inside and, having paid the admission fee, made his way to Virgil's lair.

Later that night, Scotty hoped to meet Virgil and Nick Di Nobile at Caffé Vecchio to finalize the deal. Scotty hadn't told Virgil the whole story. He left out an important part, one even the thieves didn't know. The part the entire plan depended on and that he was counting on to keep him alive.

As promised, Sophia greeted him at the landing. She stood behind a hostess stand, a practiced but genuine-looking smile on her face. She walked around to greet Scotty as if she had been expecting him. The lounge was dark, and Sophia's face was bathed by the spotlight that illuminated the stand. As she turned to escort him to his table, her profile triggered a spark of recognition in Scotty. He viewed all faces he encountered as potential subjects, and this one was exquisite. Reminiscent of da Vinci's *Lady with an Ermine*, except she held a drink menu in the crook of her arm instead of a weasel. Her resemblance to da Vinci's subject, the Duke of Milan's mistress, was striking. Scotty studied the contours of her jawline as it met her earlobe. This was how Scotty coped with a world of otherwise terrifying stimulations—he synthesized them into living, breathing paintings. Just as Caravaggio had rendered the most gruesome of scenes into works of tear-evoking beauty, so had Scotty arranged a sometimes-intimidating South Philadelphia neighborhood into a menacing yet beautiful landscape. And as he studied his newest subject, he remembered where he had seen that regal jawline and predatory mouth before. It was at Caffé Vecchio Saturday night. Those innocent-looking lips had been firmly affixed to the jugular of Joey "The Kid" Musante.

Virgil smiled at his old friend's approach, his grin broader still when he eyed the gift bag in Scotty's hand. White and wispy, his hair stood up wildly, having seen neither brush nor comb for days. It blended with the cigar smoke that encircled him, making it unclear where follicle ended and vapor began. Virgil had been wearing a blue surgical mask long before it had become prudent, let alone mandatory. It had become optional once more, but he wore it still, albeit draped about his chin while he smoked and drank. Virgil wasn't impolite or disrespectful, but he didn't readily pick up on cues and social convention, so he remained seated while Scotty made his way around the table to shake his paint-specked hands. Scotty was well aware of Virgil's various quirks and eccentricities, so he took no offense. In Scotty's estimation, it was the price the man had paid for his genius. For someone who had himself paid so dearly, it wasn't hard to understand.

FRANK AND DINO

Frank's flight was delayed, and he was in a foul mood when he finally arrived in Philly two hours ten minutes behind schedule. He was seated in 16 F and cursed the fifteen rows of passengers who seemed to take their sweet time walking off the plane. "Cocksuckers," he mumbled under his breath. He grabbed his carry-on from the overhead with his good arm. It was one of the few instances where his old handicap became evident. The withered arm was how Frank first got the nickname "Stone Crab," and why he always sported a long sleeve shirt no matter the weather. He hustled to the first men's room in the terminal, barely avoiding pissing his pants in the process.

Dino had been tracking his flight and pulled up just as Frank walked out of the terminal, before he even had a chance to light up a Marlboro. Frank tossed his bag in the back seat of the Mercedes as Dino had made no move to pop the trunk.

"Mind if I smoke in here?" Dino knew Frank from the old days, so he smiled when he answered, "No."

Frank placed the cigarette in his mouth.

"But Andy does." Frank slipped the pack back in his pocket and stashed the loose cig behind his ear for the short ride to Caposecco's Fruit and Produce.

"How's Andy doing?"

"Andy's Andy," Dino muttered his non-answer.

Real conversationalist this guy, Frank thought as they made their way down 95 and the city rose in the distance. Somewhere in the space between Frank and those high-rise buildings sat the swath of rowhomes, bars, and churches that composed South Philadelphia. This incubator that gave life to all the drama that eventually spread south until it parted the palm trees and rudely roused them from their lounge chairs and barstools. *I'm gonna fucking die here one day*, Frank couldn't help thinking. "But not today," he murmured in response to his thoughts.

"You say something?" Dino asked.

"Nah, just talking to myself."

"Already?" Dino snickered. Feeling a little bad about denying the old man his cigarette, he hit the accelerator aggressively and merged toward the Broad Street exit. "Let's get you a drink and that smoke. Andy's been waiting for you."

They pulled up to the loading dock off Pattison Avenue in minutes, and Andrea Caposecco stood there waiting for them. In a show of graciousness, Andy walked down to help Frank with his bag, remembering his bad arm but not wanting to make it look obvious. He hugged his old friend and kissed him on the cheek.

"Frankie Stone Crab. You haven't changed a bit."

Frank had always liked Andy. He was a class act all the way back to when they were teenagers together. Frank remembered a gin tournament in the back room of the Paradise back in the early '80s when the two of them were the last players standing. Andy was the superior player, and the pot was over twenty thousand dollars. Frank was down on his luck, as always. So when Andy generously offered to split the pot and call it a day, everyone, including Andy, was shocked when Frank refused and sat defiantly at the table instead.

Predictably, Frank lost. Sometimes he felt like he'd been losing ever since.

They stood out on the loading dock, watching a truck being loaded up with pallets of produce. Frank retrieved the Marlboro from behind his ear and lit it. He took a deep drag, closed his eyes, and held it in for a long time. Andy looked on, surprised at how long Frank stayed like that, holding his breath, considering he was still recovering from a heart attack. He reminded Andy of a Houdini copycat he once saw at Steel Pier in Atlantic City. *The Great Gabagool,* or whatever the fuck he called himself, had opened for the diving horse and did a cut-rate variation on Houdini's underwater box escape. It was pretty obvious the box and handcuffs were rigged, but it was risky nonetheless, as evidenced by the Gabagool's eventual drowning. As Andy remembered all this, Dino wheeled out a crate, not unlike Houdini's box, and loaded it onto the truck. Its contents were integral to the plan sketched out by Andy and Nino Scopa in the back room of the cheese shop and just as risky. Nino had used whatever was on the table to map it out. A sugar packet signified the Paradise, Tony Di Nobile's funeral card stood in for Caffé Vecchio, a wine glass, matchbook, saltshaker, and

Zippo lighter all became game pieces in Nino's deadly version of South Philly Monopoly.

When he had finished laying out the plan, he asked Andy to commit the gameboard to memory before clearing the table with a sweep of the back of his hand. The scheme was ambitious in its reach yet nuanced in its intricacies. *This could work*, Andy had thought as he walked out of the shop. *They don't call him The Wizard for nothing*. The plan was dependent upon an illusion, and an illusion is predicated upon the willingness of the audience to believe in it. The willingness, as in all good schemes, exploited a fatal flaw in the target, which in this case was the most reliable of them all—greed.

REMEMBRANCE OF THINGS PAST

"No sooner had the warm liquid mixed with the crumbs touched my palate than a shudder ran through me and I stopped, intent upon the extraordinary thing that was happening to me. An exquisite pleasure had invaded my senses, something isolated, detached, with no suggestion of its origin. And at once the vicissitudes of life had become indifferent to me, its disasters innocuous, its brevity illusory – this new sensation having had on me the effect which love has of filling me with a precious essence; or rather this essence was not in me it was me. ... Whence did it come? What did it mean? How could I seize and apprehend it? ... And suddenly the memory revealed itself. The taste was that of the little piece of madeleine which on Sunday mornings at Combray (because on those mornings I did not go out before mass), when I went to say good morning to her in her bedroom, my aunt Léonie used to give me, dipping it first in her own cup of tea or tisane. The sight of the little madeleine had recalled nothing to my mind before I tasted it. And all from my cup of tea."

— Marcel Proust, *In Search of Lost Time*

Nick hesitated before walking into Caffé Vecchio. While he had committed to return days ago, this moment, more than any, signified the crossing of the Rubicon. Beyond that door was everything he had left behind, even ran from. Now, for the second time in twenty-plus years of self-imposed exile, he was breaking the promise he had made, first to himself and eventually to Grace. He had come back home.

"Are you coming in, Uncle Nick?" Joey asked gently.

It wasn't a challenge, but Nick didn't want to appear indecisive, especially in front of his nephew, so he charged through the door Joey held open for him. And that's when it hit him . . .

The first blow that landed was the smell. Of all the senses, smell is the most reliable and the most evocative when it comes to triggering memories. Nick was having his own Proustian moment of what has been referred to as involuntary memory. For Proust, it had been a soupcon of tea mixed with the crumbs of a madeleine. In Nick's case, the peppers roasting in the kitchen transported him to countless lazy afternoons when he had run to the Caffé directly from school, throwing his bookbag behind the bar and taking a seat near the corner table where his father held court. When it had come time for him to list extracurricular activities for his grade school graduation, he scribbled in "Hanging at Caffé Vecchio," then thought better of it and rubbed at it with a worn-out eraser that only served to tear up the paper, so he had just left it blank. As the years passed, he had given up on rewriting the history of his misspent youth, seeing it eventually for what it was—not some nostalgic romanticized upbringing (a story he had sold himself for far too many years), but a dysfunctional, motley apprenticeship administered by a rotating cast of questionable role models whose alcoholic ruminations he had once mistaken for wisdom. Nick had come to reject all that he had once embraced, and as tasty as those peppers might be, he had long since lost the ability to digest them.

Next came the sounds. The kitchen chorus—transistor radio playing Latino Top 40, the cacophony of pots and pans, jingle of utensils being sorted and polished.

Nick gripped the bar, running his fingers over the grooves and notches. He sank back into a cushioned barstool that was in need of re-upholstering. Alberto leaned over the bar and gave Nick a playful pinch of the cheek. He placed an ice-cold Peroni in front of him, just like he had once served him hot chocolate all those years ago.

"Welcome home, Nicky."

He allowed his eyes to dart around the room's perimeter, trying to detect any changes but finding none. Like vigilant sentinels, his father's paintings hung in their appointed spots. The newest, Virgil Corrado's interpretation of Rembrandt's *The Prodigal in the Tavern* featuring the likeness of Tony Di Nobile as the Prodigal, retained its place of honor above the jukebox. Nick had retrieved the painting from the A.C. Antiquary, a used book and antique shop in Atlantic City where his father had brought it to be framed before his death. Nick had stumbled across it in his pursuit of *The Return of the Prodigal Son*, the first Rembrandt he had found himself reluctantly hunting.

The jukebox . Like a newspaper comic page puzzle from an old *Daily News*, Nick had found the piece of the Caffé that was different. The vintage jukebox was missing. In its place was a tech-friendly internet machine that was just a glorified search engine with flashy graphics. You could even play it from your phone. *When did the whole world become an app?* Nick bemoaned. He had to remind himself that he had begrudgingly caved in to the same upgrade at the Tuscan Tiki.

Nick sipped his beer and wrestled with all the sentimentality rising inside him, steeling himself against the old seduction, the temptation to wade into an idealized version of the past. He couldn't afford to have that particular emotion interfere with the decisions he would be called upon to make in the coming days.

Blame it on the peppers, but it was one of those alcoholic South Philly truisms delivered by a forgotten Caffé philosopher that came to mind: *Always remember, kid, nostalgia killed more guys than cancer.* Like countless other whiskey-soaked nuggets of Caffé wisdom slurred in his adolescent ear, he'd had no idea what it meant at the time. But as he sat at the Caffé's bar, running his fingers over its once comforting imperfections, Nick couldn't think of truer words.

"Pretty boy!"

Gary's booming voice preceded him into the Caffé, and the kitchen door swung open violently as he burst through, his frame blocking out both light and sound. (Actually, Carlos, the dishwasher, had turned down the radio at the approach of Gary's Yukon). The big man moved across the floor with surprising grace, and he had Nick in a bear hug before he had a chance to rise from his stool. Gary left his arm draped over Nick's shoulder and showed no sign of retreating as he motioned for Alberto to tighten them up with something worthy of the moment.

Nick started to detect within himself a vague sense of guilt he couldn't readily explain. Later that night, lying awake and tossing restlessly, he would put his finger on it, whispering a prayer for forgiveness into the darkness. He would remind himself that not all his role models had been drunks and brigands, and not all the advice had been worthless.

Alberto poured a round of Don Julio 1942, including himself and Beto, who had been elevated to executive chef during Gary's illness. Gary made the toast.

"To Tony—none of this would be possible without him." He raised his shot glass toward Virgil's portrait of Nick's father. The magic of Virgil's rendering ensured that Tony always returned the toast, his arm raised in perpetual salutation. Nick joined and knocked back the elixir, allowing the burn to fade to a comforting warmth. He held his father's stare longer than he ever had during his life, reconciliation having eluded them both. He had come to know his father better in death and vacillated between resentment and regret. *Maybe Grace was right*, he thought. *I really should be in therapy*.

"Joey stepped out back to make a call," Gary said.

"I guess we wait on him these days," Nick replied. "Remind me to kiss his ring."

Gary shook his head and blew out a breath that made a low whistle.

"What, I said something funny?" Nick asked.

"That depends. I was just thinking I used to say the same thing about you twenty years ago."

Nick was about to come back with a stinging rebuke but thought better of it. Instead, he signaled to Alberto for an encore. His turn to make a toast, Nick locked eyes with Gary and raised his glass. "I love you, big guy."

Nick was caught off guard by Gary's response—the big man audibly choked. The two men had a bond that assured both would lay down their life for the other, yet it wasn't a sentiment they frequently voiced. Gary cleared his throat and regained his composure.

"I love you too, Nick." Gary clicked glasses with him.

The room was silent, until Beto and Alberto added their glasses to the toast. Gary had barely placed his glass back on the bar, his face still grimacing from the shot, when Nick responded.

"Good." Nick extended his arm toward Gary. "Now kiss my fucking ring."

Gary erupted and feigned a frontal attack, pinning Nick against the corner of the bar like it was a turnbuckle. Beto pretended to break it up, stifling a laugh, and the remaining kitchen staff gathered at the door, curious to see what the uproar was about but hesitant to come out into the dining room.

Gary squeezed Nick tight. Nick wouldn't have stood a chance if it had been a real tussle. As he felt Gary's grizzly mitts press tight against his rib cage, he sensed that the attack had morphed into a genuine hug. The big man was already breathing heavily from the exertion. He gently placed his forehead against Nick's before he released him from his grip. Nick felt Gary's sweat transfer to his own brow. As he stepped back, he tapped Nick on the chin with a playful but lightning-quick jab that he pulled back at the last moment. Even so, it caused Nick's teeth to click together, and he rubbed his jaw.

"What did I miss?" Joey had walked in from the kitchen just in time for the love tap.

"Nothing, young boy, have a seat. You next," Gary replied.

"You're up," Nick said to Joey, nodding at the jukebox, trusting the kid to punch up a suitable soundtrack for their meeting. Beto took that as his signal to return to the kitchen. Gary walked over to the corner table, setting up court where Tony Di Nobile had presided for so many years. Joey quickly punched up a few tunes and joined them. Gary rapped on the table with his knuckles, unofficially bringing the sit-down to order. A kingly bassoon heralded The Delfonics' "Didn't I (Blow Your Mind This Time)," followed by a funky sitar. For the first time since his arrival, Nick began to feel at home.

"When does Frank get in?" Gary asked.

"Pretty sure he's already here," Nick responded.

"Should we wait for him before we get down to the dirty details?"

"Well, that's just it," Nick said. "Frank *is* the dirty detail."

"I don't get it," Joey chimed in.

Gary waived over to Alberto for a refill. Nick clarified that he was switching to Peroni, and Alberto brought over their drinks. Nick's premonition was coming true; he hadn't been back for a day, and he was already half in the bag. *When I get back, I need to dry out for a while*, he vowed, knowing he was kidding himself. He sipped the crisp lager, which cleansed the residue of the tequila, and continued.

"If I'm not mistaken, he's already meeting with someone from De Rosa's crew."

"That scumbag from the sticks? Why would he be anywhere near that clown, especially after what happened to his rat uncle?"

Gary shot Joey a stern look, like he had breached some unspoken underworld etiquette. Nick stepped in to save him but only managed to turn up the heat.

"Frank's gone over to the other side."

Joey jumped out of his seat. "What? After everything you did for him?" Joey hiked up his pants and pushed his chair in like he was headed for the door to settle the matter right then and there.

Gary's furrowed brow gave way to a smile as he leaned back in his seat far enough to put the chair on its rear legs. Nick feared it would give way, but Gary leaned back forward, averting disaster, and the single clap of his mitts went off like a gunshot.

"Whoo hoo! Ain't that a bitch?" Gary shook his head slowly.

Nick smiled back in admiration and raised his glass to the big man.

Joey spread his arms wide, fingers splayed open. He was already halfway to the door. "What am I missing?"

"What you're missing could fill a book," Gary answered. "Sit the fuck down."

"Excuse me?" Joey looked to Nick for some clarification.

Nick pointed to the empty chair in response. "Have a seat. You just might learn something."

"And live longer," Gary added.

"Yeah, that too."

Joey sat back down under protest. He pushed his chair back from the table and leaned forward with his legs wide open, arms draping between like he was ready to change his mind at any second. "So?"

Gary was looking straight at Nick, like Joey wasn't even in the room and they were having their own conversation. He was icing Joey a bit without directly reprimanding him.

"Ralph's idea?" Gary asked.

"All the way," Nick answered.

"Nice." Gary was rocking back and forth now in time to the music. The manicured fingers of his right hand tapped the table along with the bass line. His mind made the calculations as he envisioned the moves playing out on the gameboard. The streets were *his* canvas, and he was no less an artist than Virgil or Scotty when it came to applying the finishing strokes.

Joey begrudgingly slid his chair back up to the table. He plucked a sugar packet from its holder and slowly began to shake it between his thumb and forefinger, complementing Gary's percussion.

MONEY NEVER MISSES

Fenway Phil sat at the end of the Paradise bar watching his Guinness cascade inside its pint glass. He would have preferred a house-grade Chianti poured from a jug, but the stout better suited his current role. Originally hailing from New Haven, Connecticut, from a half Italian father and a half Irish mother, the remaining half a jumble, Phil had learned to adapt to his surroundings from an early age. Adopting the genealogy most suitable to the prevailing winds, Fenway Phil (occasionally going by Flatbush Phil) fancied himself something of an underworld chameleon. So complete were his adaptations, he actually convinced himself that each was authentic in its own right, the hallmark of the consummate con man—believing his own bullshit.

His present mutation: Boston-based old head, vaguely connected to either the IRA or a Charlestown crew (no one cared enough to check, nor did it really matter), was going over without a hitch. The Thorn's crew were all either too stupid or too greedy to question this shaky pedigree. All The Thorn cared about was that Phil looked the part, and that he did. Phil Ragusa had an uncanny resemblance to the actor George Raft; this alone gave him credibility enough. Moreover, Fenway Phil was always working on some big score. Naturally, none of these scams had panned out, but he always had a perfectly reasonable explanation as to why they fell through at the last second. Up until now, that is.

This collection of miscreants had actually managed to stumble upon an epic score, the true value of which none of them fully comprehended. Being the misfits they were, they had no idea how to unload it. Phil had assured The Thorn he had the perfect fence but had been stalling until he could devise a way to steal it for himself. So when Dino Graniti reached out with a proposal, Phil was more than receptive. He was barely eking out an existence from the crumbs that fell onto the floor of the Paradise. Everybody knew Andy Boy controlled everything that generated any real money in the neighborhood, so they were reduced to scrounging around the periphery, where the prey didn't know any better.

Dino appeared at the rear door, the "Ladies Entrance." He waved at Phil, but with a come here motion, indicating he needed some help. Phil made his way over, careful not to look too eager. It was important to keep up appearances, and he had strived to give Dino the impression that he wasn't desperate, though desperate was an understatement. Phil drank at the Paradise three nights a week. The remainder of his time he spent in the Marina District of Atlantic City bouncing between the Borgata, Harrah's, and the Golden Nugget, making the rounds of the poker rooms, sports books, and various lounges. As for where he laid his head on any given night, he liked to say he had a waterfront residence at the Jersey shore, which was technically accurate. Phil's 2001 Econoline van was permanently parked on deflated Michelins in "A" lot of the Frank S. Farley Marina at the Golden Nugget. The van faced the bulkhead and had a perfect view of the marina filled with the kind of vessels he would never own.

Phil had scored an extra vehicle hangtag and boat owner's access card from Bigeye Billy, the captain of a Viking sportfishing yacht. Billy was a regular at the Borgata's race book and a nice enough guy. One afternoon over a few drinks, he had bought Phil's Flatbush act hook, line, and sinker. Phil slept in the van most nights and made use of the marina bathrooms and showers, commandeering the BIGEYE's cockpit for late-night cocktails. In the off-season, things were a great deal easier. He could usually score a comped room or at least find a deal on Hotel Tonight or Trivago for about $49.00 a night when he needed to sleep in a real bed and take a real shower. In this fashion, Phil arguably maintained a waterfront residence at the Jersey shore.

Phil had to step aside as one of Dino's guys jostled past him with a hand truck. Dino was standing on the lift gate of a box truck and was lowering a wooden crate.

"What's going on?" Phil asked.

"Just a few changes around here. You'll see," Dino answered.

The man who had passed Phil was now pushing the Paradise's Dodge City poker machine out the door. When he got to the top of the steps, it toppled forward, crashing onto the sidewalk like a day drinker who overstayed his shift. The machine shattered, pieces of it spreading into Passyunk Avenue. Phil feared what was about to happen next, Dino undoubtedly erupt at the man for his clumsiness. Instead, he just laughed and stepped down from the lift gate.

"Give us a hand, will ya?" Dino said, and the three of them lifted the machine, tipping it into an Athens Hauling dumpster. "These are the next things to go." Dino pointed at the dumpster. He snorted up some phlegm and spat it onto the Athens logo.

Phil didn't ask any more questions. He didn't have to. Dino had made his move. Andy was out, and Dino was in. Dino handed him a crowbar, and the two of them pried open the crate. Instead of the *Great Gabagool*, a sparkling new poker machine revealed itself. *Presto!* The first part of Andy Boy's illusion was introduced.

"This is the first of many. We split this one, you and me. The rest belong to Frankie Stone Crab and me, but I want you to service them. For that, you get a flat $2,000 a week. Any new ones you originate on your own, we split 50/50 with you after the house gets their cut. You whack up your end however you like."

Phil knew that he was referring to The Thorn. Two thousand was more money per week than he had ever earned in his life. The right thing would have been to thank his lucky stars and cut The Thorn in on this miraculous windfall, but being the con artist he was, Phil immediately started to scheme how he could cut Lenny out of the equation. This was the second part of Andy's trick—the misdirection. Andy knew he could always count on the two great motivators when performing his sorcery, but this particular sleight of hand was Nino Scopa's idea.

The Wizard had a philosophy when it came to these matters, a refinement of Andy's old adage. He shared it freely in the back room of his cheese shop to any who had ears to listen.

Pussy is powerful, but money never misses.

SALOME

Now Herod had arrested John and bound him and put him in prison because of Herodias, his brother Philip's wife, for John had been saying to him: "It is not lawful for you to have her." Herod wanted to kill John, but he was afraid of the people, because they considered John a prophet.

On Herod's birthday the daughter of Herodias danced for the guests and pleased Herod so much that he promised with an oath to give her whatever she asked. Prompted by her mother, she said, "Give me here on a platter the head of John the Baptist." The king was distressed, but because of his oaths and his dinner guests, he ordered that her request be granted and had John beheaded in the prison. His head was brought in on a platter and given to the girl, who carried it to her mother. John's disciples came and took his body and buried it. Then they went and told Jesus.

Matthew 14:3-12 (NIV)

"What time is he getting here?" Nick was growing a little impatient.

"What's your hurry?" Gary responded. "You got somewhere to be? Besides, I haven't seen you in almost a year. I was hoping we would catch up. You know, reminisce about the good old days."

Nick was used to adhering to a fairly tight regimen back in Lauderdale and had to think about it for a second. Why was he feeling so stressed and hurried now that he was back at the Caffé with no real schedule to keep—unless you counted having to report back to Dmitry at some point. As for the second part, well, as much as he genuinely loved seeing Gary, he had a distinctly different recollection as to how *good* the good old days had been. He couldn't escape the fact that returning to Caffé Vecchio always meant revisiting the failed, sometimes tortured relationship he had with his father, a relationship that would never be mended. Closure, if such a thing even existed, had eluded Nick when it came to his father. Any such notion had turned out to be a phantom, running through his hands like grains of sand, vanishing from his sight like ashes in the surf.

The sound of the back door slamming shut mercifully delivered Nick from further rumination or, heaven forbid, self-examination. Charles Scottoline emerged from the kitchen in a breathless state. He was lugging a brown paper-wrapped package in the shape of a painting.

"Hope you don't mind. I told him to park out back and come through the kitchen. Didn't want anyone to see him traipsing up the Avenue with your *present*." Gary dragged the word out, taking some indistinct pleasure in sounding it out.

Nick was never a big fan of receiving gifts, especially from strangers. Even with Grace, he much preferred being the gift giver. Despite her constant assurances she didn't want or need any presents, her face always betrayed her, her eyes lighting up like a child on Christmas morning. At those times, Nick could glimpse the little girl in her, and he felt unworthy, certain that she was better than he deserved. Now, a man he had never met before was standing in his Caffé bearing an unsolicited gift. His suspicion was so high that it morphed into an amused curiosity.

"Charles Scottoline." He extended his hand to Nick, removing his cap with the other and giving a nod of acknowledgment to Gary and Joey. "My friends call me Scotty."

Nick shook his hand and invited him to the bar for a drink. Scotty had leaned the package against a table, and he retrieved it before joining Nick and taking a seat at the bar, one hand still draped over the top as he propped it against his knee.

"That looks a little uncomfortable. Not to appear forward or anything, but Gary said you had something for me?"

Alberto poured 1942 all around in anticipation of the reveal as Scotty began to tear at the paper.

"Yes, of course, pardon me. It's just that I know your father was a great appreciator of art. Jilly always spoke so highly of him, and Virgil's painting." Scotty was nodding in the direction of Virgil's rendering of Anthony

Di Nobile as *The Prodigal in the Tavern*. "My old friend doesn't paint such things lightly. Your father must have been an extraordinary man to warrant such a tribute, and I thought it only fitting that you have one of your own."

Scotty had peeled back enough of the paper for the painting to begin to reveal itself. Gary and Joey were gathered behind Nick, and even Alberto couldn't help leaning over the bar to get a peek.

Scotty paused. "I'm sorry. How rude of me. You should have the honor."

Gary nodded in agreement, and Nick reluctantly got up from his stool, tearing at the paper, impatient to get at the root of this strange little man's folly. He wasn't prepared for the image that awaited him beneath.

The first face to emerge from beneath the paper was that of Salome, in the likeness of Angie Romano. Nick had randomly torn at the paper in a way that exposed her eyes first. Her stare was piercing. Not because of any malevolence, but far more sinister due to its indifference, as if the executioner's handiwork was so mundane as to be anticlimactic. Like a child throwing a rock at a bird, shocked by having struck it, its dying breath inspiring not terror but ennui.

Next came the executioner. His face was downturned and in shadow, perhaps revealing a modicum of shame for having had to swing his sword for a child's whim.

The last character, Caravaggio himself in the original, wasn't exactly a person at all. Set upon its side, facing forward and resting on a platter, was the head of John the Baptist, which Salome had requested from her stepfather, Herod. Nick did his best to mask his shock at seeing his own face depicted on this disembodied skull, but Gary's eyes practically bulged out of his own.

"What the fuck is this?" Joey spoke first. "Your idea of a joke?"

Scotty stood there, hat gripped with both hands in front of him, spinning it nervously but apparently unrepentant.

"Take it easy, Joey," Nick said. "It's a gift. I'm sure Scotty has his reasons. Beauty, after all, is in the eye of the beholder."

"Well, I'm beholdin' some fucked up shit then." Even Gary couldn't maintain his usual diplomacy.

"Caravaggio was wanted for murder. While in exile, he frequently painted his own face in various beheading scenes. It was his plea to patrons and benefactors for their protection. I painted this scene in that grand tradition. And now, I'm humbly requesting your protection," he said to Nick.

"Well correct me if I'm wrong, but then shouldn't that be your old mug on that platter instead of my boy here?" Gary plucked the toothpick from his mouth and flicked it with his thumb and middle finger with surprising accuracy at Nick's head—on the painting, that is.

"I . . . I took certain artistic liberties," Scotty replied.

"What does that mean?" Joey inquired.

"Well." Scotty paused for a long time, as if he was about to share some deep insight that only a master painter could comprehend. "I'm much too shy for self-portraiture, and he's much better looking than me." Scotty pointed at Nick with a craggy, paint-stained finger.

Scotty's self-deprecating explanation seemed to defuse the situation. Gary shook his head and signaled Alberto for backup. Joey retreated to the jukebox to punch up something to improve the mood. Nick was still fixated. Not on *his* face, oddly enough, but on Angie's languid gaze, captured so accurately by Scotty. She had somehow followed him back from Florida, and now here she was, poised to be immortalized in Caffé Vecchio.

"Wait. What about the girl in the painting?" Nick asked.

Scotty went on to describe the picture taken at Caffé Vecchio on New Year's Eve a few years prior. Nick remembered, of course. It had been the last time he had seen Angie. That is until she turned up at the Tuscan Tiki a few days ago. Nick was starting to have that sensation that challenges you to question whether you are stuck in a dream, like this all had happened before and he could predict the next thing someone would say.

Just then, the opening notes of "Not on the Outside" by the Moments kicked in, just like Nick's subconscious predicted, and the effect was complete. A second later, the sensation faded, and Nick returned to the real world, uncertain of where he had been or for how long, but his focus regained. His gaze shifted to the chilling image of his own head staring back at him from a platter.

Nick walked over to Scotty to thank him. The painter shrunk a bit as if uncertain of Nick's intentions in approaching. He put out his hand sheepishly, but Nick ignored it and wrapped him up in a hug.

"Thank you, Scotty. It's beautiful. Virgil was right. You're a master of your craft."

"You're welcome," Scotty replied. "And the other part?"

Gary answered for Nick. "Ain't nobody gonna hurt you long as you here." The big man walked back toward the kitchen to get a hammer and hardware to hang the newest addition to Caffé Vecchio's increasingly eclectic art collection. When he returned, he looked to Nick for guidance on where to place it.

"Well, let's not put it next to the other beheading scene," Nick said, referring to the other Caravaggio reproduction, *Judith Beheading Holofernes*, Virgil had painted for Nick's father.

"Aren't they the same scene?" Joey asked

Nick looked to Scotty. "What do you think?"

Scotty carried a stool to the front and took a seat. He sat there quietly for a few moments, taking in the entirety of the paintings hanging around the perimeter and absorbing them in their unnatural habitat.

"Are you familiar with the story of Judith?" His question was to the group, and when no one volunteered an answer, they began to gather around him for the story to come. "It's quite intriguing."

JUDITH

Finally, when it got late, the guests excused themselves and left. Bagoas then closed up the tent from the outside and prevented Holofernes' servants from going in. So they all went to bed; everyone was very tired because the banquet had lasted so long. Judith was left alone in the tent with Holofernes who was lying drunk on his bed. Judith's slave woman was waiting outside the tent for Judith to go and pray, as she had done each night. Judith had also told Bagoas that she would be going out to pray as usual.

All the guests and servants were now gone, and Judith and Holofernes were alone in the tent. Judith stood by Holofernes' bed and prayed silently,

O Lord, God Almighty, help me with what I am about to do for the glory of Jerusalem. Now is the time to rescue your chosen people and to help me carry out my plan to destroy the enemies who are threatening us.

Judith went to the bedpost by Holofernes' head and took down his sword. She came closer, seized Holofernes by the hair of his head, and said,

O Lord, God of Israel, give me strength now. Then Judith raised the sword and struck him twice in the neck as hard as she could, chopping off his head.

Judith 13: 1-10

"She seduced the Assyrian general who was waging war on her people. He invited her into his tent, and the result was not what he had hoped for." Scotty appeared more relaxed now that he was talking about paintings. His discomfort in navigating the real world began to fade. He gestured to Alberto with his glass, requesting a refill before continuing his dissertation. "The story has been told many times over in various forms. The actual history is fuzzy, and it's debatable whether there is any historical truth to it, but the story has inspired artists from Botticelli to Klimt."

"I like that Klimt," Gary interjected, eliciting some inquisitive looks.

"Thanks for sharing that," Nick jabbed.

"What, I can't have an opinion? Fuck this." Gary feigned insult and jostled Joey as he got up from his stool and took his turn at the jukebox. Nick and Joey knew he was just playing his role in their decades-old drama, but Scotty looked genuinely alarmed. Nick gave him a reassuring nod and a half smile, signaling him to continue. Scotty took a sip of his drink, cleared his throat, and continued addressing Nick directly.

"In the Baroque period, Cristofano Allori painted the head of Holofernes as a self-portrait, while imagining his former mistress as Judith. That concept also influenced my present work."

"Yeah, I noticed." Nick raised his glass. "Thanks."

"Please, I meant no offense. I simply wished to convey that some themes are universal and the dynamics are timeless. That's why we repeat the same mistakes over and over."

"What are you trying to say here?"

"Only that the purpose of all art, in my humble opinion, is to make the lonely feel less alone, the shunned less isolated. At least that's what it did for me. Knowing that others shared both my dreams and afflictions, sometimes centuries ago, has given me great comfort when I was at my lowest, maybe even saved my life." Gary had cued up Marvin Gaye's "Distant Lover." Scotty pointed one finger to the sky. "Which is why songs about heartache never go out of style."

"Art should comfort the disturbed and disturb the comfortable. Anyway, I think that's how the saying goes," Joey said.

"That's exactly how it goes, Joey. Good for you." Scotty raised his glass.

Even Gary paused and looked up from the jukebox to indicate his approval. He raised a glass to Scotty. "Well, you come to the right place, my man. We all disturbed here."

"Can't argue with you there, big man," Nick said.

"It should go *there.*" Scotty pointed at a spot on the wall to the right of *Prodigal in the Tavern*, Virgil's take on Rembrandt's self-portrait with his wife Saskia, with

Anthony Di Nobile sitting in for the Old Master. Scotty's decision was certain, like the answer had been there all along but only revealed itself at that moment.

"Works for me." Gary walked over with the tools.

"Fine with me too," Nick said. "But may I ask why you're so sure?"

Scotty got up from his stool and started walking around, beginning at the front and working his way clockwise, pausing only momentarily at each painting—he breezed past the focal point of the room, the copy of *Christ in the Storm*, the memory of the burglary and the incomprehensible loss too raw for him to revisit—until he came to a reproduction of Titian's *Rape of Europa*.

"This painting is part of a poesie—a visual translation of a poem. Titian was commissioned to create a series of paintings for Prince Phillip, and this is one of them. Each is beautiful standing alone, but together they form a cycle, a series. They refer to mythological stories and are Titian's visual translation of Ovid's 'Metamorphoses.'"

"That's some deep shit," Gary said.

"Is it really, though?" Gary's face registered surprise at Scotty's curt response. "Is it any deeper than the choice of songs you gentlemen play on that jukebox? Each song is meaningful in its own right, but strung together, they form larger themes. Did you think I hadn't noticed?"

Gary's expression went from surprised to stunned.

"So, you're saying our music is a kind of a… poesie?" Joey asked.

"Maybe, Joey. Tell me, how does this make you feel?" Scotty nodded toward the jukebox, referencing the current selection, "Try a Little Tenderness." Otis Redding's voice was kicking in on the second part of the song, the part where it shifts into a higher gear.

"It makes the hair stand up on the back of my neck."

"Exactly." Scotty appeared exceedingly pleased by Joey's description. "That's precisely what I'm referring to. There's a word for that, Joey. It's called *frisson*. You can experience it from a song, a painting, sometimes even while reading a novel."

"How 'bout this?" Gary was hip thrusting his way through the end of the song.

"Yes, that too," Scotty answered.

Nick shook his head, not only at Gary's gyrations but also at the absurdity that had brought this disparate crew together. He concluded that, in a weird way, it seemed not only perfectly natural but inevitable. He conveyed that sentiment by mumbling, "Fuck my life."

"What I'm saying is this. These paintings, the order in which they are arranged, maybe they're not so random, maybe they form a little poesie of their own. Take this one, for instance." Scotty stood before a print of Vermeer's *Girl Reading a Letter at an Open Window*. He pointed at a large blank section of the wall in the upper right-hand quarter of the painting. "See this?"

"I don't see anything but a wall," Nick answered.

"Exactly. But that's not how the restored original looks today. For years, it was accepted that Vermeer had overpainted this section, which is not uncommon, but science caught up. X-ray imaging revealed an image beneath the overpainted section, an image on the wall—a painting within a painting. Vermeer had originally included a framed painting of Cupid on the wall over the girl's shoulder. Eventually, it underwent a restoration, and conservationists removed some of the varnish. Tests were performed, and the paint used to cover Cupid was found to be different from the rest of the work. Also, layers of dirt were discovered between the overpaint and the Roman god of love lurking beneath. The conclusion was that it wasn't Vermeer who executed the overpaint but a foreign hand, perhaps even after his death. This led to restoring the image back to Vermeer's original intent, and Cupid reappeared."

"This is fascinating, Scotty. Really, it is," Nick said. "But what's it have to do with us?"

"That's a question only you can answer, Nick." By this time, Gary had finished hanging Scotty's painting next to *Prodigal in the Tavern*. "May I ask a question?" Scotty pointed to the Saskia figure sitting on Anthony Di Nobile's lap. "Who is this woman?"

She was beautiful, but unlike Rembrandt's Saskia, her hair was raven black. Her piercing stare gave her a severe look that contrasted starkly with Anthony Di Nobile's good-natured grin.

Nick looked at the painting as if for the first time. It was a lighthearted, whimsical composition in a style Virgil had described as a "genre" painting depicting everyday peasant life. He had been so moved and focused by his father's countenance, the broad smile on his face and the raised glass, that he hadn't paid much attention to the woman in the background. He felt guilty for not having given it more thought before now.

"I really don't know. It's not my mother, that's for sure. How about you?" Nick looked to his father's oldest friend for an answer.

"I got nothing," Gary responded.

Nick stroked his chin as he examined the painting more closely. The hair began to stand up on the back of his neck.

"I know who it is," Joey spoke up, confirming Nick's suspicions.

Joey couldn't believe he'd walked past it all this time, practically leaned on it each time he played the jukebox, but had somehow never noticed. She appeared to be in her late twenties in the picture, but the eyes were timeless, and unmistakable.

"It's my grandmother," Joey said.

AURORA

Texas Avenue Beach, Atlantic City, NJ
1976

Tony Di Nobile was never much of a beach person, claiming he disliked the sand. He preferred tinkering on his boat, *Tony Rome*, a Bertram Flybridge he was perpetually repairing and tweaking. So, it was a rare day when Tony pulled Nicky out of school on a steamy, early June day for an impromptu day at the beach. It was Nick's Uncle Frank who came to get him out of class. This was long before the days of heightened school security. Virtually any adult family member or neighbor could pull a child out of school.

"Family emergency," Frank stated to the principal. Nick's mother had passed away a few years prior, and Sister Mary didn't inquire further.

Frank drove him to a candy store on Passyunk Avenue. The woman behind the counter seemed familiar in a neighborhood way. Frank kissed Nick on the top of his head, sat him on a wrought iron chair at a small table, and told him his father would be along shortly. He blew a kiss to the woman behind the counter, who was by now walking around to Nick and taking off her apron in one graceful movement. She smiled at Frank but didn't return the kiss. Nick remembered feeling like this was all perfectly normal. The air conditioner over the door hummed loudly, and the candy store felt delightfully cool. The woman took the other seat at the small table. She reminded Nick of a woman from a movie his father had taken him to see at the Colonial. In the film, he was shocked to see the woman's breasts and felt ashamed sitting there with his father next to him, like he was being tested. Later in the movie, the woman was blown up in a car. Nick had wanted to cry.

In that dark theater, in the short space of those scenes, he had a realization that stuck with him throughout his youth, maybe still lurked in some dark recess of his brain; *This is what it feels like to be in love.* He hadn't seen a woman so beautiful and captivating since then... until that day in the candy store.

"You must be Nicky." She stretched out her slender arm and gently took his hand. His palm felt sweaty against her cool grip. He looked down at his hand. It was marked with ink from a pen, and his fingernails were a little dirty. The woman smiled as if she was reading his thoughts. She placed her left hand over the back of his hand. It felt comforting and seemed to say, *it's okay.*

"My name is Aurora," she said just as the bell jingled above the door and his father walked in. He pulled his hand back quickly, as if he were afraid to be caught doing something wrong. He felt exactly like he had that day in the Colonial when the lady on the screen dropped her nightgown, and he'd pretended to focus on his popcorn.

Tony was carrying a bag with a change of clothes for Nick. He went into the back of the candy store, which turned out to be a living room, and Aurora directed him to a bathroom to change into his beach clothes. When he came out, Aurora had changed as well. She took Nick's school clothes and folded them neatly back into the bag. When they walked back into the front of the store, Aurora held his hand and walked him over to the counter.

"Pick out anything you like, Nicky," she said.

The counter was stocked to the gills with every type of candy, lollipop, and gum. He looked back at his father to see if it was really okay, but he was already holding the front door open for them.

"Go on, Nicky, it's a gift. Help yourself," Aurora said. Nick settled on a pack of gum with a zebra on the wrapper. He had never had this particular gum before, but he had seen the commercial and it seemed like magical stuff happened when you chewed it. "Good choice," Aurora said. "That's my favorite too." Nick wasn't sure if she was being serious, but it made him feel good.

Aurora flipped the sign to *Closed*, locked the door behind her, and they walked out together. Tony's Cadillac was parked at the corner. It was still early, and the Avenue was quiet. They walked the half block with Aurora still holding his hand, and Nick noticed that his father was holding her other hand. It was painfully brief, but Nick would later recall thinking in those fleeting, precious moments, *This is what it feels like to be a family.*

Nick sat unbuckled in the back seat. Aurora slid over to play the radio, retrieving an 8-track cassette from the console like she'd done it many times before. The front of the cassette had a picture of a man with long hair and a guitar. She pushed the tape into the opening, and it made a satisfying clicking sound. They drove the length of the Atlantic City Expressway like that, Aurora occasionally smiling back over her shoulder at him. Nick liked the weird sound the man made with his guitar. It wasn't like anything he'd heard before. In the years that followed, Nick could never hear that song, "Show Me The Way" by Peter Frampton, without thinking of that day—the sweet taste of the zebra gum that faded so fast, Aurora's smiling face looking back at him from the front seat, the smell of the Coppertone suntan lotion Aurora applied so gently on his back (not like his father, who slapped it on like spackle). Those sensations eventually became all jumbled up and intertwined in his recollections. It became impossible to encounter one without evoking the others. Now, every time he heard that song, he changed the channel.

They spent one glorious day like that. Nick and his father splashed in the waves while Aurora watched from a beach chair, clapping and shouting when either body surfed a wave. She wrapped Nick in a towel when he finally emerged, fingers pruned and fingernails flushed spotless by the saltwater. They walked the boardwalk after and played Skee-Ball in an arcade. Later, they had pizza for dinner and fried dough sprinkled with powdered sugar for dessert. It was the happiest day of his young life. It was also the last day he ever saw Aurora.

Now, she stared at him from a painting, frozen in time, looking much like she had that day. Before everything went bad. Before the light went out in Tony Di Nobile's heart.

THE HONEY TRAP

Frank had been holed up in the apartment above Smokey Joe's Tavern for the past few days. He didn't want to risk running into Nick until the plan had been set in motion. Ralph held on to the apartment for use by the Tasker Morris guys, and for occasions like this. Frank got a text from Dino this morning and headed down to the bar around noon so he could perch up someplace with a good view of the street. He also needed a few drinks to take the edge off and help channel the old Frankie "Stone Crab" Valletto persona.

Smokey Joe's was still the way he remembered it. Unlike most of the other businesses on the Avenue, the new owners were from the neighborhood. They knew the value of leaving some things the way they were. Most importantly, it was dark, like a proper bar should be. Frank could never understand the appeal of a brightly lit taproom. It was like drinking in a hospital cafeteria. The drinker should feel like he escaped from the outside world, with its prying eyes and judgmental looks. Smokey Joe's did not disappoint in this department. Frank groped his way to a corner stool while his eyes adjusted. In this environment, a man could plot and plan. In the dimly lit haze of the early afternoon, a drinker could dream that life still contained endless possibilities. A longshot could still cross the finish line, and a beautiful stranger could wander in from the sunny Avenue. *Who am I kidding*? Frank checked himself. *I haven't hit a longshot in years*, and beautiful strangers? *They're not so beautiful anymore, just strange.*

Frank ordered a Maker's on the rocks, which turned out to be just one extra-large rock, a massive sphere of ice that he swirled around the glass in a satisfying orbit. The whisky hit just right. The first few always did. This was the good part.

Dino walked in, bringing a slashing burst of sunlight with him. It cut across the bar and pierced Frank's perfect sphere, threatening to melt it like a laser. Dino paused in the doorway, taking a quick inventory of the room before wading in.

"You mind?" Frank said.

An old-timer at the back of the bar wasn't so diplomatic. "Shut the fucking door!"

Dino smiled, allowed the door to close behind him, and sat next to Frank without really looking directly at him. "How's it feel to be home?" Dino asked.

"I wouldn't know," Frank answered. It was true. Florida might not have been home for Frank, but *this* no longer was either. "I'm kind of a man without a home these days."

"That's not so bad." Dino pointed at Frank's drink as the bartender looked up from his *Racing Form*. "Sometimes . . ." Dino waited for his drink to arrive and clicked glasses before finishing his thought. "Sometimes home is overrated." Dino's face was incapable of forming a smile and displayed a look of perpetual disgust that most people found scary. Conversely, when he uttered something genuinely witty, the effect was one of exaggerated hilarity.

"Fuck home." Frank raised his glass and joined Dino in downing his as a voice rose up from the back of the bar.

"Fuck home." The old-timer echoed the toast and raised his glass.

"Nice fucking place," Dino said. "Smells like the exterminator just left."

"It's not so bad," Frank said. "Besides, they're good kids that took it over. It might be the last real taproom left on the Avenue. I heard even the Paradise has a gluten-free menu now. Ain't that some shit?"

"Yeah, Frankie, that's some shit. But you can try it for yourself. I set up a meeting with Phil and De Rosa. The Thorn wants to meet the famous Frankie Stone Crab."

"You don't think he knows about… that thing."

"I don't know what you're talking about, Frankie, and I'm sure he doesn't either. Not that it would matter. I don't get the impression they were very close. Besides, that crew is running on fumes, and we just backed up a tanker."

"What about the painting? Whaddya hear?"

"Stashed away somewhere until they line up a buyer. I doubt Phil knows where despite what he wants me to believe. De Rosa trusts him as far as he could throw him, and I don't think they know exactly what they got."

"So, what's the play?" Frank said.

"That's the fun part. I got a call from Ralph this morning. Looks like Dmitry sent in the honey trap."

Frank's eyebrows jumped, and his face registered a look that mingled fear and delight. He ordered three more Maker's, counting in the old-timer. "When does she get in?"

Dino was facing the window looking out at the Avenue. Instead of answering Frank, he said, "Make that four." Frank figured he was just buying one for the bartender, but then the door opened and the daylight intruded once again. The old-timer opened his mouth to deliver his standard greeting, but thought better of it after looking up at the petite silhouette backlit in the doorway.

"Hello, boys," Anastasia said. The honey trap had arrived.

The door closed, blotting out the sun and revealing the most exotic creature to step into Smokey's since Angie Romano attended her grandfather's funeral luncheon there in '94. Frank was blinking to adjust his eyesight, but he kept seeing her figure projected on the inside of his eyelids, like that St. Theresa prayer card they used to stare at as kids until she appeared against a blank wall. Dino offered her the stool between him and Frank, but she walked right past him and threw her arms over Frank's shoulders while planting a passionate kiss on Frank's thin lips. She released him with a playful finger to the chest that pushed him back in his stool.

"Careful, Frankie, mind your ticker. And you must be Dino."

Dino straightened up and licked his lips a bit.

"Yes," she said as she gripped his hand in a chaste shake. "Ralph was right; you do look disgusted about something. Not me, I hope."

Frank laughed, puffing out his chest and feeling pretty good about Anastasia's little display. "So, can I still call you Donna?" Frank asked, referring to the alias she had used on her last visit.

"You can call me whatever you like, my love. But for our purposes, yes, Donna will do just fine." She knocked back the whisky and settled in for the debriefing. Ralph had filled her in on the target, but she needed to hear it from Frank. She trusted his insight and opinion. He had a knack for speaking the truth in an unvarnished manner that only a man who had suffered greatly could manage. His suffering, she thought, had purged him of ego.

"Just get me close," she said, "and when the time comes, I will do what needs to be done. But first, I need to study him."

"How're your bartending skills?" Dino asked.

Donna studied Dino for a moment but didn't respond. Instead, she walked around the bar, slid past the bartender with a rhetorical, "May I?" and sauntered over to the ice machine. She picked up a rocks glass, turned her back to the gallery and bent over in a prolonged, exaggerated movement, stretching her Lululemon yoga pants to their limit. "Sorry," she whispered to the bartender. "Just needed some ice."

He backed up to let her through. The old-timer's tongue was practically on the floor. Frank decided that maybe life still contained some possibilities, and even Dino lost his look of perpetual disgust, if just for a moment.

Donna sat back down next to them. "How was that?"

Dino composed himself. "You start at the Paradise tomorrow. Be there at six."

"That's what I thought," she said. "Frankie, it's too quiet in here. Why don't you play some music?" Frank walked over to the jukebox, his head still swimming with possibilities. "And make sure you play *our* song."

Frank had no idea *they* had a song, much less what it was, but he'd be damned if he wasn't going to play it.

AL AMIN

Victor Baldassare was a patient man, or at least he maintained the outward appearance of one. But like a duck gliding serenely across a pond, his mind was paddling furiously below the surface. And that was how he came to the conclusion that Lenny De Rosa was jerking him around. The break-in had gone off without a hitch. Predictably, Charles Scottoline didn't open his mouth about the stolen painting given that he had stolen it in the first place. Now, however, Victor was getting reports that Scotty was spending time at Caffé Vecchio with the De Nobile crew. Most infuriating of all, De Rosa was getting squirrely about the exchange and blaming it on *an abundance of caution*. Victor suspected the real reason had more to do with an abundance of greed. *The Thorn is trying to cut out the middleman and find his own buyer.* Victor occupied himself with these thoughts as he sat in the back seat of an Escalade that was barreling down I-95 like a cruise missile fired out of the North End of Boston and headed for Philadelphia.

"Pull over here," Victor directed his driver, Mickey, as they approached a rest stop. He needed to take a piss and make a few calls outside the interior of the Escalade, for which he had developed a growing distrust, and out of earshot of Mickey, whom he trusted even less.

Victor relieved himself, considered grabbing a coffee, but thought better of it. He was trying to minimize the stops on his way to his destination, North Atlantic Aviation, a fixed base operator and refueler at Philadelphia International Airport. Al Amin, his buyer, had sent a representative, Nasir, on a Gulfstream G650ER from Monaco. Nasir operated as a sort of first lieutenant for Al Amin. He had been in Monaco making arrangements for his boss's arrival at the upcoming Monaco Grand Prix, an undertaking that rivaled preparations for a papal visit. The fact Nasir had been diverted to Philadelphia sent an unmistakable message that didn't need to be spoken out loud—Al Amin expected the painting to be on the plane before it departed for Riyadh.

Victor tried De Rosa on the burner—no answer, as he expected. Just then, a text came through from a number he didn't recognize. The text began with HZ, denoting the tail number of a private jet registered in Saudi Arabia. It was the number he needed to recite at the North Atlantic security gate. His stomach started to turn, and Victor's legendary patience began to evaporate. *This is when mistakes are made,* he thought. Still, he was running out of time and had no good options left. The priest was out of the way, and the sextant, Scotty, was next. The painting, last he knew, was stashed safely. He just didn't know where. And now The Thorn had gone rogue. *When I get a hold of that motherfucker . . .*

He knew how Al Amin operated. There would be no further complaint. Al Amin's plane would land in Riyadh, either with the painting on board or without it. The first alternative ended in a five million-dollar payday, the second with a bone saw. Victor pulled out his regular phone and scrolled his contacts to W. Using the burner, he punched in the number of an old friend from Philly he knew from his time as a guest of the feds in Ray Brook but hadn't spoken to in years.

"Scopa Cheese, how may I help you?" The voice was feminine and formal, almost British. More like a law firm receptionist than a counter worker. Victor wasn't even sure if it was the right number after all these years, but he figured he had nothing to lose. Still, he felt a bit silly repeating what the man had told him to say if he ever needed something in Philly.

"May I speak to The Wizard, please?"

The woman on the other end didn't flinch. "I believe he's finishing up his nap. May I ask who's calling?"

"Big Vic from Boston," he said, adding as an afterthought, "and Ray Brook."

"One moment, please."

Victor could hear the sound of a landline receiver being placed on a counter. A few moments later, someone fumbled with the phone, and Victor pictured someone old and infirm trying to figure out which side to talk into. *Maybe this is a mistake*, he began to think, but then a gruff voice from the past announced itself on the other end and dispelled any momentary doubts he may have had.

"What took you so long?"

When he returned to the Escalade after a very brief conversation with Nino Scopa, who gave off the comforting impression he knew exactly what Victor needed, he gave Mickey a new destination—the address to a cheese shop on Passyunk Avenue.

BLUEBERRY VIAGRA

It didn't take Anastasia long. "Donna," the new bartender from Ukraine, started at six. By nine, she could have had her pick of any of the men at the bar, and half the girls. But she only had eyes for one.

Lenny De Rosa had no game to speak of. His methodology was as blunt as it was corny. Donna pretended to swoon at his witticisms and double entendres, all of which would embarrass any self-respecting teenager. And when he slid her a fifty like it was surely more money than a Ukrainian refugee like herself had seen in her whole poverty-stricken life, she gripped his hand like he was her savior. She even mustered a tear, which she would have liked to credit to method acting, but had to admit was the result of her suppressed laugh at how much fun it was going to be watching this pig writhing on the floor and foaming from the mouth.

"What time do you get off?"

Another original line, she thought, but answered dutifully with an exaggerated pucker of her lips. "Two."

The Thorn wrote down the address to a South Philly apartment he kept for occasions when he didn't want to drive back to Hammonton for the night. Of course, no one knew about the apartment, not even Phil. Which also made it an excellent place to hide a certain invaluable painting until Phil's buyer materialized.

Could this guy make it any easier? She was almost a little disappointed.

"I'm sorry," Lenny said. "What was I thinking? You'll need a ride."

What a gentleman, she thought. "No, is okay," she said, pointing to her phone. "I have the Uber." She laid the accent on a little thick, and it had the desired effect.

The Thorn couldn't believe his luck. Maybe the websites were right. He had struck that lucrative deal with Dino—even with Phil giving him a haircut—and now this exotic beauty couldn't deny his charisma. The Blueberry Prince drove to his non-descript apartment above a body shop on Bancroft Street. There, he popped a Viagra, washed it down with a Glenlivet, showered, and settled into the sofa to wait for his little Ukrainian conquest. Poor thing. He almost pitied her ignorant ass.

As soon as he left, she texted Frank to come get her after her shift—her first, and last, night bartending at Paradise. Frank and Dino were waiting outside in a car by 1:45 a.m. They went over the plan on the ride over and dropped her off at the corner of Bancroft and Snyder at 2:10 a.m. Anastasia would go first, leaving the door open behind her if possible. Then, if she didn't come back down by three, or if she flashed the upstairs lights, they would go through the door.

It didn't take that long.

REMBRANDT'S EYES

(Forty minutes earlier)

The Thorn was at the refrigerator fishing around for a beer when he heard a gentle, almost apprehensive knock at the door. He glanced at his watch. *One thirty; she was early.* He practically jogged to the top of the landing, leaving the refrigerator door open in his haste, and had to restrain himself from sliding down the banister.

He looked through the peephole, but Donna was so petite that he couldn't see her, although he could make out her Uber, a black Escalade idling in the street. Poor kid must have asked the driver to wait until she went in, just in case he had given her a bad address or something. The blood was pulsing in his temples from the Viagra, and his head was swimming with the things he was going to do to his poor little Ukrainian concubine. He swung the door open, and time stood still.

Lenny had opened that door with all the anticipation of a spoiled kid on Christmas morning. But instead of sugar plums, a ball-peen hammer wielded by Victor Baldassare impacted his head. It's funny what a man focuses on at such a moment. Time froze, and Lenny could actually make out the ball side of the hammer as it closed in on his orbital bone. It seemed like it was suspended there for a long time, giving him sufficient time to contemplate why his face was about to be pummeled by a hammer instead of the Ukrainian beauty's grateful kisses. Then his survival instinct kicked in and he began to figure it out. He turned to run up the stairs, but by then, it was already too late.

Victor hadn't put in this kind of work since the '90s, and it felt liberating. He swung the hammer with gusto, having secured it in his fist with electrical tape, an old trick he had developed after losing a pipe from his bloody grip on a collection job back in '93. That debtor was a pretty rough customer and had recovered the pipe, which he began to use on Victor. Ever since then, Victor had taken the extra step of wrapping his weapon with electrical tape, which he then weaved around the outside of his closed fist. This left his other hand free to grip and hold the target in place. It worked like a charm.

Victor followed his retreating prey up the stairs, scoring blows on the back of his head as they climbed. About halfway up, the ball head became lodged in the back of De Rosa's skull, and was it not for the tape, The Thorn might have run up the rest of the steps with the hammer dangling from his head. Victor was able to extract it and managed to twist his grip just enough to switch to the flat-headed face. The next blow landed with a satisfying thud that sent De Rosa sprawling across the floor. The Thorn stopped moving—would never move again.

Victor didn't have to search very hard. The Wizard had been right about everything. De Rosa kept the painting right out in the open, where he could admire it. It was still in its frame, leaning against the wall with a slight tilt. A slash of light spread across the center of the painting, illuminating the eyes of a figure in the center of the boat. Of all the disciples in the picture, this was the only one staring directly out at the viewer. Victor didn't know it at the time, but Rembrandt had painted the man as himself, a little self-portrait in the tempest. A small conceit the Master had allowed himself to indulge in. Victor stood there mesmerized by the man's eyes, losing track of time. The painting had that effect on people, and Victor could almost understand why De Rosa kept it out in the open. He reminded himself why he was there and snapped out of the trance. He was standing over a dead body and needed to get out of there quickly. But first, he would indulge a small conceit of his own. He traced the light's source to a partially open refrigerator door. He used the head of the hammer, still taped to his hand, to open it the rest of the way, finding the perfect medium within. He took the pint of blueberries out, leaving the door the way he found it, and completed the forgery by putting another artist's signature on his work.

When he finished, he took a moment to step back and admire his work. His gory composition rivaled anything Caravaggio might have conceived of. He unwound the electrical tape from his hand, placing the sticky ball in his pocket. Victor slid the hammer into his belt loop like a little kid playing pirate. He retrieved a sheet from the bedroom and wrapped his treasure as best he could, then picked it up from both sides of the frame and maneuvered it down the stairs. He tried to pull the front door shut with his foot, but it didn't close all the way. *Fuck it*, he thought. *I'll be long gone by the time someone finds him.* The lift gate of the Escalade rose at his approach, and he laid the painting carefully inside.

Victor was breathing hard from the exertion, and it felt good—good to know he was still capable, still lethal. *The greedy prick had brought it on himself,* he thought, and there hadn't been time to delegate. Besides, there were fewer witnesses this way, other than the driver, Mickey, and he would take care of that as soon as they got back to Boston. He had been getting on Victor's nerves anyway. Sometimes, he felt like Mickey hit potholes on purpose, especially when Victor took a sip of coffee or punched in a number on his cell phone. Anyway, there was no shortage of drivers waiting to take his place.

For a split second, Victor entertained a crazy idea. What if instead of heading to the airport, he directed Mickey to drive back to Boston? He could dig in, insulate himself, stash the painting, disappear for a few years. It was a momentary fantasy, but a powerful one just the same. No doubt Lenny De Rosa had entertained a similar fantasy. *And look at him now. No, stick to the plan.* Five million was a lot of money, and the alternative behind curtain B was, in all likelihood, the bone saw. *No, this was the smart move.* Just like The Wizard had counseled right before he handed him the hammer and tape.

They drove west on Passyunk Avenue, the sights and sounds of South Philadelphia fading behind them as they crossed the Schuylkill River toward the airport. *Good riddance*, Victor thought. He vowed right then and there that as long as he lived, he would never return to this crazy neighborhood with its casual killers and ancient grudges.

For reasons he couldn't then imagine, he would keep his vow.

CLEAN UP IN AISLE FIVE

Anastasia pushed at the door, which was open a crack, with a gloved hand. The door led into a small hallway landing, but something was wedged between the door and the interior stairs, preventing it from opening all the way. She slipped past and found the obstruction—a shoe. One of those horrid slip-on affairs favored by mall walkers. She picked up the offending loafer and noticed it was speckled with an umber pattern. As she walked up the stairs, the pattern spread onto the walls, and she felt an occasional pebble crunch into the carpet beneath her feet. When she got to the top of the landing, she found the source of the mess. She was filled with mild disgust, and a feeling of disappointment at having been denied her amusement. She flashed the lights twice.

"Jesus, that was fast," Frank said.

Dino was already out of the car and walking briskly toward De Rosa's apartment. Frank walked on the opposite side of the street, keeping an eye on the second-floor window, a .38 held down low by his side. The apartment was dark, but he saw Anastasia's silhouette standing alone when she flicked the lights. Even at a time like this, the first thing he thought of was how hot she looked in that silhouette. *I need to have my head examined*, he thought as he followed Dino through the door and up the stairs.

What was left of Leonard De Rosa was spread out on the living room floor. It looked like it had started at the front door and he was either dragged, or more likely had managed to retreat upstairs. His skull was smashed open and gray matter and blood littered the area around his body.

"Did anybody touch anything coming in?" Dino asked. Frank shook his head, and Anastasia held up her gloved hands. Dino handed Frank a pair of surgical gloves and donned a pair himself. "I want everybody's shoes when we leave," Dino added.

"How am I supposed to get home?" Frank asked.

"Walk fucking barefoot. Who gives a fuck? I'll drop you off right outside."

"Where's the painting?" Frank said.

"By the look of things, I think somebody beat us to it," Dino said. The three of them quickly searched the one-bedroom apartment with predictable results.

"It was here," Dino said.

"Can you feel it?" Frank asked.

"Are you fucking nuts? Look." Dino shined his cell phone flashlight at an area on the rug by the living room wall. The pile of the old carpet still displayed an indentation.

"How wide—" Frank began to ask, but Anastasia cut him off.

"One hundred twenty-eight centimeters. He's right. It was here."

"Let's get the fuck out of here," Frank said.

It was then that Dino noticed Lenny's pants were pulled down around his knees. "What the fuck?"

They had all been so fixated on the gore around his head that it hardly seemed important until Dino flashed his light on the area. The only other light came from a cracked refrigerator door, like someone quickly tried to shut it and failed.

"What the fuck is that?" Frank said.

There was a small box and some bluish matter smeared on The Thorn's ass.

"Blueberries. Somebody jammed a pint of blueberries up his ass."

Anastasia chuckled. "That's a new one even for me. What does it mean?"

"It means someone from out of town did this," Dino said.

"How do you know that?" Frank asked.

"Think, Frankie. It's a message. Lenny was an outsider. Whoever did this wanted it to look like it was us."

"What do we do? It's too risky to move him." Frank said.

Anastasia knew what needed to be done and had already walked to the kitchen sink. She came back with a wet rag and a waste basket. Squeamishness was a luxury her upbringing had not afforded her. She cleaned the mess as best she could, placing the intact berries back in the pint, which she neatly dropped into the kitchen trash bag. She wiped the remainder in a workmanlike fashion and disposed of the rag. She had done far worse for far less, and this particular unpleasant act had the added motivation of being necessary to protect her friends.

Dino had his suspicions about who was responsible, and if he had a four-leaf clover handy, he would have happily shoved it up The Thorn's ass in place of the blueberries.

They slipped out as quietly as they had entered, shutting the door behind them. Later, they disposed of the bag, along with their shoes, in a dumpster behind Stella Wholesale Seafood. The stench provided added assurance that no one would be digging through it.

Dino dropped Frank off first. "I'll meet you at the Caffé tomorrow. We need to tell Gary and Nick."

"I'll meet you there around one. Get some sleep." Frank threw a kiss to Anastasia, and she threw one back.

The Rembrandt was in the wind—that could no longer be helped—but at least they had dodged a possible frame. Dmitry wouldn't be happy to hear the news. If there was one thing the Russian hated more than losing, it was losing to the Saudis. Once again, Anastasia volunteered for an unpleasant task.

OUT OF THE PAST

Nick hadn't heard from Grace in two days. Her last text suggested she was giving him room to do whatever he had to do back in Philly. The text wasn't threatening, that wasn't Grace's style, but it was truthful and to the point, which was much scarier. The last line read, *Call me when you get back.* Nick had thought about calling her right then, but figured maybe she was right and he should just wait till he was clear of all this shit. Then, he would show up at the Tiki, sweep her up in his arms, and walk off into the sunset just like in the movies . . . or something like that.

Nick sat in the Caffé, staring at *The Prodigal in the Tavern* and the woman sitting in his father's lap—Aurora. Finally, he called Joey's mother, Tina.

"Hello, Nicholas," she answered.

"You sound like you were expecting my call."

"I'm psychic, remember?"

"So then, I guess you know why I'm calling?"

"Yes. I'm home, and yes, you can come over. How's that?"

"Pretty fucking good, actually. Fifteen minutes okay?"

"I'll make some espresso."

"No drinks?"

"Nah, sounds like you already had too many. See you in fifteen."

Tina was Jimmy's girl, and the four of them had been inseparable. Jimmy and Tina, Nick and Angie. But that was a long time ago. Before Angie broke his heart, and before Jimmy turned up dead in The Paradise. Tina had been working the bar that night, and by the time Nick got the call, Jimmy was gone. Nick never bought the suicide angle, and Tina had her reasons for keeping her mouth shut. Eventually, the neighborhood figured it out, and so did Nick. It took twenty years, but Bobby "The Rose" De Rosa finally paid the price. The revenge was served so cold that it no longer had any taste. That was the funny thing about revenge. The smart move never felt quite as satisfying. Ronnie Cruz, Nick's trusted bartender and right-hand man in Lauderdale, had taught Nick that lesson many years ago.

Ronnie had been a fearsome operator in the Badlands area of North Philly back in the '90s. He ran his empire from a strip club on Allegheny Avenue. Nick and Jimmy were regulars on the nightclub circuit when they met him in an after-hours club in a neutral area of the city. What Ronnie lacked in height, he more than made up for in charisma and wardrobe. Ronnie was about 5'2, but he dressed like he played center for the Lakers. That is, if the Lakers' center was also a pimp.

They became fast friends, trading stories from their respective neighborhoods, making toasts, trading insults, and basically having a great time. They ended up at the Melrose Diner for a drunken breakfast. Even for a place that was used to seeing its share of characters, Ronnie's purple four-button suit, matching gators, and fedora caused a bit of a stir. A few guys looked up but quickly looked away when Jimmy shot back a hard stare.

"Easy, homie," Ronnie said. "Who cares what they think? I know who I am, and I know what I'm capable of. You can't go around proving shit over and over again to everybody you meet. Always remember, the hundredth guy don't believe you killed the first ninety-nine."

Nick had never met a person so certain of himself, so sure of who he was.

"You see this?" Ronnie whipped out a switchblade at the table and snapped it open with a loud crack that could be heard throughout the diner. "This is my *cariño*." He began to heat the blade with a lighter until it became red hot.

Jimmy looked at Joey like *what's this crazy fuck doing?*

Ronnie plunged the fiery blade into the seat cushion next to him. "See that? That's revenge. Feels fucking good, right, bro? But that's not the right way." Ronnie withdrew the blade, dipped it in a glass of ice water, and it made a hissing noise. He then stabbed the cushion on the other side of him. "Now that didn't feel half as good, but believe me, that's the right way. Every time. You feel me?"

Jimmy and Nick had both nodded, not knowing what else to say to this lunatic. Then they were politely asked to get the fuck out and never come back. But Nick never forgot that lesson, and Frank saw to it that Bobby De Rosa learned it the hard way. Now, Ronnie was older and mellower, bartending for Nick at the Tiki, but he still carried his *cariño* with him everywhere he went.

Nick was thinking of all this on the walk over to Tina's. He climbed her step to ring the bell, but the door opened and Tina stood there smiling, a steaming cup of espresso in her hand.

"Hello, Nick. I knew you'd come eventually. Come on in, make yourself at home."

Tina still looked good, and Nick remembered how crazy Jimmy had been over her. Their countless double dates blurred into one long, drunken bar crawl. They were some of the happiest memories from the first act of Nick's life. Even the craziness of the "Nick and Angie Show" had mellowed and taken on a nostalgic patina, burnished by time and polished by sentimentality.

"It's good to see you, Tina. It's been a long time."

"Has it? It seems like only yesterday you were standing right there, nursing a broken heart and asking my advice."

"Yeah?" Nick defended himself halfheartedly. "Did I take it?"

"Of course not. Brokenhearted lovers are incapable of taking advice." Tina sat on the sofa and patted the cushion next to her. Nick could do little else than sit obediently. "So I'm gonna give you the same advice today because you've obviously learned nothing in the twenty-plus years since."

Nick gave Tina an offended look. "Don't you think you're being a little presumptuous? You don't even know why I'm here." Nick took a sip of his espresso but was starting to feel like he needed a drink. "And it's not about Angie if that's what you're thinking."

Tina smiled. "Who said anything about Angie?" She started to feel a little sorry for him and decided to let him off the hook for the moment. "I'll be right back," she said as she walked upstairs. "I have something for you. Make yourself a drink if you like."

Nick was beginning to regret his visit but went to the kitchen, poured two glasses of bourbon, and sat at the kitchen table while he waited for Tina to return. When she did a few minutes later, she was carrying a shoebox, which she placed on the seat beside her. They sat there like that for what felt like an uncomfortably long time—for Nick at least—until Tina broke the silence by stating the obvious question.

"Aren't you gonna ask me what's in the box?"

Nick felt like he was being toyed with. He had come here in good faith, in the spirit of friendship. Okay, that was only partly true. He also came because he had questions and hoped Tina had the answers. Now, however, he was feeling defensive, so he changed the subject. "Let me ask you something. Don't you get lonely here?"

She looked at him for a beat before responding. "Lonely? No, I'm not lonely. Joey still stops by to see his mother. And I can have company anytime I wish. Besides, a wise man once said the only cure for loneliness is solitude."

"Oh yeah? And who, may I ask, was the great philosopher who imparted this wisdom?"

"You know, for an allegedly nice guy, you can be a real asshole sometimes. He's the very same man you came to ask me about. And everything you want to know about him, and my mother, is in this box." She drummed her fingers on the lid as she spoke.

Nick sat stunned for a moment, his gaze fixed on the box. *She's fucking with me*, he thought. *There's no way*. "Look, I'm sorry, Tina, it's just . . . I was looking at a painting in the Caffé earlier today and—"

"The one with my mother sitting on your father's lap?"

"You knew?"

"Of course I knew. How many times did you walk by that painting, Nick? You just figured it out? My mother told me all about it before she passed."

"I'm sorry, Tina. I was wrong. I shouldn't have come here the way I did."

Tina reached across the table and grasped Nick's hands, looking him in the eyes. "She loved him, Nicky. And he loved her. It just . . . it just wasn't meant to be. But she never stopped loving him. Even toward the end, she would call out his name like he was in the room."

"Jesus Christ, then it's true." Nick sank back in his chair, his hands slipping from her grip.

Tina looked at him quizzically. "What's true?"

"I went to the beach with them when I was just a kid. You were probably a toddler. What year did your father go to prison?"

It took a second for Tina to figure out what he was getting at, but when she did, she erupted in laughter. Then, when she finally caught her breath, she got up from her chair, walked around the table, took Nick's face in her hands and kissed him gently on the forehead.

"You really are adorable. I can understand why Angie was so crazy about you all those years." The last part still made Nick's stomach jump a little. "But if you came over here thinking we were going to have a Luke and Leia moment, I'm sorry to have to disappoint you."

Nick suddenly felt pretty stupid, and Tina sensed it. "Here." She sat next to him with the box. "Open it up. Let's look at it together."

Nick looked at the box and hesitated. Tina got up and poured them two refills before she sat back down and nudged the box a little closer. They clinked glasses.

"To Anthony and Aurora. Here's hoping they're finally together," Tina proposed.

"To Anthony and Aurora," Nick reciprocated. They both drank. Nick blew out a breath meant to clear his head and removed the lid. ..

Most of the items were mundane little trinkets, the flotsam of lazy summer days and steamy summer nights, boardwalk postcards, and kitschy souvenirs. Nick dug around, and Tina helped sort the relics into some order on the kitchen table. The two of them unearthed the artifacts of Tony and Aurora's love affair: a ticket stub from a Four Top's concert at Bally's Casino; a cocktail napkin with some smudged writing; an old-school motel key with instructions to drop in a mailbox if found (postage paid); even some faded Skee-Ball tickets, all of which Tina began to assemble into a sort of collage. A pocket square separated those surface items from what lay beneath. Nick peeled back the silky fabric, revealing a paper layer consisting of cards and notes written on lined paper, each carefully folded into tidy squares.

"Do you really think we should be reading these?" Nick asked. "I feel like maybe we're intruding here."

"I don't think they would mind. Besides, I've already read them; there's nothing too racy in there." Nick registered a look of surprise. Tina continued. "I read them out loud to my mother at her request. They were the only things that eased her pain on those final days. They're poems, written to her by your father. They're— Well, let's just say no one ever wrote anything like that for me. They're beautiful."

Tina began reading from one poem about a barefoot girl from a small town in Sicily. It told of a sailor who arrives at the port and becomes enchanted by her beauty. He begins to paint her portrait, but before he can finish, he's killed in a knife fight with a group of robbers. They take the unfinished portrait and sell it to a merchant, who brings it back with him to Denmark. Years later, when the girl has grown into a beautiful, sophisticated woman, she sees the portrait in a New York gallery—"

"Stop," Nick said. "I've heard enough."

"What's wrong? You don't like it?"

"No, it's not that. It's just . . . here's yet another thing I didn't know about my father. So now he's a poet? I mean, come on, Tina. You were around my father growing up. Would you have thought he was capable of writing something like that?"

"I don't know. Love makes people do incredible things. He shared things with my mother, and she shared them with me."

"Sure, everyone but me." Nick poured himself another bourbon.

Tina allowed him to drink and sulk for a minute.

"Listen. You're a good man, maybe even a great one, but you've got to let shit go at some point. Not everything in life has an answer. Not everything requires closure. You got abandonment issues? Join the club. But you need to stop fixating on resolving the past. Did it ever occur to you that maybe the past doesn't want to be resolved? That applies to you, to me, to your father, to this whole fucking city." She hesitated for a second, not wanting to hurt him, but felt she had to add, "And I'm sorry, but it especially applies to Angie."

That jolted Nick out of his trance of self-pity. "Maybe you're right. It's just that every time I think I've done just that, things seem to come back from the past to haunt me."

"Yeah, well, ghosts have that advantage over living people. They don't have to go on living regular lives like the rest of us—doing laundry, getting old, becoming boring. But if that's the way you want to see it, then that's gonna be your reality. So either the whole universe got together to conspire against Nick Di Nobile, or maybe, indulge me here for a minute, maybe you're attracting things and perceiving them in a way consistent with that belief. Now you tell me, which one is more likely?"

Tina's words hit hard. He knew she was right, of course, but it still didn't stop the hurt.

"Look, I have my own demons. You think I don't miss Jimmy every time I look into Joey's eyes? It's okay to be brokenhearted. Brokenhearted people have empathy for others. We're kinder, more patient. We see the best in people."

Tina moved to an old turntable that Joey liked to play. She slid a vinyl record from its jacket and dusted it off before carefully placing the needle down. The record came to life with a crackle that filled Nick with a soothing sensation. Tina sat next to Nick and fished around the bottom of the box, finding what she was looking for. She placed it before Nick as Eddie Kendrick's voice kicked in on "Just My Imagination (Running Away With Me)."

It was one of those black and white photos you take in a booth on the Boardwalk. Four squares in a vertical strip, four poses, each showing two people who were clearly in love. She sat on his lap in the last one, and they gazed into one another's eyes. Nick thought they looked just like Robert Mitchum and Jane Greer in a movie poster for the noir classic *Out of the Past*.

"My mother told me something your father shared with her. I think it's important you know this. Your father wrote stories as a kid. Silly stuff, science fiction, I think, about aliens and other worlds. He had this wild imagination, until one day . . . well, you remember how your grandfather was."

"Yeah?" Nick was beginning to figure it out.

"Well, he found the stories in your father's room. '*Those were different times*.' That's how your father explained it to her. Let's just say your grandfather wasn't very supportive. Your father never wrote again. Not until he wrote those poems for my mother. And he loved her for that, Nick. Loved her for bringing that spark of imagination back into his life. That was enough for them. Life isn't like the movies. Not everything has to end with a ride off into the sunset. Just because it doesn't last forever doesn't mean it wasn't real. You, especially, should remember that. But what broke my heart most about that *those were different times* story was even then, even after being robbed of his creativity for all those years, he was still trying to make excuses for your grandfather with that bullshit. I guess what I'm trying to say, Nick, is I don't think he would want you making those same excuses for him."

Nick stared at the photos the whole time Tina was talking. His father looked so young, younger than Nick was now. So handsome, so full of hope. He had always seen his father as the swaggering lord of Caffé Vecchio, confident and wise. Now, all he could see was a sensitive young man, wounds still fresh, not yet having abandoned his dreams, and perilously in love. He remembered the story Frank told him of how his father had wept when he first laid eyes on Rembrandt's *Return of the Prodigal*, and now he finally understood why. Just like Dmitry, his father had realized he would never know the love of a father. Nick's thoughts drifted back to the notebook he'd begun scribbling in at the airport. He resolved to finish the story he had started.

"I know you're right, Tina. I get what you're saying." He gestured to the items spread out on the table. "I especially appreciate you sharing all of this. It's just that sometimes I know the right thing to do, but I just don't know how to pull it off."

"Sure you do." Tina smiled as she took a pair of scissors and cut the photo strip in half, handing the bottom two to Nick and keeping the top two for herself. Then she made a slight voodoo motion with her fingers as she said, "Use *the Force,* Nick."

That cracked them both up, and Nick propped up his two photos against the bottle of Maker's. They clicked glasses, then Tina draped her arm over Nick's shoulder and leaned her head against his with sisterly love and affection.

Nick's phone buzzed, and he took it out of his pocket. It was a text from Frank. A breach in protocol that could only mean one thing—the charade was over.

LEAD WHITE

Frank's text read, *Meet me at the Caffé.* Nick's suspicion something had gone wrong was confirmed when he walked in to find Frank, Dino, and Gary gathered around the bar.

"I'm assuming this isn't the victory party," Nick said.

"You would be correct," Frank confirmed. He introduced Nick to Dino and continued. "Lenny De Rosa's dead."

Nick made a gun with his hand and squeezed an imaginary trigger while raising his eyebrows at his uncle.

"Nah, somebody else got there first. Looks like they got the other thing too."

Nick took a seat. Alberto poured him a double Don Julio 1942 without him having to ask.

"Any idea who?" Nick sipped his tequila. It burned in his chest as he tried to plan out his next move, and how he was going to explain the failure to Dmitry. He stared at his likeness in Scotty's painting, his gaze inevitably drifting upward to Angie's indifferent countenance. Scotty had captured her perfectly. He had to give him that.

"Something tells me the Arabs maybe made a friend in Beantown," Dino answered.

"Maybe it ain't gone yet," Gary said.

"No way. It's probably on a container ship leaving Boston Harbor already," Frank said.

"Do we know somebody with the longshoremen who could maybe reach out?" Dino asked.

The banter was interrupted by Nick hurling his rocks glass across the room. It struck the frame of Scotty's painting, splattering it with the remnants of his tequila. Everyone but Gary was caught off guard by Nick's outburst.

"Just stop," Nick shouted. "It's gone, and that's the end of it. We missed our chance."

Alberto came out from behind the bar to retrieve the glass, which remarkably hadn't broken, and did his best to dry off the painting, gently wiping it with a bar rag at first but stopping when he sensed he might be smudging it. He returned to the bar, whispering to Gary that perhaps he should call Scotty to come over and have a look at it. The tequila had begun to streak down the painting, making it appear that Salome, finally, had shed a tear for the Baptist. Alberto had quickly grown fond of the painting, and it made him sad to think it might be damaged.

Frank walked over to his nephew. "You okay, kid?" Nick nodded unconvincingly. "Fuck it. It's just a painting. We don't even know if it was the real thing. You know how that shit goes."

"Scotty knew it was real. That's enough for me."

"Where's he been anyway?" Frank asked.

"I don't know," Gary said as he held his phone to his ear. "I ain't seen him in days, and he ain't answering. I'm gonna go check on him. Nick, why don't you give Virgil a call, see if he knows anything."

"I'll go with you," Dino said, and the two of them walked through the kitchen and out the back door. They got in Gary's Yukon and headed to Scotty's house.

Nick called Virgil, who also wasn't answering. "I don't like this. Frank, take a ride with me to Virgil's." Nick had his father's old Fleetwood parked out front. "Have you seen Joey?"

"Not today. I think he's with the Persian broad. They've been inseparable these days."

"She's Persian?" Nick asked. "I thought she was Lebanese."

"Ain't that basically the same thing? You know, like Sicilian and Calabrese?"

"Come on, Unc, you know better than that. I know some Sicilians who don't even consider themselves Italian, like they're a separate nationality."

"Yeah, like when you get introduced to somebody in Florida. Guy says, 'Meet so and so, he's from Philly too,' and it turns out he's from Quakertown or something."

"Or Hammonton," Nick added.

"Yeah." Frank laughed. "Or Hammonton."

Nick rang the bell for Virgil's apartment. When there was no answer, Nick started to fear the worst. Then, just as he was about to try to force it, the door cracked open and Virgil appeared in the space created by the chain. His eyes looked crazed, and even through that small space, the heat and smell that emanated from within suggested that Virgil was in the midst of one of his manic spells.

Virgil let them in without a word and returned to the canvas he had been working on nonstop for the last eighteen hours. The heat was turned up oppressively high, and Virgil's hair was plastered to his head. Paint, brushes, and jars of liquid were scattered everywhere, and music was blasting. Virgil resumed painting as if they weren't even there as John Lennon sang "Watching The Wheels" on a continuous loop. An old-school ashtray stand was overflowing with half-smoked cigars. As Frank cracked a window to let in some fresh air, Nick approached Virgil with care. He had seen his old friend like this before and knew to handle him gingerly.

"Hey, buddy. Whaddya say you get cleaned up, then I take you to the Caffé for a bite to eat?" Virgil either didn't hear him or was ignoring him. He continued to paint furiously, one brush clenched in his teeth as he made tiny refinements with another, applying lead white touches to an absolutely stunning version of Vermeer's *Girl with a Pearl Earring*.

"Jesus Christ," Frank couldn't help himself from saying as he walked in front of the canvas and took in the painting for the first time. "It's fucking beautiful."

"Watching The Wheels" started over again.

"How long have you been at this?" Nick asked.

Virgil didn't answer, but he had stopped painting. He put down his brushes and stared at the girl in the painting for a long time. Frank and Nick kept a respectful distance, giving the man some space. Virgil began to weep. Tears ran down his face, but he didn't make a sound or move to wipe them. With the spell starting to show some signs of breaking, Nick placed his hand lightly on his shoulder, guiding Virgil toward the bedroom.

"Virgil, have you heard from Scotty?" Virgil angled his head down and shook it in response, his runny nose causing him to sniffle. "How 'bout you shower and get dressed, and we'll wait for you out here?" Virgil nodded slightly, and Nick waited until he heard the water running in the bathroom.

"You ever seen him like this before?" Frank asked.

"No, but Gary has. He said it usually lasts a few days, then he's back to normal. Well, normal for Virgil. I think he's coming out of it."

"Do you think he painted this in the past couple of days? I mean, it's friggin incredible." "Yeah, well, Virgil's a pretty friggin incredible guy."

"Only in South Philly," Frank said. "Never fails. If they made this shit into a movie, no one would believe it."

"You got that right, Frankie."

Nick felt around in his breast pocket for the little notebook, even though he knew it wasn't there. He had an overpowering urge to write something down about what they had just witnessed. He wasn't sure why or who he would be writing it for, but he felt the need just the same. He pulled out the photos of his father and Aurora instead, reflecting on what Tina had told him. It was the closest he had felt to his father since grade school. He passed the photos to Frank. Like Virgil, Frank didn't say anything. He just nodded and smiled ever so slightly, the corners of his mouth turning up at the image of his old friend captured in black and white—and he understood.

Virgil emerged from the bedroom looking—and smelling—a good deal better. His usually unruly hair was still wet and framed his face, giving him a childlike appearance. The shower seemed to have soothed him a bit, but he was struggling to line up the buttons on his shirt with their corresponding holes. Nick walked over and assisted, using the opportunity to tell Virgil about the damage to Scotty's painting. Nick had also calmed down, and he began to feel foolish for his outburst. He was experiencing feelings of guilt. *Guilt for what?* Somehow, throwing that glass at Angie's face in that painting made him feel like he had cheated on Grace. He knew that wasn't exactly accurate, but was glad Grace wasn't around to witness it just the same.

Nick described the damage to the painting, and Virgil looked at him queerly. Perhaps he was offended that Nick had desecrated the work of his brother painter. Virgil retrieved some tools and materials from his trolley and tossed them in a canvas sack that he swung over his shoulder.

"Hey, Virgil," Frank said "This painting, it's beautiful."

Virgil looked at the painting like it was some foreign object he had never seen before. He looked from the picture to Frank, watching his face as he said the words. Virgil took a brush and, with the bag still over his shoulder, contorted his lanky body in a stooping move and affixed his signature in the lower right corner. *V Corrado.*

"You can pick it up tomorrow," he said to Frank.

Frank put up his hands and was about to protest, but stopped when he saw Nick shaking his head at him. "Thank you, Virgil. I'll treasure it always."

Virgil smiled and tossed a few Opus X cigars in the bag as they headed for the door. The notes of the piano signified another round of "Watching the Wheels."

"Hey, Virgil, how do I stop—" Nick thought better of it. "Fuck it."

They got in the Fleetwood and headed back to Caffé Vecchio.

RED UMBER

When Gary and Dino arrived at Scotty's place, they found the front door unlocked, and as they climbed the stairs, it became clear someone had beat them there, just like at De Rosa's apartment.

The place was in shambles. Furniture was overturned and the painter's belongings were strewn across the loft. What looked like paint the color of burnt umber, but might also have been dried blood, was spattered on the walls and smeared across the hardwood floor, like something, or someone, had been dragged across it.

"This don't look good," Dino said.

"Ya think?" Gary replied as they moved through the rest of the loft, finding a similar scene but no sign of Scotty. All of his paintings, together with his tools and pigments, were gone as well. A dog dish was overturned, but Frank could make out the name *Leonardo* in the upside-down script. Kibble was scattered across the kitchen floor, and it crunched underneath their feet as they turned to leave. The freezer door was left ajar. Someone had likely rifled through it looking for valuables. It was a terribly obvious hiding place, but Dino knew many people still hid money in their freezer, wrapping it up like meat. He looked inside, and sure enough, someone had torn through the contents, which explained the freezer paper and defrosted food in the sink and on the countertop. He reflexively closed the freezer door with his elbow. It was a silly thing to do, as it certainly didn't matter if the freezer door remained open under the circumstances.

A small magnet clung stubbornly to the face of the refrigerator, an image of da Vinci's *Lady With An Ermine*. The magnet had spun counterclockwise, giving the lady's head a quizzical tilt, as if she were considering Dino a potential suitor and questioning his motives. Dino pulled his hand back into his sleeve, and with a nudge of his sheathed finger, he righted the image.

"You done?" Gary asked.

Dino paused for a second before answering, still looking at the Lady now that the image had been righted. "Yeah, I'm done."

They left Scotty's house and drove back to Caffé Vecchio to report what they had found. Gary turned on the radio, and they listened silently to Blue Magic's "Stop to Start."

Dino couldn't get the image of the Lady out of his mind. Her inquisitive stare combined with the heartbreaking falsetto coming out of the speakers transported him back to a simpler time—before he had given up on the dreams of his youth. Before he had put on the white jacket for Andy Boy and left those dreams behind forever. *Something doesn't seem right*. Dino began to assemble the events of the past weeks: Andy's visit to the cheese shop to meet with that old fossil they called The Wizard; his insistence that Dino reach out to The Thorn's crew and make it seem like he had his own agenda with the whole poker machine *tarantella*. How could an outsider get the information necessary to pull off the theft, De Rosa's murder, and Scotty's disappearance in such short order?

A picture began to emerge, and for the first time in his life, Dino began to question his blind loyalty to Andrea "Andy Boy" Caposecco.

LA SANTA CARIDAD

"HZ . . ." Victor's driver started to recite the tail number to the guard at the security booth of North Atlantic Aviation, but the gate began to rise before he could get past the prefix. Victor should have felt relieved. He had the painting in the back of the Escalade and was about to drop it off to Al Amin's guy, Nasir, and collect. But now, when he was so close to the end, he was more anxious than ever. Victor never felt any anxiety in moments of violence. On the contrary, he was comfortable in that world, confident in his ability to adapt and improvise. The events of the evening had been exhilarating and life-affirming.

It was *this* phase, the handoff, that had his mind racing with scenarios and caused him feelings of dread. *Everything's fine*, he reminded himself. He'd had these guys checked out thoroughly. Victor's people had even tracked the G650ER from Nice Cote d'Azur to Philly. Al Amin's superyacht was moored outside the port of Monaco under the flag of the Cayman Islands, according to marine traffic websites, all of which was consistent with Nasir's representations. Still, his thoughts kept drifting back to an FBI sting in the early '80s where the agents impersonated Arab sheiks and set up some Philly politicians in an operation called Abscam. *What the hell did that one guy say on tape?* Victor quizzed himself. *'Money talks and bullshit walks.' Kinda hard to cross-examine that shit.*

Two of Nasir's men stepped out to direct them to a hangar. There, they were greeted by two more, identically dressed, mercenary-looking types. Victor's stomach grumbled as they pulled into the hangar, but he cracked his knuckles and the tacky residue on his right fist gave him an odd sense of comfort.

Nasir was seated at a metal desk set up in the corner of the hangar. Victor's driver moved to open his door, but the big man had already sprung out of his seat in a surprisingly quick move and was bounding over to the desk with an urgency meant to convey that he was all about business. In reality, Victor had mustered all the courage he had left and was charging headlong to his fate. Whatever awaited him, he was resigned to getting it over with. He knew intuitively that Al Amin and his people had little fear of some washed-up racketeer from the North End. His apparent confidence and seeming indifference to his life expectancy was the only armor he had. The same technique had kept him alive in Walpole and Ray Brook, where he had met Nino Scopa all those years ago.

Nasir greeted him warmly, grasping his outstretched hand with both of his and recoiling only slightly at its stickiness.

"I am so glad to see you are safe, my friend. My employer sends his regards and wishes for me to convey that he has been praying fervently for your well-being."

I fucking bet he has. "Please tell him I have been praying for him as well." *As much as a guy with a 450-foot yacht needs prayers.*

"I assume you have the acquisition in your possession," Nasir inquired in that unique language of provenance-speak meant to avoid calling the painting what it really was—stolen goods.

It was the same type of language that allowed Murillo's *Return of the Prodigal Son* to be proudly displayed in the National Gallery in Washington, DC, with only a cryptic, 'Removed by government decree,' which should more accurately read, 'Looted from the *Hospital de la Caridad* by the French during their occupation of Spain in 1810.' Indeed, back at the Caridad, it is listed as 'stolen,' along with four of the other six paintings in the series Murillo painted for the *La Santa Caridad* brotherhood. But unlike the empty frames on display in the Isabella Stewart Gardner Museum in Boston, four copies hang in their place at the Caridad. Perhaps after a sufficient passage of time, Al Amin's heirs will be able to display *Christ in the Storm* with equal impunity.

Nasir's men made their way to the rear of the Escalade, and Mickey hit the button to raise the lift gate. They removed the painting, still hastily wrapped in the sheet De Rosa had hoped to ravage his Ukrainian conquest on only a few hours prior. They laid it down at Nasir's feet and carefully unwrapped it. Once liberated of the sheet, they propped it up for his inspection. Nasir examined it closely, feigning an expertise he did not possess, noting the craquelure and accumulation of dirt expected of a painting almost four hundred years old. He even wielded a magnifying glass at one point, focusing in on the image of Christ, ignoring Rembrandt's mini self-portrait gazing out at him and taking his measure. The work had an overwhelming physical effect on Nasir. The seascape drew him into the maelstrom, and a queasiness snuck up on him. He had to look away, but nodded to the men, indicating his approval.

"It will be evaluated further once it arrives in the Kingdom. The second half of your payment will be disbursed to you after the auction."

"Wait a minute," Victor said. "That's not the deal we made, and I don't know nothing about no auction."

"Things have changed." Nasir spoke with the certainty of someone in control of the situation, which he was. Once Victor had barreled into the hangar, the dynamic had shifted and Victor knew it. He turned to see Nasir's men tossing a duffel bag into the back of the Escalade and closing the lift gate. Victor considered his options—they weren't many or particularly good. Right then, he would be grateful to get out of the hangar alive. Still, he needed to preserve a shred of dignity, as a showing of total capitulation would not bode well for his prospects of ever receiving the second half of his payment.

"Count it," Victor barked at Mickey, using a tone he only wished he could direct at Nasir. Mickey popped the gate, walked around, and unzipped the duffel bag. After what seemed like an excruciatingly long time, Mickey reported back.

"Two million five."

"Half. As I said." Nasir was becoming impatient.

Victor paused only long enough to cause Nasir to study him for a moment, perhaps consider another scenario, but Nasir knew men better than he knew art, and he didn't need a magnifying glass to detect that Victor was bluffing. Nonetheless, he decided to end the standoff diplomatically.

"My employer will be very pleased. I will see to it that you receive the balance of your compensation without undue delay upon authentication." Nasir extended his hand, which Victor took. He resisted the urge to tear out of the hangar, happy to leave with all his limbs, but he gripped Nasir's hand firmly and held it for an extra moment. Nasir smiled and placed his other hand atop Victor's, uncertain of the source of the tackiness but confident in his own prowess in the art of the bone saw. "I look forward to being present when you are paid in full."

Victor got in the back of the Escalade, and only after the door was shut and he was shielded by the tint, gave the hurried command. "Get us the fuck outta here."

Mickey drove them out of the hangar, past the gate, and onto I-95 North.

"I hate this fucking city," Victor murmured to himself.

PENTIMENTO

Noun. (plural; pentimenti)

1. **Evidence of earlier painting evident beneath an existing paint layer.**
2. **Indication of change in a book or other literary work. Origin; Italian — repentance or contrition.**

By the time the three of them arrived back at Caffé Vecchio, Gary and Dino were already there. Gary got up from his stool when they walked through the door and pointed toward the kitchen while looking at Nick.

Nick joined him, and they walked out back by the dumpster.

"Virgil says he hasn't heard from Scotty. That's all I could get out of him until he levels off a bit."

"Yeah, that don't surprise me. It didn't look too good over there," Gary said.

"What do you mean didn't look good?"

"I mean, somebody got there before us, and I think Scotty might be reunited with Jilly."

"What? Are you fucking serious? How can you be sure?"

"I mean, I didn't do any DNA test or nothing, but it's definitely a yellow tape situation."

"Jesus Christ. That poor fucking guy."

"There was nothing else left around either, just a big mess like somebody was looking for something and couldn't find it."

"I don't think we should break the news to Virgil yet. He's not up to it."

"Yeah, I was thinking that. Best wait a while."

"Agreed."

Joey suddenly appeared at the back door. "Hey, Unc. I just got here, but I think you better come inside. There's something you need to see."

"What is it?" Gary said.

"It's Virgil. Just come in. I can't explain it."

They walked back through the kitchen, where Frank was at a cutting board slicing a Spanish onion in half.

"What are you making?" Nick asked.

"I'm not making anything. It's for Virgil." He poured some extra virgin olive oil into a bowl and handed it to Nick. "Here, carry this for me."

Nick took it, knowing it was senseless to ask what this was all for. When they returned to the dining room, Virgil was animated, practically dancing around the painting. He had a bar rag wrapped around the first two fingers of his right hand, and Nick noticed that it was stained with paint. He reminded Nick of the shoeshine man from a shop on 10th Street where his father had taken him years ago to get his parochial shoes buffed. Virgil took the onion half and dipped it into the olive oil. He began to move it in a circular fashion over the surface of the painting, followed by a dabbing of a solution that he dipped the bar rag in. He alternated those applications, refitting the bar rag to a clean section when it became full of paint.

"You're making it worse." Nick couldn't help stating what seemed obvious. The painting was indeed becoming a smeared mess. Virgil ignored him and continued executing his craft like a major league pitcher being heckled by a drunk.

"Lock up," Gary said to Joey. "We're closed for business."

Joey went to the front door, turned the bolt, and with a smile of satisfaction, retrieved the "Member's Only" sign that had been retired behind the hostess stand at Gary's insistence. He slid it behind the half curtain along the front windowsill, dusting off his hands as if he'd just finished digging a ditch.

Scotty's painting of *Salome with the head of John the Baptist*, like Caravaggio's original, was a dark composition consistent with its subject matter. Only the faces stood out in stark contrast to the shadowy background. Scotty had been faithful to Caravaggio's technique, using an underpainting of linseed oil and earth, the so-called *mestica*. Virgil began to narrate as he worked, his voice now booming with authority.

"Scotty applied an underpainting coat to this canvas to prepare it, then sketched the figures in burnt umber. That's what you see on the towel now. There are forms and strokes beneath that. Ordinarily, I would think they are what's referred to as *pentimenti*, his initial lines and figures that he later decided to paint over, but this—this is something else."

"What makes you say that?" Nick asked.

"It's a faithful reproduction, other than the faces, of course." Virgil snickered. "There is no need to be indecisive when you are copying something. Besides, the figures are in an area of shadow, the space between the subjects. This is more like Vermeer's Cupid—something that has been painted over entirely."

Virgil moved his focus to the lower portion of the painting, just left of center. He worked mainly with the onion, using the solvent solution only sparingly.

"Sorry about that, Nick," Virgil apologized as he reduced Nick's likeness to a grotesque mask more resembling the subject of Munch's *The Scream* than Caravaggio's John the Baptist.

"That's okay, Virgil. To be honest with you, I was never crazy about it. Just promise to work on Salome next if you don't mind."

Gary got a good laugh out of that one. Joey had lost interest and drifted over to the jukebox, Peroni in hand. "I think youse are all crazy with these fucking paintings," Joey mumbled as he studied the usual selections. *What the hell goes with this bullshit?* he thought as he struggled to come up with a few numbers to complement Virgil's performance.

Virgil continued to dab at the area until another layer began to emerge. A layer of ancient varnish that served to protect the paint beneath it. He put down the onion, closed his eyes, and used his bare fingertips to trace a raised section that had been concealed by Scotty's overpainting. "*Impasto*," he exclaimed.

"What's *impasto*?" Nick and Frank asked in unison. They were all glued to Virgil's work and hanging on his every word. All except Joey, who had finally decided that Tavares's "Check it Out" was the perfect accompaniment to Virgil's restoration.

"It's a technique where the paint is laid on thickly, sometimes with a brush, or in this case maybe a palette knife. It reflects light differently, giving the work dimension. The smoother strokes are in contrast, like another version of light and shadow. It was employed by some of the Renaissance Masters."

"Which ones?" Nick asked.

"Oh, quite a few. Titian." Virgil worked even more carefully now. A small face peeked out at him from beneath Scotty's painting. "Vermeer." Virgil spread out his hand. He drew an imaginary line to the right of the face, approximately the distance from the tip of his thumb to the tip of his pinkie. He resumed his work there.

"Anyone else?" Nick continued to nudge him.

A second face began to show itself. Unlike the first, which looked straight out at the viewer, this one was in profile, turned to the left. A face of comfort, of calm, of peace. The Galilean—savior of the world.

"Rembrandt," Virgil stated, both in response to Nick's question and as a revelation of what he had uncovered.

"What about him?" Nick asked, as if he were inquiring about a guy from the neighborhood.

Virgil pointed at the small figure staring out from the painting. "This is Rembrandt."

"What are you saying? Scotty painted a little Rembrandt under my face?"

"Oh no, Nick." Virgil took a step back, viewing the canvas in its entirety, imagining the painting hidden beneath, his mind's eye more accurate than any radiographic imaging. "That's not what I'm saying at all."

Little Anthony and the Imperials' "Going out of my Head" kicked in as the Mad Painter of Rittenhouse Square rendered his finding.

"This is a self-portrait."

As Virgil continued his work, Nick instructed Alberto to fix up a giant charcuterie board for everyone, and a pot of espresso for Virgil.

There was a clanging ring that Nick hadn't heard in years. Gary called Nick over to the bar and handed him the receiver to a beige, old-school landline phone. The line ran from an upstairs apartment and was in the name of a widow Nick's father had allowed to live there for the better part of a decade until her death in 1987. The line survived both the widow and Bell Telephone and had continued to be paid ever since. It was so rarely used, however, that Nick had forgotten all about it. It sat beneath the bar like some relic, reduced to a conversation piece. Except it had rung—a literal phone call from the past.

"What?" Nick smiled as he took the receiver from Gary like it was a joke.

"It's for you, slick."

He searched Gary's face for signs of a prank but, finding none, put the receiver to his ear.

"Hello?"

"Congratulations, kid," a gravelly voice stated.

"You got the wrong number. I never won anything in my life."

"That ain't how I remember it, kid. You did some pretty nice work with the skirts back in the day."

"Well, that settles it then. Where do I go to collect?"

"That's simple. Follow the yellow brick road."

"That's funny. Listen, this has been really entertaining, but I'm a little busy and—"

"I bet you are. I saw the Member's Only sign in the window."

"Good, then you got the message."

"Easy, kid, I'm just breaking your balls. I don't need a membership card to a club me and your father founded. Besides, how many people do you know still remember this number?"

The mention of Nick's father unnerved him. "Listen, I don't know who this is, but—"

"Sure you do, kid. I've been supplying the Di Nobiles with mozzarella for decades."

Nick looked over to the charcuterie board and then back to Gary for some guidance, but the big man just moved the toothpick from one corner of his mouth to the other and shrugged.

"Okay, I know who you are, but why would I come to meet you? Are we behind on the bill or something? I'll have Gary send a check out in the morning."

"The Caffé is never late on a payment. Besides, your credit is good with me. Let's just say we have a mutual friend, and I just got off the phone with him. There's been a slight change in plans."

"I'm sure we have dozens of mutual friends. It's a small neighborhood."

"This guy is a bit out of the neighborhood. Are you sitting at the bar?"

Nick hesitated. He walked to the door, stretching the cord until the coils straightened. He parted the curtain and looked outside to see if maybe there was a car idling across the street, but the Avenue was quiet.

"Yeah, I'm at the bar."

"Good. Look up at the top shelf. See the tallest bottle, the one in the center?" Nick looked up at the bottle of Stoli Elit. "That's what he likes to drink."

"Lots of people drink that, including my uncle. So what?"

"He told me a story about you, about how much he respects you . . . even though you threw up on his boat."

That stopped Nick dead in his tracks. No one knew all the details of what had transpired that night on the *Mishka*. He hadn't even told Gary.

"Okay, fine. But let me tell you something my father taught me. I'm sure you'll remember it, what with the two of you going way back and all; 'Broad Street runs two ways.' So why don't you hop on that yellow brick road and come over here, alone. And in case I'm not being clear, well, you heard the voice that answered when you called right?"

"You're really living up to your billing, kid. Too bad you didn't stick around back in the day. But take it down a notch; we're all rowing in the same boat. Capisce?"

"Yeah, capisco." Nick hung up. He filled Gary in on the call. The big man nodded and toyed with his toothpick, but he took it all in. Whatever it was, Nick just wanted to get it over with. "Let's move Virgil back in the kitchen. I don't want this thing sitting out in the open when the cheese man walks through this door."

"Me and Dino are going to head over to the Paradise, you know, keep up appearances and such. I'll let you know if we hear anything about Scotty," Frank said. "Call if you need us, okay?"

"Yeah, I suppose that's a good idea," Nick answered. "Just be careful and check back later tonight."

With Joey's help, Nick and Gary moved the canvas back into the kitchen and cleared off an area for Virgil to continue his work.

FOR WHOM THE BELL TOLLS

Therefore, send not to know
For whom the bell tolls,
It tolls for thee.

"For Whom The Bell Tolls" — John Donne

"Where are you going *now*, baci? We have a big day tomorrow." Gloria was packing up some last-minute items. It had all happened so suddenly, and she had that sickening feeling that she was forgetting something really important.

"Don't worry, baci, I won't be long. Just tying up some loose ends before the trip."

Instead of alleviating her fears, Nino Scopa's comment only served to heighten her anxiety. "But we're getting on the road by 4:00 a.m. You said it yourself; you want to get around the beltway before rush hour."

Nino had one hand on the doorknob and had opened it enough to make the little bell ring. The look on Gloria's face made him pause. He stood there for a moment, taking in her beauty as if for the first time. His heart was as full as the first day he had laid eyes on her. *What did I do to deserve such a woman*? he asked himself. But of course, there was no answer. The world didn't always work like that, no matter what the Church would have you believe. *Sometimes, magical things happen to undeserving people,* Nino reasoned. So there he stood, at the age of seventy-seven, about to embark on one last adventure. Nino had done what he had always threatened, but no one, not even Gloria, really believed he would do. He had signed over a ten-year lease on the cheese shop and put the building in trust for the kids. The new operators were a young couple from the neighborhood. Nino felt good about that. It had all come together over the course of three days.

They'd packed up the Sprinter van with what they needed for now and put the rest in storage. He immediately felt ten years younger. Gloria didn't fully believe it until he put the engagement ring on her finger.

"Are you crazy? We're too old to get married."

"Love knows no age," The Wizard said from one creaky knee. "I should have done this years ago." Gloria'd had to help him up, but she said yes.

"We'll stay at The Royal Palm until I find us a place. It won't take long. I have an old friend down there looking for a house for us, something on a golf course."

"You're going to golf? I don't believe it." Gloria was almost in hysterics at the thought of Nino Scopa in a country club.

"Sure, why not? I used to golf when I was a boy." Nino mimicked a golf swing. He was lying, of course, but Gloria went along with his little charade.

"I don't care if we live in a trailer, baci. You've made me the happiest girl in South Philly."

"Not for long."

"What do you mean?" Gloria looked confused.

"I'm about to make you the happiest girl in Boca Raton." Nino grabbed his new fiancée and dipped her a little before kissing her passionately.

That had been earlier that afternoon, and now Nino had to venture out for some unexplainable reason. It filled Gloria with dread.

"Don't go," she stated abruptly. "What could be so important? Let's go to bed early and watch TV. I'll make it worth your while," she added with a wink.

It was a sensible offer, and Nino considered it for a moment, but he knew he needed to see Nick Di Nobile before he left. He had promised Dmitry, and more importantly, many years ago he had made a promise to his old friend. *Look after my son when I'm gone.*

That's the only thing the man had ever asked of him, and Nino Scopa wasn't the type to break his word, even when no one else would know, even if it meant putting himself in danger.

He kissed Gloria. "I'll be back soon. How 'bout you go to bed early, and when I get back, I'll make it worth *your* while."

Gloria knew there was nothing else she could say. His stubbornness was part of what she loved about him. She would busy herself making a list of all the things she wanted to do once they got to Florida, and hopefully that would pass the time until her baci returned.

The little bell rang again as Nino left.

RIYADH

Al Amin's Gulfstream touched down at the King Khalid International Airport in Saudi Arabia. The pilot, a member of the General Intelligence Presidency, taxied the G650ER to Saudia Prime Jet Aviation. The seventy-million-dollar jet was carrying an extra passenger since arriving in Philadelphia the previous day. This passenger stood 160 cm high and was purportedly worth more than the plane itself.

The plan was for Nasir to transport the painting to the Islamic Port of Jeddah, where it would be loaded onto *Perseus*, the slightly smaller superyacht in Al Amin's fleet, for transit through the Suez Canal and across the Mediterranean Sea to Monaco, where it would meet up with *Serenity*.

Upon arrival, the painting would be transferred to *Serenity* and, after further analysis, displayed next to *Salvator Mundi*, Al Amin's prized da Vinci (although some, including the Louvre, would take issue with this attribution). Al Amin would not be deterred. He planned to build a museum and cultural center in Al-Ula that would rival anything in Europe. The idea was to auction off both paintings aboard the *Serenity* in Monaco during Grand

Prix weekend. His previous plan to have *Salvator Mundi* displayed at the Leonardo exhibition at the Louvre was scuttled when the French experts expressed an opinion that the painting was more likely "From the Workshop of" as opposed to by the Master himself. One of the more generous attributions was that da Vinci had contributed some retouchings to a work primarily painted by an assistant, Giovanni Antonio Boltraffio. The 450-million-dollar painting had not been seen in public since, save for a select few who knew of its new home, a temperature and humidity-controlled vault specially installed on *Serenity* by Fincantieri Yachts.

Al Amin had invited a select group of bidders for the proposed auction. Each had their own reasons for currying favor with Al Amin and agreed to his conditions that neither painting be subjected to any independent studies. Further, although they would be the titled owner, they would, contemporaneous to the sale, lease it back to the Kingdom indefinitely for display at Al Amin's proposed museum at Al-Ula in return for the sum of one Saudi riyal. Al Amin would funnel the proceeds (after a hefty cut for himself) to the Saudi Sovereign Wealth Fund for the construction of the Al-Ula Cultural Center, cementing his place in history as the ruler who brought the Kingdom triumphantly into the post-oil future.

The world would just have to get over the origins and provenance of the paintings. They were authentic because Al Amin said they were. And as to the "stolen" asterisk some would attach to Rembrandt's *Christ in the Storm on the Sea of Galilee*? In time, the world would forget it like they did the theft of Murillo's *Return of the Prodigal.*

What right did the US have to protest when they themselves displayed Murillo's looted work in the National Gallery in their own capital? He had written the proposed provenance text himself: "Rembrandt's sole seascape, saved from destruction by His Royal Highness Prince Al Amin, Crown Prince and Deputy Prime Minister of Saudi Arabia, and returned to the world at the Al-Ula Cultural Center."

THE CHEESE MAN

Nino walked at a brisk pace, hands jammed in his pockets, shoulders hunched up around his ears. It was only two and a half blocks from the cheese shop to Caffé Vecchio, and Nino had walked the route since he was a boy. However, the thought this might be his last time strolling along the Avenue caused him to slow his pace and look around, taking in the sights as if through the eyes of a tourist. Soon, he would be trading in the telephone pole-lined avenue for a palm tree hugged stretch on Camino Real.

He was close enough to hear the music pumping from the jukebox when he sensed a large figure on the periphery of his vision. The figure stepped out from between two parallel parked cars as Nino passed. Nino had one foot on the first step and was about to reach for the door when he heard a vaguely familiar voice.

"Yo, cheese man."

Nino felt foolish for allowing someone to sneak up on him like that. *What was I thinking? Looking around the neighborhood like some white bread tourist.*

He wasn't afraid as he turned to face the man behind the voice. Instead, he felt guilty—guilty for not listening to Gloria and leaving her all alone just as they were ready to start their new adventure together. "Baci," he whispered to himself as he turned.

"Who?" Gary laughed at Nino's slipped utterance. "I'm flattered and all, and don't take it the wrong way, but you ain't my type."

Nino breathed a sigh of relief. All his life, he had been steady as a rock, but now that he was so close, he was a bundle of nerves.

Gary sensed his apprehension. "Easy, Nino. I just gotta show you some love before I let you in—you understand." Gary took The Wizard in a bear hug so that to any passerby they would look like two old friends greeting each other, except the hug was just one long pat down. "You know, you can hug me back if you like . . . baci." Gary couldn't resist one last playful jab, just like he couldn't resist sliding his hands down to Nino's ankles. "Just being thorough, Nino, no offense."

Nino had regained his composure. "None taken. I'd be insulted by anything else. But I haven't carried a piece since '93," Nino said with a wink, making a statement without really saying what he meant.

But Gary got the message. He held the door and Nino stepped into Caffé Vecchio.

Nick was seated at his usual spot at the bar, and Joey had taken the stool next to him. Nino approached Nick with an outstretched hand, and Joey sprung to his feet to intercept him.

"He good," Gary spoke up, and Joey sat back down.

Nick took his hand and offered Nino the stool next to him. Gary made introductions all around, and Alberto took the drink orders. Nino ordered a Peroni, seeing that was what everyone was drinking. He raised his bottle and clicked its green neck against the bottle in Nick's hand.

"Nice work, kid. You're standing on third."

Nick sipped his beer before responding. "Don't tell me; you're here to bring me home?"

"That would be correct," Nino answered with authority. The fog from his little jaunt down Passyunk Avenue was beginning to lift, and The Wizard of old had returned.

Over the next hour, Alberto kept the drinks flowing, Joey kept the songs playing, and Nino laid out an audacious plan that required equal parts balls and luck. All the while, Virgil continued his work in the kitchen. Gary had sent the cooks and dishwasher home early so the volatile painter wouldn't be interrupted. Of course, some portions of the plan Nino wasn't comfortable divulging just yet. He needed to preserve the illusion, even among his co-conspirators—a wizard never gives away all his secrets.

"This just might work," Nick weighed in once Nino was finished.

"And it will," Nino added, "as long as everyone holds up their end."

"I can vouch for my guys," Nick responded. "How 'bout you?"

"The only thing I vouch for is human nature. And I've never been wrong about that. You know, Nick, I sat in this very spot with your father many years ago. I know you probably don't want to hear this, but you sound just like he did back then."

Nick squirmed a bit, looking for some distraction that would serve as a pretext for bailing on the conversation.

"Stop," Nino said bluntly. "You think I don't know it's a sore subject? That's why I don't raise it lightly. But I have my reasons." Nino's forceful delivery was tinged with just enough kindness to put Nick at ease. "Listen, we can run only so far from our DNA, no matter how much we might want to. Take my jerk-off son, for instance. He's ashamed of me and won't admit to his high-class friends that he grew up on top of a cheese shop on Passyunk Avenue, like there's something wrong with that. Last week, my accountant asked me if I was interested in a loan package secured by some monstrosity in Bryn Mawr. It was a sweet deal, so I funded it. Turns out one of them high-class friends got in a little over his head this football season."

Nick considered where Nino was going with all this but gave the man his respect and let him continue.

"My point is this, Nick. Things ain't always what they appear to be. As much as it might hurt me that my son wants nothing to do with me, I would take everything I own, put it in the middle of the street, and fucking burn it if I thought that would ease his pain. And believe me, your father was no different. And I'll tell you another thing; I funded that deal *hoping* that blueblood cocksucker goes bad, cause the minute he does, I'm taking him down and giving that property to my ingrate son."

"I think I get it," Nick responded a bit too summarily.

"You don't get shit." Nino paused, realizing that was a little harsh. "Look, all I'm saying is your father and me went through shit we don't tell nobody. When your mother passed"—Nino blessed himself—"God rest her soul, your father was left a young single parent. He was crushed, but he had to put on a brave face for you. Your mother . . . I'm so sorry you never got a chance to really know her. She was an angel on Earth. I think that's why he never remarried. I mean, he found love again, especially with that beauty from the candy store—*madone*, what a woman—but I think he felt it would be disloyal to her, and in a crazy way disloyal to you, to remarry."

Nick took the Boardwalk photos out of his pocket and placed the half strip on the bar. "Is this the woman you're talking about?"

"Jesus Christ." Nino put on his reading glasses for a better look. "That's her alright, and look at your father." Nino smiled mischievously at the sight of his old friend. "Fucking Casanova. So, you knew?"

"Yeah. I've been learning a lot of things these last few days. And I want to thank you."

Nino looked up from the photos.

"I appreciate what you just said. I've been wrong about plenty of things, but I'm trying to make things right. It's just, well, I miss him. I miss them both and what might have been. Mostly—I know this doesn't make sense—but I think I blame myself."

"Makes perfect sense, kid. It's human nature. And I'm never wrong about human nature."

Alberto opened some fresh Peronis as Nick waved Gary back over. He had retreated respectfully when the conversation had veered to the personal. Nick ordered a round of Crown Royal all around. Nino proposed a toast to Nick's mother and father, and they all drank.

Nick stood to escort Nino back to the kitchen. "I suppose you'll be wanting to have a look at it."

Nino didn't budge. "What makes you think that?"

"Well, I just figured you would want to confirm it."

"Nah, that's where everybody goes wrong. They trust this"—Nino pointed at his eyes—"when they should trust this." Nino stood up and grabbed his balls, giving them a vigorous shake for emphasis. "I know what's back there because I did my homework, not because my eyes tell my head what to think. That's how guys get jammed up with broads. And it's how we're gonna give his Royal Highness a good ass fucking."

"I don't get it," Gary said.

"Think about it. How long you think it's gonna take them to figure out they have a fake?"

"Oh," Nick said. "You're probably right, but then what?"

"Do you really think Al Amin's gonna admit he got outplayed by some paisans from South Philly?"

"I don't follow," Nick said.

"It's only a fake if he says it's a fake. Same as that other painting, the *Salvator Mundi*. Nobody's gonna tell the emperor he has no clothes. He'll just put it on display in the Kingdom and no one will be the wiser. Unless…"

"Unless what?" Gary asked.

Nick's eyes lit up as he began to put the puzzle together. "Unless the real one turns up."

Nino smiled at his new apprentice. "Now you're thinking, kid."

"But how does that help Dmitry? He's not going to be able to sell it like that," Gary said.

"Maybe our friend doesn't want to sell it," Nino answered. "Maybe he'll just be happy to get one over on Al Amin."

Gary looked puzzled, but Nick's mind was firing away. "But maybe *we* could."

Nino dismissed the idea immediately. "Sell the painting out from under Dmitry? No way, kid. You might as well sign your own death warrant. Besides, that's not how I operate, and neither should you."

Nick smiled, savoring the moment, then he laid out his own plan. Nino had a little trouble following it—the concept was a bit foreign to him—but it sounded like it had promise.

"You ready for a road trip?" Nick said to Gary.

"Born. I'll gas up the Yukon."

Nick looked to Nino. "How 'bout you?"

"Way ahead of you, kid. I'll be on the road before you get out of bed."

Nick hugged The Wizard. "Thanks again — for everything."

"Don't mention it, kid, thank *you.* You helped me keep a promise to a dear friend."

Gary saw him to the door, but not before asking Joey to walk the man home. He took a seat at the bar next to Nick.

"You really think this could work?" Gary asked.

"Only one way to find out." Nick took out his phone and made a call to the man they called Gates.

TRAFFIC PERMITTING

Frank and Dino's visit to the Paradise had turned out to be relatively uneventful. There was no word about Scotty, the new bartender was a no-show (no surprise there), and Fenway Phil was nowhere to be found.

Nick filled them in on most of the plan and booked them on the 8:20 a.m. on American.

"We'll meet you at Blaine's by midnight," Nick said to Frank, "traffic permitting."

Dino stood there for an extra moment, the look on his face even more disgusted than usual.

"What?" Nick finally asked.

"I need to talk to you about something."

"Sure, what is it?"

"This is hard for me to say but . . . bear with me here."

"Just say it. You can speak freely here," Nick said.

Gary was furiously switching the toothpick back and forth in his mouth, sensing this might be bad.

"I don't trust Nino. Or my boss, for that matter."

"Okay, you have my attention. That's a pretty serious accusation."

"It's not an accusation, just an observation. This whole thing just seems too convenient. I think the two of them have been working together with Boston. And God forgive me—I don't have proof, mind you—but I think maybe Andy's been talking to the FBI."

"Whoa. That sure sounds like an accusation to me," Gary weighed in.

"Let me finish. Like I was saying, I can't be sure. Look, I love the old guy. I hope to God it's not true. But I can't sit here and go along with this without speaking my mind."

"Okay," Nick said. "No judgments are being made here. You're right to bring it up. But do you have any proof?"

Dino told them about Andy Boy's meeting with Nino Scopa and his little stroll with a guy who walked and talked like a fed. He described Father Gus's visit to Angelina's on the night of his demise and Fenway Phil's story about seeing a guy in the neighborhood who resembled someone he knew from the North End—guy by the name of Big Vic.

"What do you think?" Nick asked Gary.

"Suspicious, but not enough. People have said worse things about me over the years, just not to my face." Gary was thinking about his visit from Special Agent O'Connell and wondering whether Dino was making some type of indirect insinuation about him as well.

"Okay, let's keep our guard up and leave it at that for now. I just don't see the angle. Even Andy Boy isn't crazy enough to try to double-cross Dmitry," Nick concluded.

Everyone stood silent for a while. Dino had his arms crossed in front of him, chin pointed down like he was trying to figure out the angle. Gary tapped twice on the bar to signal the powwow was over.

"We best get some sleep," Gary said to Nick. "Four o'clock comes around mighty early. I'll stay here with the painting."

"Okay, I'll go check on Virgil," Nick replied.

"I'm going to sleep over at my Sophia's house if that's okay, Uncle Nick," Joey said.

"Just don't be late," Gary said. "Four on the dot."

Joey gave a satirical salute and headed out the door. Frank and Dino knocked back what was left of their drinks and followed close behind. Nick and Gary walked to the kitchen to check on Virgil and the status of the restoration.

Virgil had cleaned up the painting about 90% of the way. "I need more specialized tools to finish. I don't want to do any damage."

"I'll drive you home, and you can pack a bag with everything you need," Nick said.

"You mean . . . I can come?" Virgil was genuinely touched. No matter how often Nick and Gary tried to reassure him, the painter was never quite sure he was one of the guys.

"Are you kidding me? You're the star of the show. None of this works without you. I mean, look at this . . ."

The result was stunning, even under the flickering fluorescent lights. The faces leaped off the canvas, especially Rembrandt's little self-portrait. He practically stole the show from the Savior.

"I can't believe it," Nick said. "Rembrandt's only seascape, missing for over thirty years, and it's here in our kitchen. I wish my father could have seen it."

"He's seeing it, pretty boy," Gary said. "Believe that."

REARVIEW MIRROR

Nino Scopa had difficulty sleeping after the previous night's events. He wasn't a man who spooked easily. A lifetime spent navigating a landscape chock full of naked ambitions, shifting loyalties, and multi-generational grudges had made him virtually immune to such superstitions. But his brush with the prospect of losing Gloria due to some 9th inning carelessness on his part, unfounded as it might have been, had him on edge. At 3:00 a.m., he brewed some espresso in the stovetop pot and woke Gloria with a kiss on the forehead. After seventy-seven years, he had an overpowering urge to leave South Philadelphia, the Avenue, and even his beloved cheese shop, in his rearview. The last thing he grabbed on his way out the door were his competing stacks of business and funeral cards. He tossed the two paper bricks, rubber bands stretched to the max, into a paper bag. The little bell rang as they walked out, and Nino Scopa, The Wizard of Soppressata, locked the door, knowing it was the last time he would ever hear that little bell. He opened the passenger door of the Sprinter van for Gloria, and they were on I-95 by 3:30 a.m.

Gloria gripped his hand across the console. She recited a silent prayer of thanks for what she considered to be nothing less than a miracle. "I love you, baci," she said.

"I love you more, baci," Nino echoed back, as always.

ARE WE THERE YET?

At quarter after four, there was still no sign of Joey.

"Give him a call," Nick said to Gary.

"I already did. Text too."

Gary was packing the last of their things in the Yukon. The painting was wrapped up in a few sheets and tied along its height and width with industrial twine in the shape of a cross. Gary topped it off with a heavy-duty moving blanket and placed it carefully in the back of the SUV. Nick was just about to suggest they swing by Joey's place when he walked through the door, a bit bleary-eyed but ready to go.

"Sorry, Uncle Nick. I was saying goodbye to Sophia," he said with a glint in his eye. "You know how it is."

"He used to," Gary answered for him.

Nick was getting impatient, and it was still a little early in the morning for that level of ball breaking. "Let's just go pick up Virgil and get this show on the road. We're already behind schedule." Nick was anxious to get the painting to Florida, but was even more anxious to get back to Grace and make things right. She hadn't responded to his late-night text that he was coming home. He had a feeling that if he had any chance of mending things with her this time, it would have to be in person. He made a silent vow.

"Yo, Nick." Gary snapped him out of his trance. "Something you want to share with us?"

Not really, Nick thought. So he lied. "I was just thinking, next time I don't give a fuck if the *Mona Lisa* is hanging from the rafters of the Wells Fargo Center, I'm staying in Florida."

"Who said there's going to be a next time?" Gary said.

I hope not, Nick thought, *but somehow there always is.*

Virgil was ready and standing outside his place. Still in the same clothes, a canvas tote filled with painting supplies was slung over his shoulder. It wasn't even 5:00 a.m., yet he was already halfway through an Opus X.

"You ain't bringing that thing in here," Gary said.

The painter looked disappointed but dutifully extinguished the cigar on the sidewalk and climbed into the back seat. They were on I-95 by five. Conversation was minimal as they passed through Delaware, stopping only once for a bathroom break. They got around the beltway pretty quickly and were barreling through Virginia in short order. Like an adolescent who couldn't help himself from constantly inquiring *are we there yet?,* Virgil was already asking if they could stop at South of the Border. Gary and Nick shot the idea down in unison with a resounding, "No." Gary glanced in the rearview. Virgil had that dejected look on his face, and Gary sensed their answer had landed more harshly than intended.

"Hey, Nick." Gary gave him a wink. "If I recall correctly, there's a Starbucks up ahead. You down for a Frappuccino?"

Virgil's face brightened, and the childlike painter momentarily forgot all about South of the Border. "I am!" he chirped.

ETHER

There lies the port; the vessel puffs her sail:
There gloom the dark, broad seas. My mariners,
Souls that have toil'd, and wrought, and thought with me—
That ever with a frolic welcome took
The thunder and the sunshine, and opposed
Free hearts, free foreheads—you and I are old;
Old age hath yet his honour and his toil;
Death closes all: but something ere the end,
Some work of noble note, may yet be done,
Not unbecoming men that strove with Gods.

Ulysses —Alfred, Lord Tennyson

The drive was fairly routine. Gary, Nick, and Joey took shifts—Virgil never quite caught on with the whole driver's license thing—enabling them to drive straight through. After stopping for gas, coffee, and bathroom breaks, as well as a brief sit-down dinner at a Cracker Barrel, the crew arrived at Blaine's Tavern around midnight. Nick had been texting with Frank, who'd arrived with Dino earlier in the day. Now, the two of them were on their way to Blaine's after picking up Gates in Boca.

Nino had arrived earlier and checked in at the Ocean Abode for the night. Gloria was exhausted but too excited to sleep. Nino left her in Ronnie Cruz's capable hands, and she nursed a pina colada at the Tuscan Tiki while Nino took an Uber to Blaine's.

The reunion was set to kick off in fine order—with the addition of an unexpected guest.

Ralph kept the interior of Blaine's blissfully dark, which in his estimation, every good bar should be. Blaine's was a dive bar that didn't care about, let alone embrace, that designation. She was an aging beauty, oblivious to well-meaning compliments like "Stately" or "Graceful." If Blaine's were a woman, she would look at herself in the mirror and say, "*I'm still hot*."

Nick felt better as soon as he stepped through the door. The dark wood and neon enveloped him like an old lover's embrace, and he started to realize how bad he wanted a proper drink. Gates walked in close on Nick's heels but didn't share his feelings. He was practically holding on to Nick's belt loops, like a kid clinging to his father in a haunted house. This was as far removed from Gates's Royal Palm ecosystem as he had ever strayed. In fact, he rarely went anywhere further than a golf cart's distance from the resort. He sensed an overpowering scent that refused to vacate his nostrils; a blend of bleach and urinal puck.

"Are you sure this is okay?" he whispered to Nick.

"Believe me, Gates, you're safer here than you are at the Royal Palm," Nick assured him.

Gary and Dino stayed in the Yukon with the painting in an abundance of caution. *You don't exactly come traipsing through a dark bar with a priceless masterpiece without at least sizing up the interior,* Nick had thought.

Joey, Nick, and Gates had a seat at the bar. Frank and Dino arrived soon after. Nick texted Nino, thinking the old man must have fallen asleep.

Where are you?

The response came a few seconds later. *We're in the back.*

"What is it?" Frank saw the look on Nick's face.

"Nino says he's here already." Nick looked at the door to the back room. He quickly ordered and knocked back a generic tequila. "You two stay here," he said to Gates and Virgil. The painter was engrossed in a pencil sketch portrait of Cathy, the bartender. His canvas was a repurposed piece of cardboard salvaged from a trashed Budweiser case. Gates looked like he was going to die. "It's okay, I'll send Frank to come get you when we're ready."

Nick opened the door and walked into a room that Ralph had set up as a combination office and poker parlor. It was a little brighter than the bar, but not much. Frank and Joey followed close behind. A single overhead light hovered low over a green felt table. It cast the faces of the three men seated around the table in shadow, accentuating their hard-earned creases in the stark relief of a film noir. Ralph was dealing cards to the other two men. One, Nick quickly recognized as Nino Scopa, but he didn't know the other man.

Frank did.

"Have a seat, Nicky," Ralph said without looking up, tilting his head toward a table to his right. "What's up, Frankie?" he added, acknowledging his old friend.

"Hey, Ralph," Frank answered weakly and took a seat next to Nick.

Joey remained standing.

"Nino tells me you have a pretty good plan." Ralph looked up at Nick for the first time since they walked into the room.

"Not a plan necessarily," Nick replied. "More of a refinement."

"A refinement," the man seated on the other side of Ralph echoed gruffly.

"I'm sorry, Nick, where are my manners?" Ralph interjected. "Let me introduce you to my mother's younger brother, Andrea Caposecco."

Andy Boy set down his cards and turned to Nick, extending his hand.

"Andy, Nick Di Nobile," Ralph said by way of introduction.

Nick leaned over and took his hand, thinking of what Dino had said. But before he could make any further calculations, Andy spoke up.

"Nice to meet you, kid. Heard nothing but great things about you. No surprise there—your father was a real gentleman. Now, if you wouldn't mind, could you send Dino in, please?"

Nick wasn't sure what to do, so he looked to Ralph and Frank. They both nodded their approval.

"Joey, do me a favor, will you—"

Joey was already moving for the door before Nick could finish.

Nick had begun putting the pieces of the puzzle together by the time Joey returned with Dino. By the time his eyes adjusted to the light, Dino looked even sicker than Gates.

Andy broke the silence. "Hello, Dino." Dino looked back over his shoulder, gauging the distance to the door. "Relax," Andy continued. "This ain't that." His staccato delivery emphasized he had no need for subterfuge. "Have a seat."

Dino sized up the situation and realized Andy was probably telling the truth. This wasn't how it would go down. He was safe—for the moment.

"I hear you're unhappy with your job, maybe thinking of going out on your own."

Dino put up his hands in protest and was about to speak in his defense when Andy cut him off.

"Stop. Just listen for a minute. You'll live longer."

Ralph and Nino laughed. Nick remained frozen. Frank fired up a Marlboro.

"You've been with me a long time, Dino, and I'm not getting any younger. We've talked it over." Andy looked over at Ralph and Nino. "You'll take over the day-to-day of the produce business and everything that goes along with it. For that, you're in for a third. You also get ten percent of the hauling. Sorry, but we have other partners in that. Agreed?"

Dino was about to answer, but realized Andy wasn't talking to him. Andy looked at Ralph and Nino, who nodded and grunted, respectively.

"Well?" Ralph asked in a way that suggested he was reminding Dino of his manners. "What do you say?"

Dino uttered the only acceptable response. "Thank you."

"Good," Andy said. "But one more thing. Don't ever question my actions again. We're playing chess here." Andy looked back and forth between Ralph and Nino. "You should stick to checkers for now."

Dino was being offered a pretty lucrative deal, but he couldn't help looking deflated. Andy noticed and threw him a bone. "For now," he repeated with meaningful emphasis. "Okay, why don't you head back to the city now. You've got a lot of work to do—and don't look so glum—a lot of money to make." Andy got up and gave Dino a hug and a kiss. Ralph and Nino shook hands with him, wishing him well.

Nick couldn't help thinking of Rembrandt's *The Return of Prodigal Son.*

Dino headed for the door, but before he reached it, Andy called out to him.

"Hey, Dino." Dino stopped and turned around. Andy reached below the table toward the empty chair next to him. "I almost forgot." Andy raised his hand back up and tossed a white package toward Dino. It hit him in the chest, and he gripped it before it could fall to the ground. It was Dino's refrigerator jacket, the red stitching spelled out *Ted* on the front. "I had it cleaned and pressed for you."

Nick let out a breath he hadn't realized he was holding in.

"Sorry 'bout that, Nick," Andy apologized. "Just a little housekeeping before we move on to the matter at hand. Now, where were we?"

"The boy wonder," Nino helpfully reminded him.

"Oh, right," Andy said. "Send in Zuckerberg."

Nick didn't correct him. He looked to Joey, who was already headed for the door to retrieve Gates. "Might as well have Gary bring it in," Nick hollered after him. "Gates is going to need to have a look at it to explain."

Joey returned with Gary, the two of them carrying the painting into the room. Gates followed close behind, bumping shoulders with Virgil as they both attempted to walk through the door at the same time. The painting was gently placed on a card table in the center of the room and unveiled. Virgil still had some work to do, but the image was unmistakable. Even Nino, who had initially passed on having a look at it, was visibly moved.

Maybe that was the real reason he didn't want to see it, Nick thought.

Gates wasn't as interested in its aesthetics as he was in the science required to bring it to market. If Virgil saw the world in shapes and colors, Gates witnessed it in formulas and equations.

"Nino tells me you have a plan to sell this without putting us all on a Russian hit list," Andy said. "You mind explaining that to us? And please, make pretend we're in fifth grade—that's as far as I went anyway."

"Has anyone ever heard of an NFT?" he asked.

Virgil raised his hand until Nick gently eased it down and whispered that the question wasn't meant for him.

As the CEO of a major tech corporation, Gates was used to speaking to a sometimes-hostile board of directors, and some people even regarded him as a visionary. So, he closed his eyes for a second and tried to imagine he was in a boardroom instead of a back room. He started slowly, but little by little he gained confidence as he gave a watered-down but compelling explanation of NFTs, the metaverse, and blockchain technology, describing how it afforded a guarantee of authenticity unrivaled in the physical art world. He told the story of the digital artist known as Beeple, who sold a collage of five thousand digital pictures he had produced over thirteen-plus years. Christie's had offered it as a single lot sale and agreed to accept payment in cryptocurrency.

"It sold for over sixty-nine million," Gates finished with a flourish.

"But I don't understand how we sell it without getting pinched," Ralph said.

"Well, we're not selling the painting; we're just selling a picture of it. There's nothing illegal about that," Nick explained.

"So what? There must be thousands of pictures of this thing. What's going to make ours so special?" Nino asked.

"None of those pictures have been taken in the thirty-two years since it was stolen," Gates offered.

"How do we prove when our picture was taken?" Andy asked.

"Technology," Gates said. "In 2020, the Rijksmuseum released a hyper-resolution image of Rembrandt's *The Night Watch*. It consists of over eight thousand individual photographs and contains more than seven hundred gigapixels."

"Fifth grade," Andy barked.

"Each pixel is smaller than a red blood cell. The amount of detail is staggering. It's like walking on the moon. Now, our digital version of *Christ in the Storm* won't be anywhere near that. Even I don't have access to that kind of equipment. Besides, that would take too long. But it will still be infinitely greater than anything that could have been produced back in 1990. You'll be able to examine every crack and brushstroke on a microscopic level. In that way, it will be self-authenticating. Think of it as the difference between Pong and virtual reality."

"What's Pong?" Nino asked Andy, who shrugged his shoulders.

"Like the difference between looking through a spyglass and the Webb telescope. The image will reveal galaxies inside the painting that were impossible to see thirty years ago," Gates added.

"Where do we sell it?" Ralph asked.

"On an online marketplace for NFTs."

"How do we get paid?" Andy growled.

"In cryptocurrency. Something called Ether transferred to an anonymous wallet."

"You okay with this?" Ralph asked Nick.

"Absolutely," Nick answered.

"This whole plan sounds like ether," Gary chimed in. "Sorry, Nick, but what happens when the real painting turns up? Won't the digital thing lose its value?"

"Not at all. If things go as planned, it should actually increase value. Don't forget, it will be the first of its kind; a present-day, high-resolution image of a stolen masterpiece."

"Won't that bring a world of heat down on us, kid?" Andy asked. "I mean, granted, the statute of limitations has long passed on the original theft, but flaunting the fact that we have it... Andy turned his palms up and scrunched his eyes. "I gotta believe somebody at the FBI is gonna be a little pissed."

"No, they won't," Nino answered before Nick, seeing the play.

Nick smiled at Nino's realization. "That brings us to the second part of the plan. The part Dmitry is going to love." Nick was now talking directly to Ralph. "If you can sell him on it."

Nick proposed a daring gambit. It was risky and dangerous but beautiful in its simplicity. If all went to plan, they would make art history, Dmitry would come off like a cultural philanthropist, and Al-Amin would become the laughingstock of the art world.

PENELOPE

"All the nobles who rule the islands about... they court me against my will, they laywaste my house... I yearn for Odysseus, always, my heart pines away."

The Odyssey of Homer 19.145-151

It was after 2:00 a.m. when Nick finally arrived back at his beloved tiki bar. Ronnie Cruz was wrapping things up, and the last of the hard-luck cases were finishing their drinks beneath the flicker of the televisions lining the perimeter. A full moon was putting on a glorious display over the ocean, but the drinkers were oblivious to anything beyond the palm thatch roof. Nick took a seat at the opposite end, where he could look out at the flat ocean and the moonlight that coated it like a silvery comforter.

"Welcome home, *jefe*." Ronnie greeted him with a Don Julio 1942 and a Peroni. The *anejo* tasted exceptionally smooth and almost erased the lingering notes of the rotgut he had drunk at Blaine's.

"Thanks, Ronnie. It's good to be back."

"So, did you find what you were looking for?"

"I'm not sure. I'll have to get back to you on that." Nick sipped his Peroni, feigning nonchalance. "How have things been around here?"

Ronnie stopped cleaning up and walked over to Nick. He placed his hands on the bar a bit wider than his shoulders and leaned close to Nick like he was doing a cheat push-up.

"You mean how's Grace."

"I guess I do." Nick wasn't in the mood for games, even from an old friend. Ronnie pushed himself back upright and resumed his closing-up routine.

"Well?" Nick followed up after a few uncomfortable moments.

"I'm not sure," Ronnie answered honestly. "I'll have to get back to you on that."

"What's that supposed to mean?" Nick could have done without the sarcasm. Here he was, finally home from a perilous journey, Grace nowhere to be found, and his trusted lieutenant was mocking him.

"Exactly what I said. I'm not sure. She hasn't been in since you left. Ethan has been covering her shifts. Wait . . . you haven't talked to her?" Nick shook his head. "Oh Christ, I'm sorry. I didn't know."

"That's okay. It's my own damn fault. I fucked up again. God knows I don't deserve her."

Ronnie walked back and reached over the bar, gripping Nick gently on the back of the neck in a gesture of brotherly affection. "I love you, brother."

"I love you too, Ronnie."

"But I ain't going to give you an argument on that point—you fucked up," Ronnie said.

"Okay," Nick said. "I get it. You've always given in to me straight, even all those years ago. Remember me, you and Jimmy running wild in the clubs on Delaware Avenue?"

"Best days of my life, homie."

"What the fuck happened to us?"

"Same shit happens to everybody. We got civilized." Ronnie patted his midsection. "And fat."

"Civilized. That's a joke. I can't even make things work with the greatest woman I've ever met. Maybe I was better off a heathen." Nick's face turned serious. "I'm asking for your help, brother. How do I make things right? How do I get her back?"

Ronnie knew his old friend was hurting. He'd been in his shoes a few times and had no intention of ever feeling that hurt again. It healed slower than a knife wound, and he didn't have that kind of recovery left in the tank.

"Why don't you do what's always worked for you in the past?" Ronnie's face was compassionate and his words soft, but he wasn't looking Nick in the eyes. Instead, he was looking past him, somewhere over his shoulder.

"Thanks, Ronnie, but somehow I don't think that's gonna solve my problems."

Ronnie turned his focus back to Nick, and this time didn't speak as softly. "You asked for my advice, right?"

"Right," Nick said. "But—"

"Good. Here it is." Ronnie slid a twenty across the bar. "Go play some fucking songs." He turned away from Nick, but not before the corner of his mouth began to curl up.

Nick gave up. It was late, and all he really wanted was a shower and to sleep in his own bed, but he picked up his drink, spun on his stool and went to play some songs.

Someone had beat him to it.

She stood in a pool of purple neon, more beautiful than Salome, more inscrutable than Judith. Grace was leaning against the jukebox, one arm outstretched, bracing her as she studied the machine.

"Grace. When did you get here?"

"I heard you were back. Look, Nick. I got your messages. I'm sorry I didn't call you back. I just figured what's the point?"

"What do you mean? I've been sick waiting to hear from you and—"

Grace cut him off. "Nick?"

"What?"

"Could you please just shut up and show me how to play this thing. I mean, it seems to work some kind of magic for you and your friends; maybe it will do the same for me."

Nick desperately wanted to take her in his arms and kiss her, but she seemed so far away. And the awful truth was he had put her there. So, he just tapped on the search bar of the touchscreen. It didn't have the satisfying resistance of punching the buttons of an old-school record machine—one that seemed to touch you right back—but it would have to suffice.

"Is there a specific song you'd like to hear?"

"Oh, I don't know. How about something for a woman whose man continually flirts with greatness but takes off at a moment's notice every time some flicker of imagined past glory twinkles on the horizon? Do you have a song for that?"

From the bar, Nick thought he heard Ronnie say *ouch*, but maybe he was imagining things. Nick thought about it for a minute. He was about to say a*ctually, I do*, but wisely reconsidered. Instead, he made what he considered to be some innocuous song selections and then listened as Grace spoke, resisting the urge to regale her with the tale of his exploits and the treasure he had brought home. Something told him it wasn't the right time. He settled for playing songs and praying for a thaw that still felt far off.

Nick spent the next two weeks assisting Gates in the lab he had set up in a conference room at El Mar Tech, his corporate headquarters on Palmetto Park Road. Dmitry dispatched a security detail that stood sentry twenty-four hours a day, two at reception and two outside the conference room. Gates's regular staff was sent away on a surprise corporate retreat to Arizona. Whatever time Nick wasn't at El Mar Tech, he spent trying to make things right with Grace. Ronnie had convinced her to pick up a few shifts at the Tiki, if not for Nick, then for him. On the nights she worked, Nick always found an excuse to stop in, but mostly laid back, close to the jukebox. Grace noticed he always seemed to be jotting things down in a notebook. Ronnie noticed too but decided to pretend he didn't.

Virgil had finished his restoration, and Gates's man had finished about half of the five hundred-plus individual high-resolution photos the digital asset would consist of. Meanwhile, Gates had set up an account on an NFT marketplace that would host the auction. Nick had one final refinement to add that would start the countdown and fuel the auction, and it was scheduled for Sunday at the Tiki. Ralph had his contact at the *Sun Sentinel* committed to attend. Frank lined up a couple of retired NFL players who hung around the Ambassador Cigar Bar. Even Vinny came through with a few TikTok influencers.

"Unc, you mind if I fly my girl in?" Joey asked. "She's never been to Florida, and I told her all about the Tiki."

"Of course, Joey," Nick answered. "You don't need my permission."

"Good." Joey laughed. "Cause she gets in this afternoon. Can I borrow the Bentley to pick her up?"

"Sure. Just be careful at the airport. Tell her to meet you up at departures; it's less hectic."

"Sure thing," Joey answered.

Gates met Nick at the Tiki the night before the big event.

"We ready for this?" Nick asked.

"It's all set. Our NFT hits the marketplace at 6:00 a.m., right after our little premiere party. Then all we have to do is sit back and watch the bids."

"All hell's gonna break loose after the news hits. I'll understand if you want to make yourself scarce."

"Fuck that," Gates said, displaying some newfound edginess. "If I can handle Blaine's, I can handle anything."

"You got a point there, my friend," Nick said.

Frank walked over to the bar, an unlit Marlboro dangling from his lips. "You got a light?"

"Ronnie," Nick said. "Can you get him a light?"

Ronnie came over with a lighter and lit the old man's cigarette.

"Them things are gonna kill you, Unc. I thought you quit, you know, after your ordeal."

"I did, Nicky, but what's the sense? I'm enjoying my life. I see guys, they watch every little friggin thing they eat, they jog, they juice—fucking Peloton. That's no way to live. Besides, half of them jagoffs end up keeling over from something else." Frank pointed to the sky. "He's gonna take me when he wants me. All our names are already in his book."

It was typical Frankie Stone Crab bullshit, but it didn't stop Nick from getting a chill up his spine thinking of his own name scrivened in some heavenly tome.

"Time is of the essence with this thing, Unc. Once the news hits the wire, it's gonna go viral. I'll handle the heat here, but I need you to make that drive before anyone figures it out."

"Don't worry 'bout that, Nicky. Me and Gary got it covered. It's not my first ride . . ." Frank was about to say *and it won't be my last,* but he didn't want to jinx it. "I was just wondering though, what with all the action going on tomorrow, you still doing the pig roast?"

"Of course," Nick said. "Nothing gets in the way of the porchetta. You know that."

"Good," Frank said with a satisfied smile as he blew smoke out of his nostrils. "Save me the ears."

Nick still loved hearing crazy shit like that from throwbacks like Frank. It gave him comfort to know there were still a few around who remembered the old ways. It kept the Tuscan Tiki from becoming Disney World. "Don't worry, Unc, I think the ears are safe."

"I hope you don't mind, but I invited Blanca. She's doing good with the real estate, and I thought it would be a nice event for her to network."

"Sure," Nick said. "That's real sweet of you. It wouldn't have anything to do with something else, would it?"

"Like what?" Frank feigned innocence.

"Oh, I don't know. Maybe some old hoodlum looking for some arm candy for the step and repeat photos."

Frank spread out his arms in protest. "Hey, I know she's too young for me. She's a sweet kid, and I'm happy to help her. But if she stumbles into a few pics, well, I can't help that."

"I'm just breaking your balls. Take all the pictures you like. In fact, have Blanca blast them out on social media. Just tell her not to forget the hashtag."

"What's a hashtag?"

"Don't worry about it. She'll know. Just tell her hashtag Rembrandt recovered. She'll understand."

PLAGE BEAU RIVAGE

Nice, Côte d'Azur, France

The *Serenity* was moored at Port Vauban, Antibes, as it was too large to be docked in Monaco, or anywhere else on the French Riviera, for that matter. The *Perseus* was en route from Jeddah, and once the transfer was accomplished, she would return to Monaco to act as the world's most expensive shuttle. Twenty or so bidders were scheduled to attend the auction. In addition to the royals from the United Arab Emirates, the elite company consisted of billionaires, despots, and strongmen from Moscow to Caracas.

One billionaire who would not be attending had rented out the entire beach club at Plage Beau Rivage for Grand Prix weekend. His own 155-meter Feadship built *Yekaterina* was moored nearby, having arrived from Cyprus the week before. Although he had been somewhat unfairly labeled as an oligarch, the truth about Dmitry Ivanov was far more complex. Unlike true oligarchs, he had made the bulk of his fortune in the US. Still, the oligarch label had served Dmitry well, so he had done little to disavow it, as he found that Americans were fascinated with the oligarchy.

But like many other Russians, he had family in Ukraine. Dmitry's mother was born in Lviv, and he still had cousins there. His hatred for Putin, therefore, was personal. And though he had only met Putin once, many years ago, he had never been a fan of the dictator and his fragile ego. Dmitry was certain the man's narcissism would eventually lead to his downfall, most likely from within.

Now world events were accelerating things, and Dmitry was being painted with a broad brush by the US government. He knew it was only a matter of time before he was arbitrarily placed on a sanctions list that would jeopardize everything he had built. Dmitry was playing for the highest stakes in his life. And now, thanks to Ralph Cappello and his friends in Philadelphia, he had a chip to play.

#REMBRANDTRECOVERED

The party at the Tiki was in full swing. Gates had rented two searchlights that gave the Ocean Abode the look and feel of a blockbuster movie premiere. A step and repeat banner with the cryptic hashtag #rembrandtrecovered printed in staggered images had been set up at the beach-level entrance to the Tuscan Tiki. Joey occasionally jumped behind the deck when the DJ needed a bathroom break, playing to an audience of one as Sophia watched him from the bar. Nick was happy to see that Blanca had shown for Frank. The old man had cleaned up nicely, even lending a little old-school debonair to his date's bombshell wattage. The guest of honor was stashed in a poolside cabana, where the ever-vigilant Gary stood guard. Next to the Rolls-Royces and Lamborghinis on the front line, a lowly Yukon was parked facing out, while an NBC 6 news van idled nearby. The NBC reporter had set up her shot in front of a large easel that had been placed in the corner, next to the jukebox.

"You're looking pretty snazzy there, Unc," Nick said as Frank walked over. "I saved you the ear in case you're looking for it."

"You can pack it to go. I'll eat it on the ride," Frank replied.

The music stopped and a minor celebrity weatherman who happened to be two months behind on his Intra-coastal home mortgage note held by Tasker Morris bought himself thirty days by stepping to the mic to emcee the festivities. For no discernible reason, he was joined by a bloated '90s freestyle artist who went by a single name that Nick had trouble remembering. Apparently she was making a comeback that had eluded everyone in attendance.

Gary and Frank escorted the guest of honor from the cabana. The frame was shrouded by a red velvet curtain Nick had borrowed from the Ocean Abode's ballroom for the occasion. Ronnie Cruz, sporting a merlot fedora, was entertaining the *Sun Sentinel* reporter, and she looked like she was enjoying his company as much as she was her mojito. Intrigued by the shrouded object, most of the guests pointed their phones at the easel, sensing something exciting was about to happen. In a few moments, they would broadcast the event across their social media app of choice.

Nick was overjoyed to see Grace walk in. She made her way to his side, saying nothing but giving him a squeeze on the arm that said everything. He was so filled with gratitude that the painting momentarily took a back seat.

"Are you sure you know what you're doing?" Grace asked.

"Do you trust me?"

"With this? Believe it or not, yes, I do."

"Good," Nick said, adding after a moment, "And I'm working on everything else."

The weatherman counted down from three, and Gary pulled back the curtain. Nick kissed Grace for the first time since he had left for Philly, and Grace kissed him back.

Everyone cheered and clapped politely. It was undoubtedly a beautiful painting, but the crowd soon rejoined the party and resumed drinking their free drinks. The Tiki was known for its offbeat promotions, and most of them just regarded the festivities as some elaborate, tongue-in-cheek prank—just like Nick knew they would. A few played along, taking selfies and posting their picture with the hashtag #rembrandtrecovered. The local NBC affiliate would run it as a quirky, local interest story—a nice little time filler at the end of the evening news.

Ralph's reporter friend from the *Sun Sentinel* wasn't so dismissive, her first paid writing gig having been with *ARTnews* years ago. She walked over to the painting, mojito in hand, and had a closer look, running her fingers lightly over its surface. She took some up-close pictures with her phone before having a seat at a high top looking out at the ocean. She jotted down some notes, then made a call to her editor. "You're not going to believe this," she said, forwarding him the photos. Just like Ralph knew she would.

Gary and Frank covered the painting and hauled it back to the cabana, where Nino had been sitting throughout the festivities, much preferring his behind-the-scenes role.

Nick joined them. "How we looking?"

"The lawyers are going over some of the fine print, but those cocksuckers just need to justify their fee. Otherwise, we're good," Nino replied.

Ralph walked in. "Looks like Lois Lane took the bait. You guys better get on the road."

Gary spread his arms across the width of the frame and hefted the painting by himself. "Lead the way, Frankie," he said. They headed out of the cabana, back through the lobby, and straight to the Yukon. Nick walked a few steps behind them and pushed the button to close the liftgate once the painting was loaded.

"He's taking the first shift." Frank nodded to Gary. "I don't drive so good in the dark."

"Sounds good, Frankie. I'll make sure Blanca gets home safely."

"Thanks, Nick. One last time, are you sure this is gonna work?"

"Don't worry," Nick said. "If it doesn't, I'll be sure to put money on your commissary."

"That's what I thought," Frank said.

Gary put the Yukon in gear. "We best be on our way."

"Good luck," Nick said. "By the way, do you know the difference between a felon and a hero?" Gary shrugged. "Fifteen hundred miles." Nick delivered the punchline and slapped the top of the Yukon like it was a thoroughbred.

Gary peeled out of the Ocean Abode's driveway, barely missing a Bugatti and causing an unsuspecting valet to leap out of the way.

RAPHAEL'S CUPIDS

When Nick returned to the Tiki, Virgil was engrossed in conversation with Grace, who seemed amused. His hands were moving in front of her face as if he were air-drafting a painting in the space between them. It was nice to see Grace smile again. Nick spotted the back of Ronnie's fedora by the jukebox. He was slow dancing with a new friend by the look of things. Ronnie removed his hat and playfully crowned his new princess. Ralph and Nino were still in the cabana, and Nick thought he should check in with them one last time to let them know the painting was on its way before rejoining the party. But before he could get there, a hand reached out for him from the bar, grabbing his hand as he walked by. Joey and Sophia were all tangled up in each other, standing back one deep from the bar. The encroaching hand had peeked out from between them, petite but firm in its grip.

Nick heard her before he saw her. "Have a drink with us, Nick."

Angie Romano was seated on the stool behind the couple. Her voice was unmistakable and insistent. Joey and Sophia interrupted their embrace, making a space for Nick to slide through.

"When did you get here?" Nick asked weakly. He glanced over to check on Grace, feeling guilty already.

"I've been here the whole time. You didn't think I'd miss the big premiere, did you? Although I have to admit, I didn't quite get what all the fuss was about. Nice crowd though." Angie scanned the Tiki as she said it, briefly locking eyes with Grace, who promptly excused herself from her conversation with Virgil and began walking over.

"Here you go, Uncle Nick." Sophia handed Nick a shot glass from a round of drinks Angie had ordered. It was some trendy red-colored shot, but Nick played along, figuring he should knock it back before Grace arrived and he had to make the awkward but inevitable introductions.

Angie led the toast. "Disaster to the wench"—Angie paused for dramatic effect—"who did wrong by our Nicky. That *is* how it goes, I believe. Right, Nick?"

"Yeah, that's how it goes." Nick knocked back the shot he had been dodging for as long as he could remember. Angie knocked hers back as well, never breaking eye contact with him. The shot tasted like a high-proof sugar bomb.

"I think I have to use the ladies' room." Sophia began to speed walk toward the bathroom, or possibly a trash can.

Nick felt a bit nauseous himself. Grace was about five steps away. Angie was giggling to herself like she'd just heard the funniest story. Nick could see Ronnie approaching from the other side of the bar, the girl in the merlot fedora leading the way. Nick's skin turned clammy, and he broke out in a profuse sweat. Grace was two steps away.

A giant hole opened up beneath Nick's feet. As he began to fall, he reached for Joey, who was looking at him with amusement, probably figuring Nick was goofing around, pulling one of his pratfalls. Nick tried to speak, but he had no voice. He tried to extend his arms to brace his fall, but his limbs were paralyzed. His torso twisted as he fell. That's when he realized he'd been stabbed, a sharp poke in his thigh. Not especially painful, more like a warm pressure that slowly spread throughout his body. Things started to slow down. He saw the precise moment on Joey's face when he realized Nick wasn't playing around and was in real distress. It was at that moment Nick came to the realization: *I'm going to die.*

He landed faceup, his legs folded under him like a doll. His entire body was paralyzed, but he could see and hear everything that was happening around him. Joey screamed for someone to call an ambulance. The last thing Nick saw before he slipped away was the face of the girl in the merlot fedora hovering over him.

Anastasia had that mischievous smile on her face—and a needle in her hand.

The helicopter whooshed above him in slow motion. Nick felt himself floating up toward a circle of light that flashed rhythmically as it was interrupted by the spinning blades. Three paramedics were leaning over him. *So this is it*, he thought. Nick always figured he'd be terrified at this moment, but instead he felt relieved. He'd be reunited with his father and finally get to know his mother. This time, there would be no misunderstandings, no hurt—only love. He would miss Grace; that was the worst part. *I love you, Grace.* He tried to say it but could only manage a silent prayer. *She knows.* He comforted himself with the thought.

Fucking Frankie outlived me. The random thought gave him an odd satisfaction.

The faces of the paramedics were angelic, like Raphael's cupids. Their bows were drawn, arrows tipped with honey. His only regret, remarkably, was the unfished notebook he had begun writing in. *How odd*, Nick thought. The three angels cradled him, and he continued to rise. *I'm entering heaven now. My struggles are over.*

The blades continued to spin, and he struggled to figure out how the medevac had managed to land inside the Tiki. Slowly, as Nick's eyes began to focus, the helicopter blades transformed themselves into the ceiling fan whirring beneath the palm thatch of the hut. The light at the end of the tunnel was just the DJ's spotlight set in the roof of the Tiki. His breathing and heart rate began to return to normal. He heard a voice. One of Raphael's cherubic paramedics, the one in the center, spoke to him. She was wearing a merlot fedora, and a necklace of three interlocking gold rings dangled from her throat.

"You're okay, baby," she said.

The paramedic to the right didn't seem to appreciate her comment.

"Baby?" Her eyes flashed in a decidedly un-angelic display.

The third paramedic, the one on the left, found the whole exchange quite amusing. She struggled to stifle a laugh, that instead snuck out of her nose as a snort. A quirk Nick had once found so endearing.

This is definitely not heaven, Nick thought. *Purgatory possibly.*

"You fucking whore! You killed him." Grace swung at Anastasia, but Ronnie reacted first. He wrapped Anastasia in a headlock and pulled her back, knocking off the fedora and causing the needle to fall to the floor. Grace's wild punch missed the would-be assassin and landed square on Angie's jaw. Angie reflexively grabbed Grace by the hair and began pulling. Joey jumped in to separate them.

Definitely purgatory, Nick thought as he started to regain feeling and use of his limbs.

"Let her go." Ralph had emerged from the cabana at the sound of the commotion. Nino was close behind. Ralph picked up the needle Anastasia had dropped. Even Ronnie knew better than to refuse an order from Ralph Cappello. He released Anastasia from his grip but reached for the switchblade in his back pocket, his *carino*, just in case.

"Thank you." Anastasia rubbed her neck. "It's an auto-injector of atropine and pralidoxime chloride—a nerve agent antidote. Don't drink or touch anything on the bar."

"But how?" Angie asked as she let some of Grace's hair fall to the floor and began rubbing her jaw. "I bought those drinks."

"It was that Persian slut," Anastasia said. "I saw the atomizer in her hand before she handed him the shot—fucking amateur."

"Sophia?" Joey looked stunned.

"If that's what she told you her name was, yes." She turned to wink at Ronnie. "I was a Sophia once."

"Sorry about the headlock."

"That's okay. I thought it was kind of hot." Anastasia raised one eyebrow. "Now please put that toy away. I'd hate for us to have any further misunderstanding when we were just getting to know one another."

Ronnie sheepishly complied, and Anastasia kissed him, giving him a playful nibble on his lower lip. He would have bit her back but noticed that Virgil was sitting alone at the end of the bar. The excitement had been a bit much for him, and he was staring out at the ocean, rocking back and forth. Ronnie went over to try to soothe him.

"Uncle Nick." Joey was almost in tears. "I'm so sorry. I—"

"It's okay, Joey. It's not your fault. You couldn't have known."

"Where'd she go?" Ralph asked.

Joey sprinted to the portico, only to be informed by the valet that she had taken off in the Bugatti a few minutes prior.

"I'm sorry too," Grace said to Angie.

"That's okay," Angie replied. "On some level, I probably deserved it. Sorry 'bout the hair."

"Forget about it." Grace was focused on Nick. He was still looking a little shaky. Joey helped him to a stool, and Grace held him until the real paramedics arrived.

"He seems okay," the EMT said after taking his vitals. "Are you sure he just had a few drinks?"

"Yes," Grace answered for him. "Just a couple shots."

"You probably had an allergic reaction to something you ate." The veteran paramedic had seen his share of anaphylaxis, and he doubted that's what this was, but he knew Nick, knew the Tiki, and thought it best to leave well enough alone. "Maybe see your doctor tomorrow. Have him prescribe an EpiPen."

"You're pretty tough to kill for a pretty boy." Ralph pinched him on the cheek. "Good thing for you, your guardian angel decided to drop in." Ralph turned toward where Anastasia had been standing, but she was already gone. "Look, there's something I've been meaning to tell you since you got back, and well, with Grace here, it's probably as good a time as any."

Dear lord, what now? Nick thought. Grace looked confused.

"It's about me and Grace's mother." He turned to look at Grace. "We're in love."

Grace laughed. "Do you really think I hadn't noticed?"

"Congratulations," said Nick. "God bless."

"So, you guys aren't mad?"

"Mad about what? That my mother smiles and prances around the house fussing with her hair and clothes like a teenager? No, Ralph, I'm not mad." Grace kissed him on the cheek. "We love you too."

"Yeah," Nick said weakly. "Me too. Now can someone please help me back to the condo? Tomorrow's a big day, and I need some rest."

Ralph helped him up, walked him to his car, and drove Nick and Grace home.

Nick fell asleep as soon as he hit the bed—just as the rumor of a recovered Rembrandt started to go viral.

BOBBY PEACE

In Nick's dream, they were lost in a fog. His father was at the wheel of the *Tony Rome*, as always. He sounded the horn as they made their way through the blanket that clung to the ocean's surface. Nick could barely see beyond the bow pulpit. *Don't worry*, his father told him. *It will lift soon.* That's when the freighter appeared. Its horn sounded, but it was already upon them. Its massive bow wake lifted the *Tony Rome*. Its hull loomed over them as tall as a skyscraper and was about to crush them. The horn sounded again. He clung to his father—

His phone buzzed for the third time, and Nick managed to pry his eyelids open. The events of the day before rushed into his consciousness all at once, and he was overcome with emotion. Grace appeared at his side, patting his forehead with a cool towel.

"You're okay, my love. Just a mild fever."

"Did all that really happen?"

"If you mean the part about you being poisoned, yes, it did." Grace held his face with both hands and kissed him. "Oh, and the part where I punched your ex in the jaw? Yeah, that happened too."

Nick had that sick feeling that is usually associated with reconstructing the misadventures of a drunken night. Except he hadn't been drunk. He reached for his phone and realized he had slept past noon. There were so many alerts on his phone—missed calls, texts, and notifications—he hardly knew where to start. He managed to pull himself up and prop a few pillows behind him. Grace reappeared with a quad espresso.

"You're going to need it," she said as she placed it down on the nightstand.

"Is everything okay?"

"Everything is fine. Ralph is on his way over. He said to tell you to take it easy and that everything is going according to plan . . . whatever that means."

"I meant with us." Nick sipped his espresso and immediately felt about 50% better.

Grace smiled but cocked her eyebrow just enough to make him a little uneasy. "Why wouldn't it be?"

Ralph arrived about fifteen minutes later. Nick heard his booming voice as Grace let him in. Nick began to recall Ralph's declaration of love for Grace's mother, Adriana, and it brought a smile to his face. *That was one good thing*, he thought.

"You look like shit, kid," Ralph announced as he walked into the bedroom.

"Let me poison you, see how you look."

"I'm just fucking with you. But why don't you get cleaned up and meet me over the Tiki? There's a lot going on."

"Gary and Frank?"

"They're fine. They should be there in a few more hours. Sounds like Gary's had just about enough of your uncle's stories though."

"How about everything else?"

"See for yourself." Ralph handed Nick his phone after pulling up the article from the *Sun Sentinel.* Nick's vision was still a little blurry, but he could make out the headline.

Recovered Rembrandt on display at Fort Lauderdale Tiki Bar?

"That ain't all. It's all over the internet."

"What about the NFT?"

"It hit the platform this morning. Gates was right. It's getting noticed. There have been some lowball bids, but Gates says once the heavy hitters do their due diligence, together with all the news, it should be off to the races."

It still sounded dicey to Nick, but he trusted Gates's acumen when it came to matters of technology and finance. "I certainly hope so."

Ralph looked at his watch. "Let's say around 1:30 at the Tiki? You should be ready for a drink around then."

Nick managed to drag himself out of bed and into the shower. He heard Ralph say goodbye to Grace as he headed for the door mindlessly whistling some old tune from his youth, like only a man hopelessly in love is wont to do.

Nick showed up at the Tiki around 1:45 p.m. Ralph was waiting for him at the bar. Gates was set up at a corner table with two laptops open in front of him. He was flanked by two young members of his staff with laptops of their own. They were the rising stars of El Mar Tech, and Gates had generously brought them in for a small cut of his end. He believed that spreading equity around was the only path to retaining talent.

Ronnie placed an ice-cold Peroni in front of Nick, and to his surprise, Ralph's prediction came true; he really was in the mood to start drinking. He had a feeling it was going to be a long day.

ARTnews had indeed picked up the story, running it as a curiosity piece and using it to rehash the old story of the Gardner heist and perhaps raise awareness. The story concluded by stating that the author had reached out to Robert Pace, Director of Security and Chief Investigator at the Isabella Stewart Gardner Museum in Boston, for comment, but at the time of publication he had yet to return the call.

"One hundred," Gates shouted.

"Is that good?" Ralph asked.

"One hundred Ether. It's about $170,000. It's a good start. But more importantly, it indicates that someone has figured it out."

Gates had listed the NFT on VastOcean marketplace and uploaded select previews of sections of the image in ultra-high definition. To a trained eye, the conclusion was self-evident. Coupled with the growing news stories and #rembrandtrecovered, which was beginning to trend on Twitter, Gates hoped to cash in on the building wave of speculation. The bid indicated that someone had put together that the painting had been recovered and felt the first digital, ultra-high-resolution image had to be worth something.

After that first bid, there was a brief lull, followed by a trickle of incrementally larger offers, and then a tsunami of bids. By 6:00 p.m., the NFT of *Storm on the Sea of Galilee* had been bid up to 500 Ether—just over $850,000.

"I still can't wrap my head around this," Andy Boy weighed in, having joined them at the bar. "I heard one of these things sold for sixty-nine million. Is that true?"

"Me either." Nino walked up to the bar with Gloria, introducing her to the boys.

"It's true. That's the beauty of it," Gates replied. "You don't have to believe. Does any serious expert really believe *Salvator Mundi* was painted completely by da Vinci? Yet that didn't stop Christie's from selling it for 450 million and it coming within a breath of being displayed next to the *Mona Lisa*."

Ralph's phone rang. It was Gary.

"We're here."

"Good. Are you around back?"

"Yeah, I just pulled up. I think we're in the right place."

"Hold on." Ralph put the phone down for a second and leaned over to whisper to Andy. Andy placed a call to Bobby Peace.

"Yeah, Bobby? They're there. You see them?" There was a pause before Andy nodded back to Ralph. "Good, thanks. What's that? You're welcome. It was our pleasure. You can thank me by answering your phone later. I'm pretty sure we're gonna have some company soon."

Andy hung up. Ralph picked his phone back up.

"Ok, sit tight. They see you. Someone should be out to get it soon. See you when you get back."

Gary's text came seconds later. *All good.*

Ralph ordered shots of 1942 all around. He pointed toward Gates and the El Mar whiz kids. "Them too." Ronnie Cruz poured the shots, including a double for himself.

Andy turned to Nick and knocked back his tequila, making a face as it went down. "You ready for some fireworks, kid?"

Nick wasn't exactly sure what he meant, but he answered anyway. "Sure, Andy."

"Good," Andy answered. "Because I think we just lit the fuse."

LA RASCASSE

Dmitry was enjoying the view from Le Bar Salle Blanche, the private bar at Le Casino Monte Carlo. The terrace overlooked the Mediterranean, but Dmitry's attention was focused on the voluptuous ingenue he had met earlier that evening at La Rascasse, the lounge named after and located at the most famous corner of the Grand Prix course. The ingenue's curves gave La Rascasse a run for its money.

He answered his ringing phone. "What is it?" His tone softened when he heard Anastasia's voice on the other end. He stepped away from the bar for a moment, and the woman used the time to fix her lipstick. Anastasia brought him up to date on the events at the Tiki the previous night, including Nick's brush with death. Dmitry had been tracking the NFT sale and had even made a few bids himself to spur things along, though he had no desire to actually acquire the image. "Excellent," he said after she confirmed the painting had been delivered according to his instructions. Dmitry watched as the woman's hand hovered awkwardly over his drink before she returned the lipstick to her purse. He sighed.

"I'll leave you to your friend, *kohana*," Anastasia said.

Dmitry spun to look around the room. "Are you here?"

Anastasia laughed. "Don't be silly. I heard it in your voice when you answered. Don't stay up too late. You have a big day tomorrow. And be careful."

"Yes, yes. Don't worry about me." Dmitry ended the call. Anastasia was the only one allowed to tease him, and he loved her for it.

"Now then." He returned to the beauty he had nicknamed La Rascasse, the French name for the venomous scorpionfish. She was young and beautiful and witty. One of the better he'd encountered. Dmitry enjoyed her company immensely. He was almost envious that she was not one of his. He considered making her an offer. Perhaps with some training she could become a valuable asset. But in the end, he concluded it was too risky. *Pity*, he thought. Dmitry invited her back to his yacht instead, and she accepted without hesitation.

"My driver will escort you." Dmitry signaled to Ramon, his head of security. "Kindly escort the lady to *Yekaterina*. And make sure she's comfortable."

Ramon nodded his understanding and extended an enormous arm toward the exit, straining the button on his tuxedo jacket.

"I'll join her shortly. Apologies, my dear. I have a small matter of business to attend to."

Ramon escorted her to one of the Range Rovers on the front line of the casino, where more of Dmitry's security detail awaited his instructions. Ramon joined her in the back seat and instructed the driver to take them to the yacht, purposefully mispronouncing its name. The driver briefly glanced at Ramon in the rearview, acknowledging Ramon's message. He pulled out of the driveway and turned in the direction opposite the marina.

La Rascasse would never get to see the interior of the *Yekaterina*—or the outside of the Range Rover.

Dmitry asked the bartender to dispose of his drink and make him a fresh one.

WALK ON BY

The NFT titled #rembrandtrecovered sold for one thousand Ether, a little over 1.7 million.

"It's no Beeple, but it's certainly a nice little score," Gates said. "Sorry, Nick. I thought it would go for more. I'll cut my commission in half."

"Are you crazy?" Nick said. "It's found money. You earned every penny."

Gary, Nino, and Andy agreed.

"Nice work, kid." Andy settled any doubt.

It was eleven, and the Tiki was in full swing. Frank and Gary had parked the Yukon at Logan and caught an 8:30 flight scheduled to land at 11:48 p.m.

Nick and Grace were at the jukebox when the first rocket went off.

"Where is it?" Special Agent O'Connell strolled into the Tiki with his gun drawn. His question was directed to Andy Boy, who barely turned his gaze away from the evening news when he heard O'Connell behind him.

"Put that thing away before you hurt somebody," Andy said.

"You heard me. I know it's here."

Grace held on to Nick's shirt to make him stay, but he pulled away and walked over to O'Connell and Andy. "What's going on here?" Nick said. "This is my place."

"I know who you are. You're all under arrest. Your black friend too."

Andy poked Nino and pointed his thumb over his shoulder. He still hadn't turned his barstool around. "You hear this?" he said to Nino. "He says we're under arrest."

"Fuck," Nino said. "I knew I should have paid those parking tickets."

O'Connell was becoming increasingly infuriated at being treated like some nuisance instead of a federal agent.

Finally, Andy turned to face him. "I have no idea what you're talking about. You're making an ass out of yourself."

"You know damn well what I'm talking about. That painting was here yesterday."

"Wait," Andy said. "That's what this is all about?" Andy turned to Ronnie. "Could you turn the jukebox down for a minute please, kid? And put the news on all the TVs if you don't mind."

Ronnie picked up the two remote controls from behind the bar and killed the jukebox. The Tiki crowd gave a collective groan. Moments later, the nightly news was on every TV lining the perimeter of the bar. *Breaking News* flashed across the screens.

"You should watch this," Andy said to O'Connell, "before you make an even bigger fool of yourself."

A man walked to the podium, flanked by a few dignitaries and a special agent from the Boston field office who O'Connell recognized as being with the Art Crime Team.

Robert Pace, Director of Security and Chief Investigator at the Isabella Stewart Gardner Museum, made the announcement to rousing applause—both at the museum and the Tiki—that *Christ in the Storm on the Sea of Galilee*, the priceless Rembrandt seascape stolen from the Gardner in 1990, had been located by a Philadelphia-based group funded by Russian philanthropist Dmitry Ivanov and returned to its home. Pace went on to add that the painting was in relatively good shape and was being readied for its return to its empty frame in the Dutch room. A partial reward of two million had been agreed upon between all interested parties. The press conference ended, and the screen turned to Dmitry Ivanov, philanthropist, appearing from Monaco via Skype.

"This is bullshit, Caposecco." O'Connell looked like he was going to have a stroke. "We had a deal."

"Deal? On what? A skid of broccoli rabe? I'm in the produce business. Besides, I don't make deals with the FBI. I'm not sure where you got that idea. *You* talked, I just listened. There's no law against that." Andy was looking at Nino and Ralph when he said the last part, as he was talking about a different kind of law.

"No law against that," Nino answered first.

"No, Andy. No law against that," Ralph added.

Andy made a phone call. "Bobby Peace," Andy barked. "Thanks for answering. Listen, somebody here would like to have a word with you." Andy handed the phone to O'Connell.

"This is Special Agent O'Connell. Who am I speaking with?"

"Robert Pace, Director of Security, Gardner Museum. How can I help you, Agent O'Connell?"

"You're not really going to pay two million dollars to these hoodlums, are you?"

"Well, yes and no."

"Yes and no? What the hell is that supposed to mean?"

"Well, I'm not sure what *hoodlums* you're referring to, but Mr. Ivanov has requested that the reward be split equally between two charities he has designated. So, yes, we are paying out the reward."

"Oh, yeah? What charities might Mr. Ivanov have designated?"

"One million is to be paid to St. Jude Children's Research Hospital and one million to Shriners Hospitals for Children. They're wonderful institutions. I'm a donor myself."

"Yeah, I've heard of them."

"If you have any other questions, Agent O'Connell, I can refer you to the Art Crime Team here in Boston. In fact, I have Agent Williams right here with me."

"No." O'Connell looked like he had been kicked in the stomach. "That's okay. Thanks." He ended the call and handed the phone back to Andy.

Gary had called Ralph during the commotion to say they had landed early and were in an Uber. Ralph gave him the short version of events. "Yeah, he said he was going to arrest the black guy too."

"Motherfucker," Gary shouted into the phone. "Always the black guy. Hey, do me a favor."

"Hey, Ronnie," Ralph called out. "Gary needs a favor." He handed the phone to the bartender.

Ronnie turned the jukebox back on and lowered the volume on the TVs. He skipped the next selections and played Gary's request.

"Hey, G-man," Ronnie shouted at O'Connell as he turned to leave. "This one's for you—courtesy of the black guy."

Ronnie turned the volume up to the max, and D-Train's "Walk on By" blasted out of every speaker as O'Connell walked out to the hoots of the crowd.

"I told you, you could trust me," Nick said to Grace.

"We'll see," Grace answered.

RUSSIAN MOON

The *Serenity* departed Port Vauban during the Formula 1 practice session. No explanation was provided to the guests who had been invited to the now canceled soiree. The *Perseus* remained in Port Hercule, and the guests would soon forget their disappointment amid the bacchanalian race day activities provided by Al Amin as a consolation prize. Although they would not get to bid on the rumored Rembrandt nor glimpse the mythical *Salvator Mundi*, each would receive a virtual gift bag of perks and privileges that would more than make up for the inconvenience: Richard Mille Formula 1 watches; nights of debauchery with barely faded pop stars; "*Bugattis for everyone!*" The canceled auction would fade into oblivion, Al Amin would simply deny there had ever been such a thing, and no one would disagree with him.

But Al Amin would remember.

On its way out of port back to the Kingdom, the *Serenity* passed purposely close to the *Yekaterina*. On orders from Al Amin, the captain issued five short blasts of the vessel's horn, the international nautical signal for danger. On the *Yekaterina*, Dmitry watched as the *Serenity* passed. He heard the blasts and received the message.

The captain of the *Yekaterina* radioed Dmitry. "How do you want me to respond?"

"Don't," he answered. Dmitry instead walked out to the helipad, raised a bottle of Dom Pérignon Rosé Vintage 1959 toward the *Serenity* and took a swig from the bottle, then turned and dropped his trousers, giving Al Amin an eyeful of his Russian ass.

Nasir and the *Serenity's* captain looked to the Crown Prince and prepared for an eruption of nuclear proportions.

Al Amin took in the view of his old adversary's wrinkled posterior and burst into a riotous laugh.

RALPH'S BIG DAY

One month later

Then he called the bridegroom aside and said, "Everyone brings out the choice wine first and then the cheaper wine after the guests have had too much to drink; but you have saved the best till now."

John 2:10 (NIV)

Ralph stood on the beach in front of the Tuscan Tiki, rocking back and forth nervously. A light breeze was coming off the ocean, but sweat was running down his face. Nick was standing at his side and handed him a tissue.

"You're sweating like a whore in church," Nick said.

"I can't help it. I'm roasting out here, and this tie is choking me." Ralph pulled at his collar. He had sworn off ties since the one he wore at his sentencing in 1977.

"Stop rocking," said Andy. "You're worse than Virgil."

"Couldn't we have done this thing inside?" Ralph said.

"I'm pretty sure the bride gets to decide that," Frank offered.

"Here." Nino offered him a bottled water. "Drink this before she comes out."

Ralph took a swig of the water. "Sorry I'm complaining so much, Nick. I don't want you to get the wrong idea. This is a big day for me."

"I understand, Ralph, don't worry. It will all be over before you know it, then we can head up to the Tiki and get drunk."

Andy nudged Ralph. "I think she's coming."

"You got the rings?" Nick asked.

Ralph searched around in the pockets of his trousers. "I think I left them back at the house."

"Are you fucking kidding me?" Nick said.

Ralph pulled a velvet pouch out of the breast pocket of his jacket and flashed a big smile. "Relax, kid. What kind of best man would I be if I forgot the rings?"

They all fell silent as Grace appeared at the top of the stairs. A dapper-looking Virgil, hair neatly combed, escorted her out onto the sand.

YETI

Do not take revenge, my dear friends, but leave room for God's wrath, for it is written: "It is mine to avenge; I will repay," says the Lord.

Romans 12:19 (NIV)

They never did find Victor Baldassare's head, although someone had been kind enough to deliver his severed limbs and torso to the Isabella Stewart Gardner Museum. His identity was confirmed by DNA conveniently on file with the Commonwealth of Massachusetts. The medical examiner concluded that the limbs had been severed with a bone saw, and that the dismemberment had likely occurred while the victim was still alive.

A month later, a container ship arrived at the Port of Jeddah. Nasir accepted delivery of a crate containing a special gift for the Crown Prince. A phalanx of Range Rovers escorted a refrigerated truck to the Royal Palace in Riyadh. Nasir's men retrieved the box from the crate, and Nasir placed a Yeti cooler at the front of Al Amin's ornate desk. The Crown Prince was on a call and seemed perturbed by the interruption. He stood as Nasir lifted

Big Vic's head by the hair, striking a pose eerily similar to the executioner in Caravaggio's *Salome with the Head of John the Baptist*.

Al Amin waved his hand dismissively, placing his call on hold for a moment. "Bury that thing out in the desert."

TAMPA OR BUST

Fenway Phil packed what little belongings he had in the Econoline for the trip to Tampa. It was late September, and the Golden Nugget Marina parking lot was ill-suited for a winter stay. Even Bigeye Billy had pulled out a few days ago. Besides, Phil had worn out his welcome in Philly. After Lenny De Rosa turned up dead, he had made himself scarce, sticking to the usual Atlantic City haunts and grifting what he could from the summer boaters and the horse degenerates at the Race and Sports Book. The Econoline was getting long in the tooth, but Phil had replaced the tires, changed the oil, and hoped it would make one last ride before puttering out.

As he returned from the restroom showers, towel wrapped around his waist, toiletry bag under his arm, Phil was outraged to find a few local delinquents monkeying around behind his van.

"Hey!" he shouted as he comically attempted to run across the parking lot in the towel and flip-flops. "Get away from there."

They looked up at him, and the biggest one gave him the finger as the other two laughed. They stopped laughing when a man approached on a ten-speed. The man didn't have to say anything, the teenagers just scattered as he rode up.

The man got off his bike and looked down at Phil's passenger side rear tire. "Ain't that a motherfucker. Looks like them boys gave you a flat."

Phil shook his head. That meant he would have to use the spare, leaving no backup for the trip to Tampa.

"I'm awful sorry 'bout that, sir. I don't know what these kids thinking these days. Give this neighborhood a bad name. I remember a time when you didn't have to be afraid to walk around here at night. Now, these youngsters don't have no respect for their elders." He put his kickstand down and placed his hands on his hips as he stared at the flat tire. "Let me give you a hand with that. Wouldn't want you to think there ain't no neighborly people left round here."

"Thanks," Phil said, extending his hand. "I'd appreciate that. I'm Phil by the way."

The man's hands were rough as sandpaper.

"My pleasure," the man said as he turned to face him, revealing a huge scar that ran down the length of his face. "Folks round here call me Chalky."

EPILOGUE

Rynek Glowny, Krakow, Poland

The man wrapped up his session in Old Town, Krakow. Rynek Glowny, the oldest medieval square in Europe, provided endless opportunities for him, especially when the light slanted unevenly across the colorful buildings situated on the curved streets spreading out from the square. The hourly trumpet call had sounded from the tower of St. Mary's Basilica. It was his signal to wrap up his work and head back to his apartment in Kazimierz, the trendy old Jewish Quarter of Krakow that he called home.

He spent his mornings either walking along the Vistula River, exploring Kazimierz's funky shops and cafes, or sometimes visiting an old friend at the Princes Czartoryski Museum. He would sit there gazing at her for hours as she looked off to the side, stroking the ermine in her hands. Occasionally, he would walk along the Royal Route, stopping in the Church of Saints Peter and Paul, lighting a candle for a special intention. As he walked down Ulica Grodkza, a canvas and easel under his arm, a tote bag over his shoulder, the spires of Wawel Castle reminded him how far he was from home.

This is home now, he had to remind himself.

A FedEx envelope with a return address of Boca Raton was waiting for him in his mailbox. He knew without opening it that it contained another in a series of checks from the sale of his works, which were in high demand of late. The sales were being administered by a South Florida brokerage he had entrusted his paintings to, and were overseen by Andrea "Andy Boy" Caposecco, who had also helpfully orchestrated his recent demise. Gossip and rumor were the engines driving the art world these days, and in death, Charles Scottoline had finally achieved what he couldn't during his life. He was referred to in *ARTnews* as "a modern-day Han van Meegeren."

If I had only known this earlier, Scotty thought, *I would have died long ago.*

The only person who had figured it all out was soon-to-be-retired Detective Jim Corey. But at one month short of his thirty, his autopilot had been set on *stay clear of trouble* mode for quite some time. In fact, he had put a deposit down on a sweet little one-bedroom condo in Pompano, not far from a certain Tiki bar.

As Scotty entered his apartment, a little Italian Greyhound whined impatiently at his human's approach. Scotty bent over to pet him, then attached a leash to his collar.

"Let's go, Leonardo," he said.

They headed out for their afternoon walk on Szeroka Street, where ancient synagogues share space with funky bistros, and friendly shop owners put out water bowls for thirsty Italian Greyhounds. The scene was vibrant and eclectic. The juxtaposition of old and new reminded Scotty of Passyunk Avenue.

It felt like home.

THE END

If you enjoyed Revenge of the Prodigal but haven't read Return of the Prodigal yet, you can purchase it on Amazon.

ACKNOWLEDGMENTS

Writing and publishing a book can be a scary proposition. So when I first published Return of the Prodigal, Book 1 in the series, I didn't know what to expect. Putting your thoughts and feelings down on the page and releasing them into the world is not easy. I'd like to acknowledge all the readers who supported Return of the Prodigal. Whether it was a call, a text, a comment, or even a "like," I see you, and I appreciate you. Without your encouragement, I may not have had the stamina to continue. This book is the product of your support and encouragement.

I want to thank some people without whose assistance and encouragement; this book would not be possible. If, for some reason, I have neglected to name someone, rest assured, I will thank you in person.

My family deserves the first acknowledgment. To my Mother, Marianne Caudo-Beck, I wish you could have lived to read Return of the Prodigal. I know you're smiling down on me. When I read it to myself, I'm reading to you.

Robert Levant, author of Finding Polaris, has been quietly coaching me for years, even when I didn't realize it. Thank you for your friendship.

Thank you to Ray Driscoll for being an advance reader and good friend.

Thank you to Ralph Frangipani of Frangipani Photography for the back cover photo and website/social media photography.

Thank you to Latte and Melanie Goldstein of River Design Books for the great cover and beautiful interior formatting.

Thank you to Elizabeth A. White for editing my manuscript. Knowing you are waiting in the wings with a padded stick has allowed me to write more confidently. (Please don't correct these acknowledgments).

Thanks to David Di Paolo of Maximus Internet Marketing Group for the website and marketing expertise over the years, but more importantly, for his unwavering support and friendship.

Thank you to my dearest friend, Chris Carvell, unofficial Mayor of the Tiki, and the entire Tiki crew at Ocean Manor Hotel and Resort and the world-famous Bamboo Beach Tiki Bar, especially Frank Talerico, owner/operator.

Thank you to the first person to read an early iteration of Return of the Prodigal, my friend J in Boca Raton. He believed in it from the start and gave me the courage to keep going.

A thank you to Lynn Rinaldi and all my extended family at Paradiso restaurant, including Dana, Roe and Jimmy Gallo, and all the other regulars who shared those special years with me.

Thank you to Frank De Pasquale for his constant encouragement. Everyone should have a friend that supports them even when they're not looking. (I peeked).

Thank you to Sophia and Santino for always asking how the book is going.

Thank you to John Takacs for his sound judgment, genuine concern, and careful reading.

Some special readers, supporters, and friends:

Chris McCrosson, Rich Klineburger, Chuck Peruto, Alan Tauber, John Walsh, Phil McFillin, Jimmy Leonard, Lou Silver, Marc Franklin, Bill Carey, Jeff Wharton. Bill Brennan (Summer Wind is dedicated to you).

To my wife Christine, none of this is possible without you. Thank you for your believing in me when these books were just a crazy notion. She gets to read these chapters as they're written, and I value her input above all others. I believe in you and me.

To my son Nick, this book is dedicated to you. A father couldn't wish for a better son. Let's write a book together one day. Love, Dad.

Thank you to Anthony Amore, Director of Security/ Chief Investigator at the Isabella Stewart Gardner Museum for his kindness in not having me arrested after my visit. I'm looking forward to returning for a private tour!

For exciting updates about the world of Nick Di Nobile and the Prodigal crew, join us in the Prodigal Cabana Club at caudobooks.com. You'll be the first to learn about events, giveaways, bonus material, and updates about Redemption of the Prodigal, Book III in the Prodigal of Passyunk Avenue series.

caudobooks.com

@michael_caudo_author
@caudobooks

Made in United States
North Haven, CT
07 June 2023

37465155R00186